My World Passes

By Donovan Harrison

Published by

Gray Hawk Publishing Company

PO Box 247
Attica, KS 67009

This book is a work of fiction. People, places, events and situations are the product of the author's imagination. Any resemblance to actual persons, living or dead, or historical events is purely coincidental.

Copyright 2009 by Donovan Harrison

Cover copyright 2009 by Jennie Green

No part of this book or cover may be reproduced, stored in a retrieval system, or transmitted by any means without the written permission of the author or artist.

ISBN: 1451596049
ISBN 13: 9781451596045

Chapter 1

WHAT A BEAUTIFUL WORLD I live in, I thought as I lay in bed and looked out the window. Outside the birds were almost deafening as they made their mating calls. I closed my eyes and snuggled down into my fuzzy den. *This must be how a bunny rabbit feels* I thought as I lay there half asleep. Then I poked my head out of the den and looked through the window again. The brown, winterkilled grass had a few sprigs of green and it soon would be time for Paul to start babying the lawn as he had every spring since we had lived here. How long had it been, and I closed my eyes and tried to remember.

Even as I struggle to remember, I reached over and felt his side of the bed. It was cold and I knew that as usual, Paul had been up for hours. I wondered if he had gone to work yet. I hoped not. Even after being married these how many years? twenty-five jumped into my mind, at times he made me feel like a newlywed bride. I closed my eyes and thought of him.

Again I opened my eyes and looked out the window. Beyond the yard was the lake. The strong south wind had the lake water churned to froth and I laughed as the thought came to me, *Stillwater isn't still today.* Yes, Stillwater, Oklahoma was the town Paul and I lived in. The home of OSU and the Cowboys. It was the middle of March and the wind was blowing in Oklahoma as usual. *Get up you lazy bum,* I scolded myself. *Get up and start enjoying the day.* But I was enjoying myself right where I was, so why should I get up? Stretching and snuggling into the covers, I closed my eyes and dreamed of the past.

Paul and I had realized that the small apartment we lived in would not be big enough when we first found out I was pregnant. Pregnant with twins as we would later find out. It was then we had bought this house, almost new, and moved. We could afford it. He was working as an engineer at Mercury Marine and was climbing the ladder of success quite rapidly. Now the twins Chris and Kris were what? Twenty-three? Yes, we had celebrated their twenty-third birthday in February. So we had lived here twenty-four years, not twenty-five as I had first thought. And I would soon be fifty, a half a century old. My, how fast time passes.

I opened one eye and again turned to look out the window. The sun was shining brightly and other than the wind, it was a gorgeous day. *Too darned beautiful to spend it in bed.* I threw off the light bedspread, the sheet, jumped out of bed, and headed to the bathroom and shower. I turned the faucet handle until the water was just right, then stepped in and closed the door. The water felt so good I couldn't help it, I burst into song. "Oh what a beautiful morning," I sang, "Oh what a beautiful day." I would like to say I could sing like a bird but I couldn't. But then maybe I could, for after all, a crow is a bird, isn't it? Besides, what difference did it make? Paul was probably at work and I doubted that Tracy could hear me.

Tracy was our cook and house cleaner, the sixth one we had had since Paul and I had been married. She was majoring in health care with emphasis on nursing. We had been married almost a year and had just found out I was pregnant when Paul had tactfully suggested we hire a cook. "Sharon, Honey," he suggested, "Why don't we hire someone to cook, clean house, and live with us? After all, we can afford it with you and me both working. I'm sure it would be easy to find someone. It would save some college coed from having to pay for a dormitory and would be ideal for her. Other than breakfast and dinner, nothing else needs to be done on a schedule. That way she could determine her own schedule to match up with her classes. I'm sure there are many girls at OSU that would jump at the chance and we would be helping them to get a college education."

I was teaching middle school math and lugging home papers every night to grade. Being a housewife, and a pregnant one to boot, it sounded like a good idea to me. I really appreciated what he was suggesting and I cherished what he didn't say. He knew and I knew my talents lay elsewhere rather than in the kitchen and doing house work. Even though I thought it was a good idea, I had to tease him. I had to say, "What makes you think only girls can cook and take care of a house. I wouldn't mind having one of those muscle-bound young hunks I've seen on campus here around the house." But he only laughed because he knew I was joking.

My shower through, I stepped out and dried using a huge, soft towel. As I dried I looked into the mirror and was startled. *What happened to the pixie,* I wondered as I looked at the old blue-eyed five foot, middle-aged woman looking back at me. Still, I didn't look bad, I thought as I looked at myself. There were gray streaks in my blonde hair. *Not gray,* I thought, *but platinum blond.* But my boobs were beginning to sag. While I was petite, Paul was a big man and we made a Mutt and Jeff team. "Why did you marry a little girl like me?" I had asked time and time again. "Because of your big boobs," was his standard answer. *Well, Paul, I hate to say this but the big boobs are beginning to droop.* I had been able to keep my weight down though, and I stepped on the bathroom scales. *But not as much as I had hoped,* and I saw the needle sitting close to a hundred instead of ninety-five.

The smell of fresh perked coffee came wafting down the hall and I quickly slipped into my panties, bra, and a pair of maroon sweats. Dressed, I went to the hall and made my way to the kitchen and the coffee.

Tracy was busy at the stove and from the smell I could tell she was frying bacon. My, did it smell good. Tracy had come from Tahlequah and would be starting her senior year at OSU this fall. She claimed to be one quarter Cherokee but looking at her, I thought she was probably more. With her doe brown eyes and raven black hair, she had to be at least half Cherokee or more. But she was beautiful, of that there was no doubt. One more year was all she would be with us and then she would be gone. A future and a new life lay ahead of her. I hoped for her the best, she deserved it.

"Good morning, Tracy," I said, startling her.

"Hi, Sharon," she said smiling. "I didn't hear you come in. A cup of coffee?"

"I'll get it. Don't let me disturb whatever you're doing. It smells too good to be interrupted. Has Paul gone to work yet?"

"This is Sunday, Sharon. Even vice-presidents of sales don't have to work on Sunday. He's having coffee out on the patio. He asked me to bring him breakfast out there. Are you going to join him?"

"Isn't it windy out there?"

"Not really. All those shrubs give it some protection from the wind," she laughed.

I knew by the way she laughed that Paul had complained to her at some time or other during her stay here. I had heard it often enough myself. 'When we moved here I could sit on my riding mower and mow the whole lawn and never get off,' Paul often said, 'but then Sharon started planting shrubs and making flower beds. I might just as well sell the riding mower and buy a push one, a bigger weed-eater and a pair of pruning shears.' And he was right, but I couldn't let a living thing die. For example, the Rose of Sharon trees planted artistically in the yard had come from the apartment building they had torn down to build the new Super Wal-Mart. The roses, on the other hand, which were also planted here and there around the yard, had came from first one house and then another which were being demolished to make way for a business or new apartments in Stillwater.

Many of the roses had been in bad shape from being run over and trampled under before I gathered them to save, but in spite of their shape, most of them I nursed back to health. Of course some of them had died but I had found replacements. The Iris beds I built had came from all over Payne County. They were now green with long stems shooting up and would soon be blooming. The beds of Surprise Lilies were also green. They wouldn't bloom until well after their leaves had turned brown and disappeared. Then one morning the flower stalks would shoot out of the ground and be knee high before you knew it. Only then would they bloom.

Cup in hand I stepped out onto the patio and suddenly stopped with my heart racing. A strange, late middle-aged man was sitting there drinking coffee and reading the paper. At his feet was Boomer, our part German Shepard with a mangled tail. Sometime before he came to live with us, his tail had been broken in three places. About five inches from his body, his tail bent sharply to the right. A little farther up the tail, it bent straight up, went for a ways and then bent to the left. The tip was gone. He looked at me and wagged his mangled tail, or what was left of it. Boomer had hobbled into our yard some years ago, starved. I fed him and he stayed.

On the man's lap lay Miss Calico, our one-eyed lop-eared calico cat. She looked at me and blinked her one eye. I would guess the strange man to be over six foot tall and bald except for the gray fringe around the side of his head. He had wide shoulders and I could see he had once been muscular, but with age, the muscles hung loose around his arms. But there was something, something about him that appealed to me and drew me to him without fear. He must have heard me approaching because he turned around and smiled at me. Smiled a most engaging smile which made my heart flutter, flutter not with fear but with love.

"Good morning, Squirt," he said as he stood. "Did you decide not to sleep all day?" He held his arms open and from years of habit I walked into them and he kissed me. A most exciting sense of thrill, excitement, and comfort passed through my body as he held me. It was then I recognized him. Recognized that this man was my husband, Paul, and I put my arms around him as far as I could reach and squeezed him tight with affection. I hoped my embarrassment didn't show. My embarrassment for not recognizing my own husband right off. Yes, it was Paul, but when had he gotten so old?

He pulled a chair out for me and I sat down, then laughing he picked up the chair and me in it and set me up to the table. "You're always the showoff aren't you, Paul," I said laughing.

"Always," he said, "But it used to be a lot easier."

"Are you saying I'm getting fat?"

"No! Not by any means. It's just that I'm getting older. No, I wouldn't call you fat at all."

We continued the nonsense banter until Tracy came out with our breakfast. She sat my plate in front of me. On my plate was one slice of bacon, one poached egg, a slice of buttered toast and a small amount of hash browns. "Are you sure you can eat all of that, Squirt?" Paul asked nodding at my plate.

I looked at his plate which was full; three eggs, what looked like a half pound of bacon, and heaped up with hash browns. I shook my head as I said, "You're a walking heart attack just waiting to happen. I know I'm going to be a young widow."

"Cholesterol's one seventy. What's yours?"

"None of your business," I replied. I hated to admit to him that it was over two hundred.

Tracy came back out with a carafe of coffee and set it on the table. "Will there be anything else, Paul, Sharon?"

"I'm fine," I said.

"Same here," Paul said.

"Then I'll get ready for church. Sharon, I've run out of ideas for something to cook for dinner. Would you please do a favor for me and look through the freezer? Whatever you want for dinner take it out and I'll fix it when I get back from church."

"Paul, how about us giving Tracy the day off and you burn some steaks tonight? I think I can bake a potato without messing it up too bad."

"Yeah, sure, Tracy. Take the day off and I'll do my magic on the grill."

"Thank you," she said, untying her apron. "I'll see you tonight. Don't worry about cleaning up the kitchen; I'll take care of it before I go to bed."

"Thank you, Tracy," Paul and I both said. Then Paul looked at me when she had left. "I think when we hire the next girl we should go ahead and have her call us Mr. and Mrs. Phillips. We are getting a bit mature for a college girl to call us by our first name."

"You're right, Paul, but it really doesn't make any difference to me."

When we were through eating, I picked up the plates and took them to the kitchen where I rinsed them before putting them in the dishwasher. Back outside I filled my cup with coffee. Paul put down his paper long enough to ask, "Do you have any plans for today?"

"Not really," I answered. "It's so gorgeous today I think I'll go take a walk down by the lake."

"It's pretty windy out there."

"I know but it's such a beautiful, wild, gorgeous day. I like wild days like this. Do you want to go with me?"

"Nope, too windy for me. I'll probably go in and pack pretty soon. I hate to wait until the last minute. If I pack this morning then this afternoon I can repack and put in the things I forgot."

"Pack?" I asked surprised.

"Yes, don't you remember? I told you Friday that I had to fly to Cincinnati to a conference in the morning. I'll only be gone three days."

"It will seem like the three days are forever," I said. I thought and thought, but no, I didn't remember him telling me.

Paul looked at me with an odd expression on his face. "Three days will be a snap. Remember when I used to be gone as much as three months?"

"No, I don't remember," I laughed. "You know I like to remember the good times and forget the bad ones as soon as I can. I think I'll go for a walk now." I stood picking up my coffee cup. As I did I stepped behind him. Standing on my tiptoes I bent over and kissed him on the top of his bald head. "See you later, dear."

"You might ought to fill your pockets with rocks so the wind won't blow you away like a straw," he said as I turned and went into the house.

In the kitchen I sat my almost empty cup on the counter and headed for my closet in the bedroom. After all it was still March and walking in the wind down by the lake would make a sweater feel good. I slid the closet door open and began looking for my maroon, zip, shaker cardigan. I didn't see it right off. I started from one end of the clothes rod and went to the other looking; no maroon cardigan. Where had I left it? I checked the chair backs in the bedroom and went from there throughout the rest of the house. *It has to be somewhere.* Not on the coat rack in the foyer at the front door, not draped carelessly over a chair in the living room, and not in the study nor the guest bathroom. Where was it? It had to be somewhere but where? Oh well, it would show up someday, somewhere. Maybe in the car or at a friend's house, but today I would just have to wear something else. It wasn't like the maroon cardigan was the only sweater I had. It was just my favorite. Back at my closet I grabbed the first thing I saw, a gray hooded sweatshirt and slipped it on over my head. Feeling I was dressed appropriately for the cool wind I stepped outside onto the patio.

"Honey, before you go for you walk, will you look in the freezer and see if we have any steaks for tonight?" Paul asked looking up from his paper. "If we don't, I'll know I have to run to town this afternoon and get a couple."

"Sure," I said, turning around and stepping back into the house. I walked to the upright freezer, opened the door and froze. I wanted to scream but I didn't. On the bottom shelf was the maroon cardigan I had been looking for. It appeared to have been bunched up and crammed in the small space. *Who did that,* I wondered, my heart knocking against my ribs. *Who did it and why. If they thought it was funny and a joke, it isn't.* Using my thumb and forefinger I pulled it out and carried it into the living room. I lay it on the back of a recliner and just stared at it. If Chris or Kris, our twin children, had been home, I would have had my answer. But they hadn't been. I had a distinct memory of wearing the sweater only yesterday and neither one of them had been here the past three days. I had worn it to Feeds & Seeds yesterday when we went to get fertilizer for the lawn. So whoever had done it had to do it after I had gotten home. But I had come home and that afternoon I had taken a short nap. Perhaps I had taken off the sweater and left it in the living room and one or the other of the twins had come by to visit us. Perhaps whichever one it was only had a minute and Paul hadn't awakened me. That had to be it. *The thought that it might be someone else, a stranger,* was too terrible to think about.

I stepped to the door, opened it, and asked, "Paul, did Kris with a K, or Chris with a C stop by yesterday while I was napping?"

"Nope," he said, "Why? Did you find a couple of steaks?"

"Not, yet," I answered as I closed the door and went back to the open freezer. A chill of fear ran down my backbone as I hesitantly looked in. *What else would I find in there?* Cautiously I approached and looked in the shelves.

After scrounging around I found two t-bones, took them out and set them in the sink to thaw. I closed the door to the freezer and stood there thoughtfully. Then I walked to the patio door, opened it and said, "I found a couple of t-bones, will they do?"

"Wonderful!" he said and went back to his paper.

I stepped outside onto the patio, crossed it and headed across the lawn to the lake deep in thought. Instead of following me, Boomer stayed with Paul.

If someone is trying to drive me nuts, I thought, *it's working.*

Chapter 2

THE LAKE WAS A WILD, living thing, gray and grumbling as it splashed onto the shore. Water splashed high into the air as the lake frolicked in the wind. Wild, wild, wild the day was. The lake ran from the northeast to the southwest and the wind blew from the south carrying spray from the waves when they hit the shore. At times a hard gust blew, staggering me and the spray blew onto me, wet, cold, and wonderful. Close to shore a fish jumped and startled me. Again, I wondered as I had many times before, 'why do fish jump?' And again the same answer came to me, 'because they can'. I understood it now. I understood the fish. The reason I was out here was because I could be.

Down a ways in the lake stood the fountain, spraying water into the air only to be carried away in a windy mist. Occasionally a part of a rainbow would appear in a flash, only to disappear again. For some reason I felt a feeling of accomplishment when I looked at the fountain.

I had left the house with the hood of the sweater pulled over my head but feeling the wind in my face, I pulled it back. With abandonment I let the wind flow through my hair. I laughed and twirled in a circle. What nonsense. Here I was a middle-aged women but I felt as if I were a kid. Perhaps not a kid, but a teenager or a young woman in her early twenties. I spied a small stone glittering in the sunlight and I bent over and picked it up. It was no bigger than the end of my thumb but it was pretty so I put it in my pocket. A little farther on I saw a shard of flint and picked it up to examine. It was flat and half the size of my hand. Time and weather had dulled its once sharp edges. Perhaps it was a flake made by a long-ago Indian as he shaped a spear point. This, too, I put in my pocket.

The lake wasn't a large body of water; though I could see only one end of it I could easily see the other side with its band of tall cottonwoods, willows and oaks. On the hillside behind the trees were the houses overlooking the lake, much as the houses on our side did. Not tract houses with all built to look alike, but houses architecturally designed. Paul had told me the lake was only a half a mile wide and I believed him. Across the lake I could see cars in the park maintained by the city, their windshields twinkling in the reflected sunlight, and people wandering through the trees and on the lakeshore. I wasn't the only one enjoying the wild, windy day.

My eyes fell upon another stone and it was half the size of my fist. I bent over and picked it up. It was oblong with streaks of red, pink and white running through it. It was hard, I couldn't begin to scratch it with my thumb nail, and it was pretty. It followed the others into my pockets. The pockets were beginning to bulge now. But hadn't Paul told me to fill my pockets with rocks so I wouldn't blow away. I would do just that.

I felt so good out here by the lake I could hardly keep from laughing. It was a wild day and I felt wild. Wild and free without a care in the world. It was then I did laugh, and why not. There was no one here to see me or hear me. No one to see or hear the crazy old woman. Up the shore a ways I saw a piece of drift wood which had washed on shore. I hurried to it and picked it up. It was heavy and by its weight I knew it was oak. A short piece of a limb from a tree. It was as long as my forearm and jagged on both ends. It was gnarled and knotty and I wondered what had broken it from its mother tree and what had broken it again. Make a good club, I thought as I carried it on down the lakeshore. But what use did I have for a club. None whatsoever---*or did I?*

I saw another flat rock and with my stick I flipped it over before I reached down and picked it up. As I examined it I saw it wasn't as pretty as it had looked when I had seen it on the ground. Circling my thumb and forefinger around it, I side armed it into the lake. It only skipped twice until it took a dive into a wave and ducked underwater. I had thrown it away more to prove Paul wrong than anything else. See I didn't keep every rock I found. Just most of them and I smiled to myself. I saw another pretty rock and then another. I only stopped looking for pretty rocks when the weight in my pockets threatened to pull my sweats from my hips.

My maroon cardigan sweater suddenly flashed in my mind and it seemed as if the sun had suddenly grown dimmer. How had it gotten into the freezer? Someone had to have put it there, but whom. Tracy? Perhaps it was her. But to be honest, it wasn't like her. She was rather serious and not much into practical jokes. But she was young and in college. More than one college student had changed and even changed personalities while they were going to school. But I knew how to find out. I knew what I would do. When I got back home I would take the sweater and hide it. Perhaps I would stuff it between the mattress and box springs on my side of the bed. Then tomorrow when she came home from classes and was cleaning the house I would tell her I couldn't find the sweater and ask her to help me look for it. Perhaps then she would laugh and go to the freezer saying 'you left it in the kitchen and you know, Sharon, everything in the kitchen goes into the cabinets, the refrigerator, or the freezer.' I knew she would laugh as she said it.

But what if it wasn't Tracy? Maybe it was Paul. However that seemed highly unlikely. Not that Paul was beyond practical jokes as I had found out early in our marriage. If it was Paul, I would find out. He had never been able to keep a secret from me. I'd pry it out of him. But I doubted it was him. His jokes were loving and funny. Placing my sweater in the freezer was neither. *Somehow it seemed sinister and evil.*

But if it wasn't Tracy and it wasn't Paul, who could it be. Neither one of the twins, they hadn't even been to the house. Perhaps it was someone else, someone I didn't even know. Perhaps he had broken into the house at night while we were asleep and put my favorite sweater in the freezer. Perhaps it was a warning. Perhaps he was telling me that I was next. Maybe he hadn't broken in; maybe he had a key to our house. Suddenly I felt a feeling of uneasiness come over me. There was no one on the lakeshore in front of me, which I could plainly see. I stopped and turned around and looked behind me. No one was there. I glanced at the trees and didn't see anyone. All I saw were the houses a short way above the lake. That I couldn't see anyone didn't mean there was no one there. I felt eyes on me. Watchful, waiting eyes. Waiting and watching, waiting for their chance.

Suddenly I felt the goose bumps and not from the wind and cold. I was thankful for the stick of driftwood I carried in my hand. Perhaps I might just need a club. I walked on down the lakeshore a way, then stopped quickly and whirled around. The beach was empty. If someone had been following me, they had darted into the trees when I had stopped. I looked into the trees, looking *for the person or thing that was watching me.* Try as I might, I couldn't see anyone or anything. But I knew it was there. As I stood there a shiver ran through me. It was then I realized that I was afraid. The day was no longer gorgeous, now it was damp evil and fear filled the air. I was no longer having fun. Suddenly I wanted the strong walls of our house around me. It dawned upon me that I was small and there were things out there much larger than me. Yes, I wanted inside my house with Paul to protect me. Only then and there would I feel safe.

I turned around and started retracing my steps. I noticed I was breathing fast and by force of will I slowed my gasping. The safety of the house I longed for seemed so far away. My stride grew longer and my steps faster, and then I broke into a jog. I wanted to be home and I wanted to be home now. Soon I tossed the driftwood aside and broke into a run; knees high, elbows pumping. My lungs were on fire and my thighs grew numb with fatigue, yet I ran even faster. It was then I tripped and fell on the rocks and skinned my left elbow and both hands. I lay there gasping and sobbing. I felt the tears running down my cheeks and I felt the wind blow sand into my face. I sat up. The path to our house seemed so far away.

I stood and started walking. I was determined not to run. An almost fifty year old woman had no business running like a child. But I felt the eyes upon me, cold and piercing. In my minds eye I could see the body and face of the man watching me. He had long, greasy hair but bald on top. He was dressed in blue coveralls with a nametag though I could not read his name from the lakeshore. He was in the trees and the distance was too far. He needed a shave. When he smiled his evil smile at me I could see missing front teeth. I could even smell him. His odor was sour and sickening and his breath stunk like rotting flesh.

My lungs hurt, my throat burned, and my thighs ached. I realized I was running again. Running for my life. Running from that awful thing. Suddenly out of nowhere, a large boulder appeared in front of me and again I tripped, skinning my right shin and knee. Fortunately I fell into the sand this time and not into the rocks. I sprawled there on my stomach gasping for breath, the windswept mist from the lake falling on me, making me damp. Sand was in my eyes and on my face.

When my breathing slowed, I rolled over and sat up. Again I looked up and down the shoreline; nothing was there. I was alone. I think I would have welcomed the presence of someone. Someone near to keep me safe. I searched the trees and shrubs with my eyes looking for him. Looking for the man who needed a shave and had bad breath. I didn't see anyone. Just because I couldn't see him didn't mean he wasn't there. Oh, how I wished that Paul had come with me. Paul or Boomer. But I doubted that Boomer would be much protection unless I was in danger from a vicious squirrel. How I wished that someone was here beside me. But there wasn't and I had to get out of this situation by my self. Alone.

My breathing slowed to normal and I jumped to my feet. I made no pretence of walking this time but took off running. Through teary eyes I watched the sand in front of me for more boulders on which I might trip. The wind was to my back and I flew along the sand. I raised my head and looked to see where I was. A long way ahead, I saw the well worn path that led up to the house. I had trod it so many times coming to the lakeshore I loved. But not now. Now I was afraid of it. Would I ever again take a walk by the lake? As I looked at the path I saw it was so far away. I became conscious of the chaffing on both legs and the weight in my pockets. I slowed to a walk, reached into my pockets and pulled out the rocks I had picked up. I flung them into the water. The path was ahead and I had to make it as fast as I could or the most awful thing imaginable would happen to me. Rid of the rocks I started running again, sobbing in fear as I went. Closer and closer came the path. But I was growing weak with exhaustion. Could I make it? Yes, I could, I had to. If I didn't I would be hurt, maybe killed. Maybe cut up and put in the freezer. I could all but feel the cold chill of its breath on my neck.

At last I came to the path and turned up it, still running as fast as my burning lungs and aching legs would allow. I could see the house! I was almost there! I was almost safe.

An exposed tree root caught my right foot and tripped me. I tried to move my feet faster and stay upright but it was not to be. I went sprawling into a pile of last fall's molding leaves. I tried to stand but I was too tired. My arms and hands were numb and wouldn't work. I looked up and saw someone was hurrying down the path toward me. I thought of jumping up, turning and running back to the lake and heading up the lakeshore. But the house was where I wanted to be. Safe. I looked at the house, so close and yet so far away. It wouldn't do me any good anyway. The man, all but running toward me, was between me and the house. I watched him as he drew near and I stifled a scream. I could see his lips moving and knew he was saying something but I couldn't understand him above the pounding of my heart in my ears. "What?" I mumbled. Then he was upon me and reaching for me. I fought him but it wasn't any use. He was too big and too strong.

"Are you alright, Squirt? What's wrong?"

Like a soothing warm shower, relief spread over me as he helped me to my feet. I threw my arms around him and the tears came in earnest. I clung to him and cried.

"Are you hurt, Squirt?" he asked as he picked me up and began carrying me to our house. I said nothing, just buried my head in his massive chest and sobbed.

I felt him climb the steps to the porch as he carried me and I felt his grasp loosen as he opened the door and carried me in. Into the living room he took me and he lay me tenderly on the couch. "Talk to me," he said. "Tell me what's wrong."

I sat up and looked at him. Then I dropped my gaze to my hands clasped between my legs. "I don't know, Paul," I said. "I was walking along the lakeshore having the most glorious time. I found some pretty rocks and put them in my pocket…"

"It figures," he said, sitting on the couch beside me and putting his right arm on my shoulders. "Go on."

"All at once I felt as if someone was watching me. I looked behind me and no one was there. I looked in the trees and couldn't see anyone. Still---I felt as if eyes were upon me. Not just any eyes, but eyes of evil. I was afraid, afraid someone wanted to hurt me. It was the most awful feeling." I turned then and put my arms around him and leaned my head against him as I cried.

"It's okay, Squirt," he said, taking me in his arms and patting me on the back. "Nobody is going to hurt you."

My tears stopped and I felt safe in Paul's arms. Paul would never hurt me, *would he?*

Chapter 3

PAUL WILL BE HOME TONIGHT. Paul will be home tonight, sang through my mind. I sat across the table from Tracy that morning at breakfast. As if she could read my thoughts, Tracy looked up and asked, "Since Paul is coming home this afternoon, is there anything special you would like me to fix for dinner tonight?"

I thought for just a moment and then asked, "Do we have Cornish game hens in the freezer?"

"I think so," she said, standing with her plate and taking it to the sink to rinse off before putting it in the dishwasher. I watched as she boldly walked to the freezer door and calmly opened the door without fear. I admired her courage. I would never be able to do that, after finding my maroon cardigan there. "Yes," she said, "We still have a half dozen. How many should I bake?"

"One for you, one for Paul and one for me. I know I can't eat a whole hen, but I'll save it and eat what's left for lunch tomorrow."

Tracy took three hens out of the freezer and put them in the sink. "Speaking of lunch, Sharon, today is my heavy day. I have an eleven o'clock class and a one o'clock lab. Can you manage lunch on your own? Or should I drive back here from the campus to fix something for you?"

"I know I'm not much of a cook, Tracy, but surely I can jam a slice of bologna between two slices of bread and open a package of potato chips. No need for you to drive clear over here just to fix me a sandwich."

"Thanks, Sharon," she said untying her apron and hanging it in a small closet at the corner of the kitchen. "I'd better be on my way, I have a nine o'clock test and it wouldn't hurt anything if I were a bit early, though I may use up my extra time finding a place to park. Just leave your dirty dishes and I'll take care of them when I get home this afternoon."

"Nonsense, don't worry about it. You just worry about making a good grade on your test this morning."

I poured myself a second cup of coffee from the carafe setting on the table and watched Tracy as she went down the hall to her room. Soon she was back with her arms full of books. She waved at me and went out the door. When I heard a car start and leave, I knew she was on her way to school. I was alone in this big house. I leaned back and relaxed, thankful that it was her heading off to take a test and not me. I knew the nervous, apprehensive feeling quite well. I'd been there and done that. I hated tests but I knew they were a necessary part of the educational system. But for a long time after I graduated I had nightmares about taking tests. Terrible dreams. Sometimes I would dream that even though I had prepared many hours for a test, when I got it and opened it, I didn't know one answer. In some dreams I knew all the answers but as I was filling it out, I noticed everyone look at me. I looked down to see I was sitting at the desk, naked, taking the test. Not a stitch of clothes on. Then there was the dream about opening my math test to find it was not a math test at all, but an English test. Thank goodness, I hadn't had such a dream in years.

I finished my coffee, rinsed my cup, plate, silverware, and put them in the dishwasher. I noticed the dishwasher was full and I started to reach for the soap and to start it, but I stopped. When I washed the dishes they seemed to always be cloudy and icky looking but when Tracy did them they came out all clean and sparkly. She would have time when she got home this afternoon while the hens were baking.

I wandered out on the back porch and looked towards the lake. Strange to say there was no wind and the lake was mirror calm. So calm I could see the tree lines and houses from both sides reflected out onto the middle of the lake.

Boomer spotted me and came running and skidded to a stop in front of me, his whole rear end wagging from side to side in joy. What a wonderful person he must have thought I was. I sat on the edge of the porch my feet on the ground. He reared up, put his feet on my lap and licked my face. I laughed as I hugged him. Soon Miss Calico came out from wherever she had been napping and sauntered to me with all the dignity she could muster. She purred as she rubbed against me and I reached over and scratched her between her ears, well, one ear and where the other ear should have been.

After a while I stood and brushed the cat and dog hair from my sweats looking at the lake. It was so beautiful down there that without even thinking I started down the path, Boomer following. Together we walked between the trees and not even a leaf was moving.

When Boomer and I reached the lake, he ran down to the edge and started lapping water as if he were dying of thirst. Then he waded out into the lake and tried another quick taste. "Boomer, I know the air is warm but the water is still cold, it's still March and hasn't warmed up yet. It's too early to go swimming." At the sound of his name, he looked over his shoulder at me and the waded farther out until water almost covered his back. "I know you have to be a half a bubble off," I said. With those words he came thrashing and splashing out, walked straight over to me and shook.

"You have the whole beach to shake on, yet you have to stand by me to do it," I said in a mock scold. He just grinned and headed on down the lakeshore. Suddenly he stopped and froze, looking toward the trees. A small shiver of fear ran down my spine. But it went away as I neared him and heard the squall of cats. "We have a cat fight, Boomer?" I asked when I was standing next to him. I looked where he was looking and saw the cats, but they weren't fighting. Far from it. A big tom had mounted Mrs. Clemens gray Siamese and she was screaming and giving him love bites as he bred her. "Mrs. Clemens will soon have a litter of kittens," I said. When she did and the kittens were old enough I knew she would be trying to give them away. Maybe I'd take one. Miss Calico was such an ugly cat. It would be nice to have a pretty cat for a change. "Would you like another kitty, Boomer?" I ask him. I know it was my imagination, but I could swear that he nodded his head, yes.

But Boomer freezing and the cat's squalling had upset me. It brought back memories of the last time I was down here. True, this time I had Boomer with me and he would protect me, and then I laughed at the idea. If something scary came out of the brush and trees, he would tuck his mangled tail between his legs and head for parts unknown. "Let's go home, Boomer," I said, turning around and heading up the lake.

I was almost to the path when I became frightened. *This is silly,* I thought. But nevertheless before I knew it, I was running. When I reached the path I turned up it toward the house. When I reached the porch I didn't bother with the steps but leaped onto the patio and ran to the door. Inside the house I turned and locked the door, and then hurriedly I went to the other doors and locked them. Once that was done I went to the living room and sat on the couch gasping for breath.

Feeling safe, I leaned my head against the back of the couch and closed my eyes. The next thing I knew, someone grabbed me by the arm and started to shake me. *He's got me,* raced through my mind. Quickly, I got ready to fight for my life, my eyes popped open and I stared into the face of Tracy.

"Are you okay, Sharon?"

"Okay? Of course I'm okay. What are you doing home so soon?"

"Lab turned out early. It seems as if they ran out of frogs and the ones of us who didn't get one, left. I'll have to work twice as long at next week's lab to make up for it."

"Lab out early?" I asked in confusion. "What time is it anyway?"

"About a quarter to two. Have you had lunch?"

"I don't remember," I said shaking my head. "I must have because I'm not hungry."

"Are you sure you're okay? When I came home I found the doors all locked?"

"Of course I am," I said trying to keep the irritation that I felt from my voice. Why did she keep asking me?

"Then I'll go change clothes and start dinner. I'll start the dishwasher and do some vacuuming while the hens are baking."

"Go ahead," I said, waving her away.

She started toward the kitchen and then stopped and turned. "If I may suggest, Sharon---"

"Suggest away."

"Paul will be coming home soon and well---well, you might want to go take a shower. Looks like you've been out playing in the dirt. What are you doing, making another flower bed?" and then she laughed.

"No, I have been walking down by the lake. But you're right. I'll take a shower soon," I said, reaching over and picking up a magazine and pretending to read. I waited until she had changed clothes, started the game hens baking and had began vacuuming before I said, "I think I'll go take that shower." That way it sounded as if it was my idea.

Showered and dressed I stepped from the bedroom and even in the hallway I could smell the delicious smell of cooking. It made me hungry. Perhaps I hadn't eaten lunch after all. "Anything I can help you with?" I asked from the dining room.

"Yes," she answered pleasantly, "You can stay out of my kitchen."

"I'm pampered, Tracy. Do you know that? You and Paul are going to spoil me if you're not careful."

"I don't think so. If anyone is being spoiled, it's me. You and Paul give me a great place to live, furnish me a car, feed me and give me a salary. When I graduate I'll never find a job that will allow me such a luxurious life. Maybe I'll just stay here after I graduate and do postgraduate work."

"That would be great," I said. "When you leave it's going to be hard to replace you."

"Thank you," Tracy said, her dark skin blushing with pleasure.

I heard the crunch of tires on gravel and turned toward the front door, "Is that Paul?"

"I hardly think so," Tracy said, glancing at the clock, "his plane isn't due into Oklahoma City until three o'clock and it's only two thirty now."

"Mom!" Chris boomed as he opened the door and stepped in. "Is dad home yet?" As usual, he, like his father, filled the room.

"No, not yet. His plane hasn't even landed. But he'll be here in about two hours."

"I can't wait that long. He asked me and Kris to look in on you while he was gone. Has Kris stopped by?"

"No, I haven't seen her."

"Good. I'd hate to be the only one that was negligent. Smells like Tracy is in the kitchen burning something good."

"Stay for dinner, Chris?"

"I can't. I have loads of work to do back at the pharmacy. Had a delivery to make in this area and I told the deliverywoman that I'd do it. I needed a break and was tired of counting pills so I did it. Then I stopped in to see you as I had promised dad. Have to go now."

"Not before you give your old mom a hug."

Laughing, he grabbed me around the waist, lifted me from the floor and I looked up to see the ceiling spin before he sat me back down. "Will that do?" he laughed.

"Very fine, thank you," I said with severity I didn't feel. "You don't have to be quite so boisterous."

He waved at me and went out the door. Soon I heard him leave and I sat in a recliner, leaned back and closed my eyes. The image of my son still burned in my mind.

He and Paul was about the same size with Chris just a little taller and Paul a small bit wider. Chris wasn't very much taller, maybe half an inch or so. But he had my blonde hair, both twins did. But Kris was brown eyed like her father and Chris had my blue eyes. His blonde hair was unruly. I wished Paul were here. I had missed him these past days. But I wouldn't think about that. I'd think of happy things. I'd think of Paul being here, holding me, kissing me, and making me feel safe. I must have dozed because I suddenly dreamed that I again could hear the crunch of tires on gravel. Then I opened my eyes and could hear the heavy steps of Paul as he reached the door. I leaped to my feet and rushed to him as he came in. My dream had come true. He came through the door, grabbed me and again I saw the ceiling spin around. Like father, like son.

I can't remember ever being so glad to see him home. I clung to him all evening but he didn't seem to mind. But that night as we prepared to go to bed, I suddenly felt shy. It seemed as if I were undressing in front of a strange man and not the man who had watched me undress these past twenty-five years. I would have turned my back on him but if I did, I wouldn't have been able to watch him undress which I was delighted to do. To cover my confusion I began to babble. "Were you able to meet a striking red-head while you were in Cincinnati?"

"Didn't even look for one," he said gruffly. "You know I'm a gentleman and a gentleman prefers blondes."

I stepped out of my panties as he carefully took off his briefs. Beyond a doubt he hadn't been with a woman since he had left Monday. Again I was awed that I could still do that to this man. "So you found yourself a cute blonde to keep you company."

"I'll show you what I found." and as quick as a wink he was across the room and before I could blink he picked me up in his arms. Laughing, we tumbled into bed. He ended up on top of me and fell between my open thighs. Without foreplay he entered me but I was ready for him. "If I had found a red-head," he said with a grunt, "or if I had been keeping company with a blonde," and again he thrust with a grunt, "do you think I'd be able at my age to do this?" he thrust again, "or this, or this."

"Nooo," I moaned. For some reason the thought of what I had seen that day while walking the beach flashed through my mind. I was a female Siamese and he was my tom. I covered his shoulders and chest with small love bites. "Noooo," I screamed and he covered my mouth with his. He knew what was coming next and it did. I shrieked into his mouth.

We hadn't even taken time to turn off the lights and after we were spent, even though I had my eyes closed as I stroked him in the afterglow, I felt his eyes on me. Quickly I popped my eyes open and saw he was staring at me. "What?" I asked.

"God, you're beautiful," he said in a horse voice.

"Even though I'm an old broad?"

"Ah, yes, we are both older. It's not often, but there are times when I wish I was young. This is one of those times."

"Why?"

"If I were younger, I could make love to you again. Oh how I want to, those big beautiful boobs really turn me on."

"You'd better look at them all you want to now because they are starting to droop.

I doubt if they will turn you on as much once they hang down past my knees."

Laughing, he gathered me into his arms and I snuggled up to him. After a while, he asked, "Squirt, would you do something for me."

"Sure, just name it."

"If you have time, tomorrow, would you go to Wal-Mart and pick me up a package of briefs? When I started to dress Tuesday morning, a pair of briefs ripped when I started to put them on. The rest of them are so damn thin that I have to be careful not to poke my finger through them and the waistbands are all stretched so much that they will hardly stay up."

"Of course I will, Paul. Can't have you dropping your drawers when I'm not around." I pushed him away and got out of bed.

"Where are you going."

"To turn off the lights so we can go to sleep."

"Better be careful how you walk across the room or you might not get to sleep right now."

Of course him saying something like that I had to swish my fanny back and forth as I walked to the door where the light switch was.

Chapter 4

ALTHOUGH I WAS DRESSED IN only my robe, I was still sitting at the breakfast table visiting. It was such a beautiful day outside. The birds were singing and you could almost hear the leaf buds popping open. It was one of those days.
I don't know why, but I still felt shy with him and last night had seemed a dream come true. He was so handsome and witty and I so much enjoyed his conversation. He made me laugh. Why hadn't I noticed it before? He was my man and I was his woman. I had almost a girlish feeling.
Shyly I kissed him goodbye at the door and clung to him for just a moment before turning him loose. It felt so wonderful to hold him and feel his arms around me. He looked at me in bafflement for just a second before he opened the door and left. I shut the door, turned around and leaned against it and closed my eyes. Suddenly I had the most terrible feeling. A feeling of impending doom. Was this the last time I was to see Paul? Would he have a car wreck on his way to work and get killed. Then I was there; the EMTs were extracting Paul from his squashed vehicle, one bloody piece of him at a time. Nooo, I whispered with my hand to my mouth. I whirled, turned the knob and jerked the door open, but I was too late. His car was already gone.
Don't think about It, Sharon. Think about it and it will happen. Paul only has two miles to drive to get to work. Nothing will happen to him unless you think about it. Think only happy thoughts. Think happy thoughts indeed. It was a most beautiful day. I had to go shopping for Paul. What was it he wanted me to get for him? Oh, yes, briefs. I'd go this morning bright and early. But first I had to shower and get dressed. Couldn't go to town dressed only in a robe. I couldn't go shopping without a shower, especially after last night.

I rushed to our bedroom and saw Tracy had already made the bed. Quickly I dropped the robe and dressed in a pair of nylon warm-up pants with pockets on the side and one on the hip and a t-shirt. I opened the door to the shower and grasped the faucet handle. Then I realized what I was about to do and laughed. I had been so anxious to go shopping for Paul that I had got things backwards. It would work a lot better if I were to shower first and then dress. Laughing at myself, but only slightly embarrassed, no one had seen me. I stepped from the bathroom to the bed where I undressed and lay my clothes carefully on it. Then I went into the bathroom and showered.

As I dressed again I looked out the window at the lake. It was blue with only a few ripples in it. I'd probably need a sweater. I slid the closet door open and started looking for my maroon cardigan. *Damn it, this isn't funny anymore.* Again I went down the clothes rod looking at every item on a hanger. *It wasn't there.* Slowly I went to the bedroom door and up the hallway. I looked at the coat hanging pole in the foyer. It wasn't there. I glanced around the living room but nowhere did I see my maroon cardigan lying on the back of any chair. *Did the sonofabitch put it back in the freezer?* Suspiciously I reached for the freezer handle and then pulled my hand back. I couldn't open it for fear of what I might find. *Don't be stupid,* and I reached out quickly, grabbed the handle and jerked the door open. Just as I squatted to look where I had found it before, I heard Tracy say, "What are you looking for, Sharon? I took a pot-roast out for dinner last night."

I didn't jump at the sound of her voice but I flinched.

"If you don't want pot-roast, I can find something else."

"Pot-roast is fine. I was looking for---*if she doesn't have anything to do with it she's going to think you're crazy if you say maroon cardigan sweater*---to see if we have any ice-cream."

"You want some ice-cream?"

"Not now, but I'll be going to Wal-Mart as soon as I put on my maroon cardigan sweater," and I watched closely to see any reaction. There was none. Either she didn't know anything about my maroon cardigan or she was a very good actress. I had given her an opening and she hadn't reacted, hadn't laughed and said something like 'Now I know why you were looking in the freezer'. I stood and took a few steps away from her and stopped. I turned to face her. "Tracy, I seemed to have misplaced my maroon cardigan sweater. Have you seen anything of it?"

"No, I haven't, Sharon. But I am going to give the house a top to bottom cleaning this afternoon and then when I put the sheets into wash, if you'll help me, I'll flip the mattress on your bed. It has been a long time since we've done that."

"Sure, I'll help you. We can do it first thing in the morning."

"Afraid not, Sharon. Tomorrow is Friday and I have early morning classes. It will have to be in the afternoon."

"Okay by me," I said as I headed down the hall. I'd just have to find another sweater to wear; I couldn't wear my favorite, since I didn't know who had hidden it or where they had put it.

I put on my blue cardigan which was my second favorite, and went outside to my car, a red Pontiac Vibe. It was a beautiful morning and the birds were singing as I got in and started it. I backed out and headed to Wal-Mart, my heart beating with excitement. I was happy and my heart sang with the birds as I drove down the familiar streets. If someone had asked me for directions to Wal-Mart from my house or had asked the directions from Wal-Mart to our house, I couldn't have told them. But I had lived in Stillwater the biggest part of my life and I just knew how to go where I wanted to go.

At Wal-Mart I got Paul's briefs first and then I began to wander up and down the aisles, throwing in an item here and there. Young girls in shorts and on roller skates met me and passed me while I shopped. The store was huge. All of the roller skaters had on were short shorts, a white blouse and the Wal-Mart blue vests as they skated along. College students no doubt, either going after something or returning something to its proper place in the huge store. At the women's section I saw a warm-up outfit like I was now wearing only it was tan and very chic. I found a set that would fit me but to make sure, I tried them on in a dressing room. They did fit, just a little tight across the boobs, but I knew that would make Paul happy so I tossed them in the cart. Soon I grew tired and went to the checkout counter with a cart full and waited in line. When I checked out I saw it was a hundred thirty-three dollars and some cents. I slid the credit card through the slot and signed. Not bad for a package of five briefs, I thought and the thought made me giggle like a young girl. The young lady, whose name, Samantha, I read from her nametag, looked at me questioningly. I didn't take time to explain since there were five or six shoppers waiting on me to move it, I just picked up my bags and left.

I was so happy with a feeling of accomplishment on my way home that my mind drifted and before I knew it I was passing car lots and farm implement companies. I had missed my corner and I was too far north. I whipped into a John Deere parking lot, made a U-turn and headed back out. It took forever to get back onto the busy highway. At last a break in the traffic and I pulled out, but still an angry driver in a blue pickup, honked at me. I thought about giving him the finger as he pulled up close behind me but the day was just too damn wonderful as I drove south. Things looked different coming from a different direction but I had driven the streets of Stillwater many, many times and soon I came to my corner, clicked on the blinkers, slowed and turned west. With a blare of a horn, the driver following me headed on south in his blue pickup. It was then I did give him the finger but he was already past and I doubt seriously that he saw me. But was this the right corner?

Soon I saw I had indeed turned at the right place as I passed familiar buildings. When I got home I saw Tracy was still at class so I took the tags from the clothes I bought and threw them in the washer. I stood there in confusion for a moment trying to remember what to do next. Then I remembered. With a turn on the dial and making the proper settings on the washer, I soon had it running. Sometime this afternoon I'd take a shower and have the new clothes on when Paul came home from work. That should please him. Again I felt like a young girl getting ready for a date instead of an almost fifty year old woman preparing to welcome home her husband. Welcome her husband of twenty-five years. I heard the washer spin out and I went to check. My clothes were washed so I put them in the dryer and on a whim I tore open the package of Paul's briefs and started them washing.

It was then Tracy came home. "I thought you had classes until noon," I said to her when she came through the door.

"I did," she said glancing at her watch. "Its twelve twenty-seven now. I'm going to fix myself a sandwich and then get to work. Do you want me to fix you one?"

"No, I still have part of the game hen you fixed for dinner last night. I'll just have it."

"Want me to warm it up for you? Won't take but a second if I nuke it."

"Sure, that would be nice. Call me when you're ready and I'll eat lunch with you."

The dryer buzzer announced the clothes were dry so I went to the washroom and hung up my new outfit before it became wrinkled. I looked at them and was delighted at how they turned out. So many times clothes look good until you wash them and then----forget it. I put Paul's briefs in the dryer and started them drying.

"Sharon," Tracy called, "I can't find your dinner leftovers. Didn't you put them in the fridge?"

"I'm sure I did. I hope I did. I'll help you look, I'm on my way." I went to the kitchen and we both looked in the fridge, but there was no game hen.

"Maybe you put them into the freezer," Tracy said. "Sometimes I slip up and do that." She reached for the freezer handle and I backed away quickly. "Nope, not in here.

No use looking any farther because if you left it out then I'd be afraid for you to eat it anyway. I'll just fix you a sandwich."

Although Tracy chatted and was good company the thought stuck in my mind like a thorn. *What happened to the game hen? Who was doing this to me and why?*

After lunch I was in the washroom folding Paul's briefs when the front door opened. No knock, no doorbell, the door just opened and someone stepped in. *Is it him? Is that whoever is after me?* I looked for Tracy but she was in the back with the vacuum running. "Mom?" I heard a voice call.

I stepped into the living room and there she was. I didn't recognize her at first, she was all dressed up with makeup on and then I saw it was Kris. Kris with a K. My, she had grown up to be such a beautiful young woman.

She was taller than I was, of course, about everyone is, but she had my blonde hair and John's brown eyes. She had my figure, thin and willowy and big boobs. I knew she turned many young man's eyes and some of their hearts. "Kris!" I exclaimed, and with her long, graceful stride she crossed the floor to me.

"Mom, look what I got," she said after we hugged and held up her left hand. On her ring finger was a ring with diamonds in it.

"It's beautiful, Kris," I said admiring the ring. "So you finally tricked JT into popping the question?"

"Oh, he'd asked me to marry him several times but I kept thinking it over. I knew I loved him but did I want to settle down and get married? Last night I finally said, 'yes'. Can you believe he had already bought the engagement ring and had it in his pocket? Before I could change my mind he grabbed my hand and put the ring on my finger. But he made a promise that after I worked just a little longer as a legal secretary, I would be able to go to OU and finish my law degree."

"When are you planning the wedding?" I asked.

"We haven't set the exact date, but it will be some time in June."

"This coming June?"

"Yes."

"But Kris, this is already the end of March---oh well, there's nothing like a long engagement."

"I know," Kris laughed, "JT and I both believe in long engagements. Two months is long enough, don't you think?"

"I suppose in this case it is. You started going with him when you were a freshman and he was a junior in college and even when he went off to law school, so
you've known him practically all of your life."

"I took a late lunch but it is time for me to get back to work. I'll see you later, Mom," Kris said as she headed to the door and out. Soon I heard the crunch of tires on gravel and she was gone.

I could still hear the vacuum running when I carried Paul's briefs back to the bedroom and put them in his dresser drawer. The bed looked inviting and it had been late before Paul and I went to sleep last night, a perfect excuse for me to take a nap. I lay down and closed my eyes.

Tracy awoke me when she came in with the vacuum. "Sorry," she said, "But it's getting late and I put off this room until last. All of the rest of the house is clean."

"What time is it?"

"Close to four o'clock."

"Goodness, I slept longer than I thought. I'd better get a shower before Paul gets home. I bought a new outfit today and I want to wear it for him."

"So you're not going to put those clothes on after you shower."

"No."

"Then just leave them on the floor. I plan to do the washing after the house is cleaned."

"My, but you are in a domestic mood today."

"This weekend is my weekend off. I plan to head out to Tahlequah tomorrow right after class."

I could smell the pot-roast cooking so I smiled at Tracy and said, "I hope the roast you're cooking is a big one."

"It is," she laughed.

"Good, we'll be eating on it until you get back. Either that or eating out."

"I've eaten your cooking before, Sharon, and I didn't think it was as bad as you make it out to be."

"No, but it's bad," I giggled, going into the bathroom to shower.

After showering and dressing in my new outfit, I went into the living room to wait. I was clean and my face was made up and I sat there waiting for my hero, my knight in shining armor, to return to our castle.

Chapter 5

SUDDENLY, I WAS AWAKE. AWAKE to a beautiful day. I glanced quickly at the clock, rolled out of bed and threw on my robe. It was seven twenty-five and if I hurried, I could catch Paul and see him before he went to work. Hug him goodbye.

Robe on I rushed down the hallway to the kitchen. Only Tracy was there. "Has Paul gone to work already? I asked.

"Just missed him, Sharon. He left not over five minutes ago. I'm running a little behind but what do you want for breakfast?"

"Don't worry about it," I said. "I'll just eat an apple and maybe a banana. Shouldn't eat too many eggs and bacon anyway."

"In that case, before you have breakfast, would you mind helping me flip your mattress?"

"No problem. Let's go do it."

I followed Tracy into our bedroom where she peeled off the blanket and stripped the sheets and pad. She threw the sheets on the floor but Paul and I had two recliners in the bedroom and she carefully placed the pad in one of them. "I washed the mattress pad just last week," she explained, "I think the sheets will be enough for today. Would you hold on just a moment and let me get these sheets washing?"

"Go ahead, you're the one on a schedule, I have all day."

I watched as she gathered the sheets and hurried away. Then she was back and at the side where I slept on the king-sized bed. "Ready?"

"Ready," I answered.

"When I get it upright, you hold it there until I can get over to you. Don't let it tip your way, it will squash you like a bug no bigger than you are. Ready?" she asked again.

"Ready," I answered.

She lifted and was repositioning her hands to lift it above her head when she looked down and said, "My word," and let the mattress down. She went to the foot of the bed, reached between the mattress and box springs and pulled out my maroon cardigan sweater and held it up looking at it.

I didn't say a word, just stood there with chills running down my spine and shaking. *So that is where he hid it. Why?* She started to hand it to me but I couldn't take it. This was *too* much. I backed away with my hands behind my back. She brought it around the bed and tried to hand it to me but I shook my head and backed away some more.

"Since we found it, Sharon, don't you want to hang it up or do you want me to wash it first?"

My mouth was dry and there was a lump of fear in my throat. I was shaking with fear. "Throw it away," I whispered

"What! But it's your favorite. It's the one you have been looking for."

"Not anymore it isn't," I said, feeling tears run down my face. "Throw it away or give it away. I never want to see it again."

She looked at me with concern as she left. I heard her go down the hall to her room, heard her door open as she went in. With tear filled eyes, I blindly made my way to the dresser where I pulled a Kleenex from the box and wiped my eyes and my face. *Who was it and what were they trying to do to me?* I was still standing by the dresser and I felt myself shaking like a leaf when she came back in.

"I put it in my room and I'll keep it for a while then when you ask for it back, I'll go get it."

"I won't," I said. "I never want to see it again."

"Ready to flip the mattress?"

"No. Let's just leave it like it is. It still sleeps well."

"Are you sure, Sharon?" Again her voice was filled with concern. Tracy wasn't in on it, of that I was sure. No one could act that well.

"I'm sure."

"If you will put the sheets in the dryer when they are through washing, I'll come back by here before I leave for Tahlequah and make the bed."

"Nonsense, I'm perfectly capable of making a bed."

"Are you sure you don't mind?"

"I don't mind, but help me put the mattress pad back on."

She grabbed it and flipped it over the bed and we started to work, pulling and tugging. As we worked I said, "As anxious as you are to go home, are you sure there isn't someone else waiting for you besides your mom and dad?

She blushed and I laughed.

"There is, isn't there? Who is it? Tell me his name."

"His name is Pete. I knew him in high school but I didn't date him. He was a geek; you know all into computers and everything. But things have changed; he has filled out and become a good looking man. Pete Christy and I have had a relationship since Christmas."

"Sounds like it's getting serious."

"It might be, but I've been trying to get him to go to school. He's very, very smart and he can make a computer do anything except stand up and salute. But you know and I know that it doesn't make any difference how smart you are, without the diploma you're not going to get anywhere." She looked at the clock and asked, "Is that clock right?"

"Of course it is. It is radio controlled. Should it get off time somehow, it sets itself to the correct time at midnight."

"Oh, my, I'm about to be late to class." She hurried to the bedroom door but stopped before she went out and looked back over her shoulder, "Are you sure you don't want me to stop by before I head to Tahlequah?"

"Nonsense, I'll be alright."

"Are you sure," she repeated, "are you sure you don't want me to stop by and check on you?"

"I'm Okay." Tracy was beginning to irritate me but I didn't let it show. Instead I smiled and said, "Head on out but drive safely and don't be in too big of a hurry to get to your man."

She went to her room and I went to the living room. As she came through the living room I saw she was loaded down. She had an overloaded backpack on her back and her books in her arms. "See you sometime Sunday," she said as she went out the door. She was gone and I was alone. Alone in the big empty house. It hadn't always been empty I remembered. Once it had rang with laughs, shouts, and cries from Chris and Kris. Oh, to have those days back again I thought with nostalgia.

I sauntered into the kitchen, took an apple and a banana from the bowl and walked out to the patio, biting into the apple as I went. Boomer and Miss. Calico joined me as I sat in a patio chair that was pulled up to the table. Boomer reared up with his feet on the arms of the chair and Miss Calico jumped onto the table. Life can't get any better than this, I thought as I held the apple in one hand and scratched Boomer between the ears with the other. My fear at finding the sweater and my nostalgia were gone. I had placed the banana on the table and Miss Calico sniffed it for only a moment then walked over, climbed down into the lap of my robe, curled up and began to purr.

When I had the apple eaten down to the core, I drew back my hand and threw it out under a tree. I laughed when Boomer went scampering after it. He grabbed it with his mouth and then looked at me, his tail wagging. "I don't want it back, Boomer. You can have it." He chomped down on it, spit it out, and came loping back. He lay on the patio at my feet as I ate the banana.

When I was through I set Miss Calico on the table and stood. "Sorry to leave such good companionship," I said, "But I have to go in and get dressed." Boomer wagged his tail but Miss Calico gave me a haughty look as if to say, 'Go ahead and leave. I don't need you anyway'.

I stopped at the washroom and saw the sheets were through washing so I took them out of the washer and put them in the dryer. With the dryer running I headed down the hall to our room to dress. My hand trembled as I opened the door to go in. I trembled in fear of what I would find there. Slowly I opened the door and peeked in. I didn't see anyone. As I stepped inside, nothing jumped out at me and nothing grabbed me. The bed room had once been such a cheerful place, such a happy place, but now it seemed cold and gloomy. So gloomy that I hurriedly slipped on a pair of sweats and a sweat shirt, put on my running shoes, tied them and hurried back out into the hallway closing the door behind me. I went back outside and thought about going to the lake, but when I thought about it I became fearful. I went to the patio and sat down to think. Of course Miss Calico soon jumped on my lap and Boomer got up from where he was sleeping and came over and lay at my feet. Boomer lying at my feet made me feel safer, but not by much. He would jump up and bark if anything threatening came near. Of course he would also bark if he saw a squirrel on the ground and that was the most likely thing he would see.

Why, why was he, she, or they doing this to me? What purpose could it serve, other than frightening me out of my wits? If they were trying to frighten me they were being successful. Here I was, a grownup woman and I was afraid to walk by the lake. Now I only went to our bedroom with fear. I didn't like it! I didn't like it at all! And I felt my cheeks grow warm as anger swept over me. Well, I wouldn't let them; I wouldn't let them do this to me. I'd show them. I jumped to my feet so fast that Miss Calico fell from my lap even though she dug her claws into my sweats and I could feel the scratches on my leg. I rushed to my closet in the bedroom, grabbed the first sweater I could find and then went back outside.

Down to the lake I went, more in defiance than anything else. *I'd show them. I'd show whomever it was that they couldn't scare me.* Boomer was at my side and it gave me a comforting feeling even though I knew he wouldn't protect me from much more than a vicious squirrel.

Of course, as soon as we got to the lake, Boomer had to try to drink the lake dry and then he walked out into it until the water covered his back. He even swam a few strokes and then he came back. And, standing right beside me he shook, as usual. I started to walk down the lake and Boomer ran out in front as I walked, sweeping the shoreline from the trees to the lake to make sure there were no dangerous squirrels ready to attack. It was a beautiful day and even though I felt uneasy, I laughed.

Boomer suddenly froze and stared at a thicket. I looked at his mangled tail and saw it wasn't wagging. There was something in the thicket, something dangerous. I stopped, my heart frozen in my chest. What was it? Was it *him* or *them*? I stood there frozen, tensed and ready to run.

Boomer yelped and turned and ran toward me. I quickly whirled to run back to the house but when I looked over my shoulder I saw what had frightened Boomer. It was a brown and white, fat, tailless poodle puppy only a third the size of Boomer. I stopped, laughed, and knelt as the puppy came waddling toward me. As it drew closer I saw it did have a tail but it was wound tightly up over its back.

'Whose dog was it?' I wondered as I knelt in the sand and it came to me. I thought I knew every dog on the street and every dog in Stillwater but I sure didn't recognize this one. But it was friendly, that was for sure. As it came within reach, I held my hand out to it. It sniffed my hand and then licked my fingers as Boomer tried to hide behind me. Then I saw it wasn't a puppy at all and it wasn't fat; it was female and very, very pregnant. What had made her look fat were the puppies she carried and in fact, she looked starved. She had burrs and sticks tangled into her long, straight hair which spoke for the fact that someone wasn't taking care of their soon to be mother dog. She lay on her stomach at my knees and I went to work pulling the sticks and burrs from her fur. Occasionally she licked my hand.

When her fur was cleaned, I stood and said, "Go back home, whatever your name is," but all she did was sit up on her haunches. I turned and started towards the house. I had gone but a short ways when I looked over my shoulder to see if she was headed home. Here she came, running as fast as her big belly would allow. I stopped turned and faced her. "No," I said sternly, "go back home." She lay down on her belly, her front paws stretched out in front of her and her back legs stretched out behind. She laid her head on her front paws and looked at me with the saddest expression on her face. "Okay, you can come and visit for a while but as soon as I find out where you live, I'm taking you home." She stood then and came to me, her whole rear end wagging frantically. I laughed as she followed us home.

When we reached the porch, she climbed the steps, discovered Boomer's food dish and quickly devoured what Boomer had left. Boomer didn't protest with threatening growls but cowered beneath a tree in the yard and whined.

When Boomer's food dish was empty she looked at me as if to say 'thank you,' and licked her lips. "Poor little thing, you're starved aren't you?" I picked up the dish, took it inside and filled it brim full. When I set it on the porch, she began to eat again. I sat on a porch chair and watched her as she gobbled the food.

When the bowl was half empty she decided she had enough and came to my feet, lay down and went to sleep. Soon Boomer came cautiously upon the porch, sat and looked at the small dog. Then he stood; cautiously he came over and sniffed her and she opened one eye and wagged her curled up tail. She closed her eye and went back to sleep.

Boomer found a warm place in the sun by my chair, lay down, yawned, and closed his eyes.

It was then Miss Calico jumped onto the porch and started her haughty stroll toward me. Then she saw the strange dog. She stopped, her fur on end. She arched her back and hissed. The poodle looked at her and wagged her tail. It was a friendly little dog but Miss Calico didn't trust it yet, and stood there with her back arched. But curiosity got the better of the cat and she began to approach the dog walking sideways. When she was near the poodle, the puppy stood and she jumped. But it reached out its nose and touched hers. This is okay, Miss Calico must have thought, because she began to walk back and forth rubbing against the little dog.

"Nice for you to be friendly to the puppy," I said, "but we can't keep it. It belongs to someone else." But it didn't make much difference to Miss Calico, the poodle had accepted her as a friend and that was good enough for Miss Calico.

I was sitting there watching the interplay between the animals when I suddenly heard the door between the house and the porch open. I jumped and turned. It was Paul. I looked at my watch and saw it was already five thirty. I turned to kiss him as he came and bent over me from the back of the chair.

"What have we here?" he asked, looking down at the poodle at my feet.

"A pregnant poodle. It followed me home from the lake."

"I don't think it's a poodle but some other breed of dog. No, you can't keep it," he said, smiling into my eyes. "Where's Tracy?"

"This is her weekend off, remember. By now she is probably in Tahlequah. As for the poodle, I don't plan to keep it. It's just visiting us until I can find out who she belongs to."

"But it's not a poodle, Squirt."

"To me it is. To me it will always be a poodle."

"But we can't keep it. I think it is an exotic breed and belongs to someone. Where does it live?"

"I don't know."

"You mean you don't know her? You don't know where she lives? I thought you knew every cat, dog, and goldfish in Stillwater."

"I don't know this one."

"She looks like a nice and friendly dog. I'll bet someone is missing her. I'll put an ad in the paper in the 'found dog' column. What are we going to do for dinner since Tracy is gone? Want to eat out?"

"We have plenty of leftovers from last night's dinner. It won't take long for me to warm it up," I said, starting to get up.

"Keep your seat, Squirt, I'll do it."

"You don't even trust me to warm up leftovers?" I laughed.

"It's just that you look so comfortable there and I'm not tired. I had a pretty good day."

He left and before I knew it, he was back at the door telling me dinner was now served.

After dinner we sat on the couch with his arm over my shoulders and watched television. I should say he watched television and I watched the colored lights on the screen and reveled in the sensation of having him near. Feeling the warmth of his body next to mine and the scent of him next to me.

Soon it was time to go to bed and he went to the bedroom first while I locked up the house for the night. Suddenly he was back and said, "The bed isn't made. Where are the sheets?"

The sheets? Had someone stripped the bed and hidden the sheets? My heart pounded and chills of fear ran down my spine. I stood frozen. Then I remembered. "The sheets are in the dryer," I laughed. "I forgot all about making the bed. Just give me a moment and I'll take care of it."

"I'll help you," he said.

Chapter 6

I AWOKE WITH A START, TURNED on my left side to look at Paul, only to find him gone. Maybe he hasn't left for work, yet, I thought and threw the sheet and blanket quickly back. I jumped out of bed, put on my robe and house-shoes and headed towards the kitchen from whence I smelled coffee brewing. There I saw Paul, dressed in a robe and unshaven. He was standing over the stove watching something cook.

"Good," I said, going up to him and putting my arms around him from the back, "You haven't gone to work yet. What are you doing anyway?"

"Cooking oatmeal, and no, I haven't gone to work today. I doubt if I will unless there is a problem."

"Not going to work? Why are you cooking? Where is Tracy?"

"Tracy is probably in Tahlequah, this is Saturday and her weekend off, remember?"

"Yes, it is," I laughed. "Now I remember." But I didn't, I actually didn't. One glorious day just seemed to follow another magnificent day and they all blended together. Tracy was gone which meant I was responsible for lunch and dinner. Thankfully Paul was taking care of breakfast. "If you're cooking oatmeal, are you cooking enough for me too?"

"Of course, Squirt."

"Good, after we eat and dress, do you think we could go on a walk by the lake?"

After a moment's hesitation he said, "Sure, if you want to. I can take my cell phone with me and then if they need me at the plant I'll be in touch."

"Wonderful, but I'm warning you, we will probably stay out until noon and have to have a baloney sandwich for lunch, then I'll warm up the leftover pot-roast for dinner."

"That would be fine but first what do you think of this? We call the kids and see if they can come over this evening. If they can, we'll go out for lunch and I'll pick up some steaks on the way back and burn them for dinner with the kids. If they're busy this evening, then we'll postpone it until tomorrow evening."

"Wonderful," I said. "I'll phone them now."

"The oatmeal is ready. We'd better eat it now while it's still warm."

As we sat down to breakfast I said, "Did you know that Kris and JT are engaged? They plan to be married in June."

"Yes, you told me Thursday when I came home after work and you told me yesterday."

"I'm sorry," I said. "I forget what all I tell you."

Paul laughed, "That's okay. At my age I usually forget what someone tells me so usually you really should tell me again."

After breakfast I rinsed the bowls and put them in the dishwasher. Then I hurried back to the bedroom to get dressed. When I got there, Paul was almost dressed. "You smell something funny, Squirt?" he asked.

I sniffed the air. "No. But that doesn't mean anything. You have a better sense of smell than I do." I went to my closet to get a clean pair of sweats and when I opened the door I caught the smell of a strange odor. It didn't stink but it didn't smell good either. It was a scent, however, that didn't belong in my closet. Oh, well, I would search it out when we came back from the lake.

It was a splendid day as we walked side by side by the lake. The sun was shining brightly and there was very little wind. Only a few ripples ran up the lake. Shyly I reached over and took Paul's hand. It was a joyous day with just Paul and me. Ahead of us I saw a squirrel getting a drink from the lake but Boomer saw it too. Barking, he took off after it and chased it up a tree. I laughed.

"There goes a lucky squirrel," Paul grinned. "He's lucky that Boomer is too fat to run fast."

"And Boomer is lucky that he didn't catch it. You can look at him and tell he's disappointed but he has forgotten the last time he caught a squirrel he ended up with a bloody nose and lip. It wasn't squirrel blood either."

"Did you call the kids, Squirt?"

I took a few steps trying to remember and then I stopped. "No, I forgot. Well, I'm pretty sure I didn't."

"Don't worry, I'll call them now." He reached into the pocket of his sweat-suit and took out his cell phone. We found a log and sat on it while he dialed. "Hey, Chris, are you counting pills today?---You have the day off---How would you like to come over for dinner tonight, I'm planning on grilling some steaks---Yeah, sure, bring Tiffany over, let her taste one bite of your ole man's cooking and you'll never be able to chase her off.---Yes about five or sooner if you want to.---see you then." Next he dialed Kris, "Yes, Kris, do you and JT have plans for this evening?---Good, why don't you bring JT over for dinner, I'm grilling steaks.---Who says red meat isn't good for you?---Of course you'll be over, that's what I thought. See you around five or earlier." He pushed the 'end' button and put the phone in his pocket. "They are both coming so we will eat lunch downtown and then all you have to do is bake six potatoes. I'll even help you with that."

We walked on down the lake shore. Out in the lake, the fountain was spraying gloriously and I felt proud. It was beautiful and I had something to do with it. But what?

Soon, all too soon, Paul looked at his watch and said, "By the time we get back to the house and shower, it will be time for lunch. Ready to go back?"

"If we must," I said looking at him. We turned around and started retracing our steps. When we left the lake shore and started up the path to the house I stopped, clutched his arm and said, "Thank you, Paul. Thank you for a most glorious morning. I've had a most wonderful time."

"You're welcome, Squirt, I had a good time myself. The only thing that would make the morning better is if you'd shower with me," he said grinning wickedly.

"Then don't lock the bathroom door. You can't ever tell."

When we reached the house, Paul went on in but I glanced at Boomer's dish and saw it was empty. I took it into the house, filled it, and set it down outside. The poodle came to me wagging her curled up tail in thanks and began to eat.

I went back into the house and feeling wicked I went to the bedroom. I could hear the shower running as I stripped off my sweats. I tiptoed to the bathroom door, opened it quietly and stepped in. With the shower running, Paul didn't hear me. I hollered "Boo!" he jumped and I stepped in.

"I was just kidding, Squirt," he said taking me in his arms and pulling me close. But he wasn't.

By the time we got to Hung Cho's, a Chinese restaurant that served an all you could eat buffet, the lunch crowd had pretty well gone and we almost had the restaurant to ourselves.

After eating, Paul and I stopped by Heartland's and he picked out six rib-eye steaks and I picked out six baking potatoes. After me throwing in an item here and an item there as we walked up and down the aisles, we checked out and went home.

At home after Paul put the steaks in the fridge, I put the six baking potatoes in the sink and he and I went to work on them, washing, scrubbing and wrapping them in tinfoil. I looked at the clock and saw it was already three thirty so we put them into the oven to bake. Paul opened a bottle of wine while I got down the glasses and he took the bottle out to the patio while I took the glasses. We were soon joined by Miss Calico, Boomer, and the stray poodle.

Miss Calico jumped onto the table, walked across and dropped into Paul's lap and Boomer lay down at his feet. The stray dog reared up and put her front paws on my leg and I reached down and picked her up. "You're a heavy little dog," I said as she tried to lick my face.

"Don't get too attached to her, Squirt. I forgot to call an ad into the paper this morning and it's too late now. Tomorrow is Sunday but Monday morning I'll call it in. If I should forget, you will remind me, won't you?"

"Of course I will," and I winked at him.

The evening passed, golden minute by golden minute. Before I knew it, Kris and JT walked out onto the patio hand in hand. Kris spotted the wine, turned and went back into the kitchen. She was soon back out with two more glasses and poured herself and JT a glass of wine. I wanted to say, 'you're too young,' but I didn't. She was twenty-three and I never thought I'd do it, but I longed for the days when she was still a teenager and in high school. Nostalgia, a lot of it going around nowadays.

Soon Chris and Tiffany came through the house and Paul had to go after another bottle of wine.

"What are we having tonight besides steaks, Mom?" Kris asked.

"We have some potatoes baking."

"Got anything in there to make a salad out of?"

"I suppose, I'll go in and see."

"Keep your seat, Mom. Come on, JT, let's go in and see if we can stir up one mean salad." Off to the kitchen they went. When they came back out they had a most beautiful salad in the salad bowl. Paul took one look at it, started the broiler and put on the steaks.

The sun set with red, gold, and purple streaks above the trees in the western sky. We ate and visited with our children and we visited with them as one adult visits with another. We shared information about their lives, hopes and dream and they shared with us our dreams. It seemed strange,

strange to accept our children as men and women in the world.

I didn't talk much, I let Paul and the others do the talking, but I listened and I was delighted with what I heard. And if a tear ran down my cheeks once in a while, it was a tear of happiness.

Too soon, all too soon, it ended. We watched a new moon set and the stars came out. A million stars in a black velvety sky. Kris and Tiffany helped carry in the dishes, rinse them, and put them in the dishwasher. It gave us a chance to talk girl talk. Although she probably didn't realize it, Tiffany dropped a word or a sentence here and there that made me realize that she cared more for Chris than Chris cared for her. I hoped my son would not break her heart. I thought I was the only one who realized it and I was surprised, after she and Chris left, to hear Kris say, "I hope that brother of mine realizes what he has with Tiffany and doesn't throw it away and hurt her."

Then JT and Kris left and Paul and I were again alone.

"Ready to go to bed, Squirt?" Paul soon asked after Kris and JT left.

"You randy old man you," I said, taking his hand and leading him to the bedroom.

"I mean, go to bed to sleep. After all I am fifty-three years old and though that's not old by today's standards, I'm not a youngster by any means."

"I'm ready to sleep, too, Paul. It has been such a splendid day."

When we were in bed, I kissed him goodnight, and after a few more kisses, I turned my back to him and he held me. I drifted off to sleep with him holding me. I drifted off to sleep feeling safe from *Them.*

I awoke when Paul got out of bed and watched him put on his robe through squinted eyes pretending to still be asleep. As soon as he had slipped on a robe and left, I jumped out of bed and hurried to the shower. When I was dry, I went to the closet for a clean pair of sweats and a sweat shirt. While I was selecting my clothes I noticed the odor in the closet had became stronger. I sniffed all down my clothes and couldn't smell where it was coming from. I then realized it was coming from the shoe boxes stacked on the floor. I'll check it out later, I thought as I quickly dressed. I don't want to spend one minute away from Paul.

"I'm going to have to change the ad for the stray dog," Paul said when I got to the kitchen where he was watching the coffee drip down into the glass pot.

"Why? Why not just put in 'A Stray Pregnant Dog Found.'"

"She's on the porch eating. Go look at her."

I stepped out onto the porch and saw that she was busily eating. I stepped back in and looked at Paul as I said, "She's not pregnant anymore. She had her puppies last night. Do you know where she had them?"

"No. I thought I'd leave it up to you to find them."

I rushed to the cabinet, found a small bowl and filled it about half full of milk. When I went out and set the bowl of milk on the porch, she abandoned the dry dog food and came to the milk. She began to lap at it greedily. "Where are your babies?" I asked when the bowl was empty. She looked at me cautiously. "You can trust me. I won't hurt them. Where are your babies? Let me help you take care of them."

She left the porch and I followed her.

Proudly she led me to where the porch joined the house and she crawled under the porch. I got down on my hands and knees and looked. Three little fur balls were shivering there in the morning coolness. She curled up around them and they began to nurse.

I jumped to my feet, ran into the house, and to the utility room. There I found a cardboard box just the right size. In the rag-pile I found three, old, worn-out towels and put them in the box and straightened them out to make a bed. Back outside, I saw the puppies had nursed but the momma was still curled up around them and they were still shivering. I squeezed under the porch where I could reach the puppies. "Those are sure beautiful babies," I said as I picked one up admiring it. That was okay with her, I could pick them up and look at them, but she became agitated and started whining when I put the puppy in the box. She was all but frantic by the time I had the third fuzz ball in the box and the puppies started whining.

I crawled out from under the porch pulling the cardboard box out with her following. She followed me into the house as I carried the box, at times walking on her hind legs trying to see into it. I took them to Paul so he could see them. "Aren't they cute?"

"What are you going to do with them now?"

"Put them in the spare bedroom. I'll just keep them there until the weather warms up. It won't be long, April will soon be here."

"Ah, well," Paul said, "puppies are better than pigs. I remember when I came home one cold winter day and found baby pigs in the bathtub. You had brought the baby pigs into the house for Ed Bogart when their mother died."

"Much better than pigs," I said wrinkling my nose.

"Do you still want me to call the ad into the paper?"

"Definitely," I answered. I felt very safe in saying so. Paul accused me of knowing every dog in our neighborhood but he was only partially right. I knew not only every dog in the neighborhood but every dog in Stillwater and the surrounding area. I knew most of them by name. I had never seen this dog before. I knew no one would answer the ad.

Chapter 7

AFTER EATING BREAKFAST DRESSED in only my robe, I saw Paul off to work and took Lady a half a bowl of milk. I couldn't call her 'the stray dog,' she was a mother now and needed to be treated with dignity, so I called her Lady. I laughed as she lapped at it. However, she only drank half of it then went to the door and wanted out. After letting her out, I stood by the door and watched her because I knew as soon as she had taken care of business she would want back in.

As I stood there looking out I saw the red streak of a cardinal as it flew from a juniper to a redbud which was about to burst into bloom. What a beautiful day, I thought, and I looked forward to getting dressed and going out. Spring was in the air and it was calling me.

Lady came to the door, sat down and raised one front paw to scratch on it. Laughing, I let her in. I followed her as she headed down the hall, turned into the spare bedroom, and jumped into the cardboard box with her pups. She sat there looking at me until I went in and looked at her babies, then she curled up around them and they began to nurse. "My, they have grown overnight and they are such pretty babies," I said and then turned and went to the bedroom to dress.

I heard Tracy's car start and she left as I hurried to the closet. I was in a hurry to get outside and enjoy the day, but when I opened the closet door the strong odor assailed me and I knew I couldn't enjoy myself outside until I found out where the smell was coming from.

Quickly I threw off the robe and dressed. I didn't bother to put on shoes but sat on the closet floor barefoot with just my socks on. I picked up the nearest shoebox and opened it. It contained my high-heels for formal wear. I had owned this particular pair for years yet they looked like new. I hated high-heels and only wore them when I had to, and then only if someone could put them on me while I was kicking and screaming. I put them back in the box, put the lid on and set them aside. The next box I opened was a pair of sandals. I lifted them out and looked at them. They were used more than the high-heels, but not by much. They were second in the category of my least favorite footwear. Like the high-heels, I put them back in the box and put them aside. I was beginning to enjoy myself looking at shoes I so seldom wore.

I opened the next box and in it was a pair of new running shoes. Why hadn't I worn them? I couldn't remember buying them. But maybe I had and maybe they were too small or too large. I slipped one on and tied the laces. It felt like it fit. It felt good. I put the other one on and tied the laces. It too fit and felt good. I crawled out of the closet and walked around the house. Yes, they felt good, why hadn't I worn them before? I went back to the closet and again sat on the floor. The next shoe box didn't have shoes in it at all, but old junk like shoe strings, rubber bands and other things I had saved. Need to sort through it, keep the stuff I would use and throw the rest away. As I looked at the tangled up stuff I wondered, what use will I ever have for a finger splint? I remembered hurting myself and the doctor made me wear it, but that had been a once in a lifetime event.

But not today, it was a cloudy, drizzly day project and today the sun was shining. I put the lid on it and put it behind me so that when I put things back on the floor of the closet, it would be on top. I lifted the next shoebox and could tell I was getting close. I put my nose close to the box and sniffed. Yes, it stunk. Probably I had put a pair of shoes in it while they were still wet and they were mildewing. Carefully I eased off the top of the box and it was as if I had taken of the lid off a stink box. I looked in, dropped it, jumped to my feet and screamed. I ran to the bathroom where I threw up. In my mind I could still see what was in the shoebox. The piteous, molding, rotting remains of a Cornish game hen.

After washing my face, I went to the kitchen and found a plastic trash bag. Steeling myself, I went back to the bedroom, picked up the horrid shoebox, holding my breath, and dropped it into the plastic bag. I tied the top tightly closed, carried it out to the trash can and disposed of it. That done, I stood there for a moment breathing deeply of the fresh air.

Back inside, I picked up a bottle of deodorizer, took it to the closet and sprayed. Then I went to the living room to sit and think. *Who was doing this to me? Why were they doing this to me? They had no right to put me through this. It was sickening.* Anger was boiling in me; hot, red lava from a volcano. I jumped to my feet, opened my mouth and screamed in rage. Lady came running to me and looked at me with concern as I stood there in the middle of the living room, turning around and around and screaming.

Finally the anger was gone and all I felt was numb. Lady still sat in the living room with me. As she sat there and looking at me I asked, "You ready for your milk, girl?"

I went to the kitchen, got down a bowl, and filled it half full of milk. She walked behind me as I went to the spare bedroom. "Why, someone has already given you milk this morning, Lady. That was sweet of them. I wonder if it was Tracy or Paul. I bet it was Paul. He has a soft spot in his heart for animals." I set the milk on the floor by the other bowl and went back to the living room.

I felt numb. I felt dead. Here I was walking, breathing, and talking, but nevertheless, I was dead. I was also tired. So very, very tired. I sat in a recliner, lifted the footrest and reclined it back as far as it would go. I closed my eyes but quickly opened them when the image of the rotting game hen flickered on the back of my eyelids. I stared at the ceiling. Slowly my eyes drooped shut but opened again quickly when I saw the rotting game hen on my eyes. I half sat and half lay there and stared at the ceiling. *Why, oh why, was someone doing this to me. I couldn't fight it much longer. In fact I wasn't going to fight it any longer. I give up.* Suddenly I heard someone scream, "I give up. I'm not going to fight you any more. Do whatever you wish, I give up." Then suddenly I realized it was me screaming. I reached to the Kleenex box on a table by the chair, pulled out a handful and began to sob. By the time I quit crying I was completely exhausted. Again I leaned back and closed my eyes. I didn't see anything with my eyes closed, only blackness.

I was dimly aware when I heard car tires crunch on gavel. *He, it, she, they are here. They have come to finish me off.* The door opened and I glance in that direction to finally see who it was, and saw it was Tracy home from class. I turned back and closed my eyes. I heard her set her books down and then she was beside me.

"Are you sick, Sharon?"

"No, I've just given up."

"Given up on what?"

"Nothing."

I felt her hand on my forehead and she said, "It doesn't feel like you have a fever. What do you want me to fix you to eat for lunch?"

"Nothing."

"I'm going to fix myself a ham and cheese sandwich. Want me to fix you one."

"No. I'm not hungry."

I heard her turn and leave and I opened my eyes to see her go into the kitchen. She was shaking her head. I closed my eyes again and saw nothing but misery. I might as well be dead, the future held nothing more for me. I had done my job here on earth. I had raised two wonderful children. What more was there left to do.

I heard Tracy in the kitchen as she made her sandwich and then it grew quiet. I knew she was eating. But I heard her when she ran water to rinse off her plate and I heard her put it into the dishwasher and I heard her close the door. Today was Monday and I heard her gathering up clothes and soon the washer was running. Then all was quiet. I lay there, doing nothing and thinking of nothing. The house was quiet, as quiet as a tomb.

I heard Lady whine at the foot of my chair and I opened my eyes and looked at her. As soon as she saw me looking at her, she ran to the door and wanted out. Wearily I got up and opened the door for her. She dashed out and I stepped out behind her. The day which had started out so beautifully golden was now black. The sun still shown and there was very little wind, but the day was black anyway.

When Lady had her business taken care of and was ready to go inside I was more than willing. She ran to her room and I went to the kitchen. I had just gotten down a bowl to give her some milk when Tracy came in. She saw the bowl and asked, "So you're hungry now? What are you making yourself?"

"No, I'm not hungry. I was just going to give the dog some milk since she's nursing."

"Sharon, she already has two bowls of milk in there. One is about gone but the other has hardly been touched."

"Oh, did you give her some milk?"

"No, but you must have."

"If I did I don't remember it. I don't know why, I haven't done anything, but I'm tired, Tracy."

"You must have done something. When I went in to make your bed, I saw shoe boxes scattered out on the floor of your closet. You must have cleaned your closet."

"Yes, I did that," and the image of the rotting game hen flashed to mind. "But that isn't enough to make me as tired as I am."

"You could be coming down with the flu or something. I'll put the shoeboxes back in your closet if you don't mind how they are arranged."

"Would you please? I don't care. I don't care how they are arranged."

"Of course I don't mind," Tracy said. Also while I'm thinking about it, I took some hamburger out of the freezer to thaw. What do you want me to do with it? I can make meatloaf, spaghetti, or hamburgers for dinner, or anything else you should want as long as it takes hamburger," and she laughed.

"I don't care. Make whatever you think Paul would want. I don't feel like eating."

"You'd better go to bed, either that or crawl back into the recliner."

"Thanks, Tracy. I think I will. But I think I'll choose the recliner." I couldn't go back into the bedroom. Alone. I just couldn't."

I sat back down in the recliner, raised the footrest and reclined it back as far as it would go. For a while I just lay there looking at the ceiling and listening to Tracy as she prepared dinner. Then my eyelids drooped shut and I didn't hear anything else until with a start, I felt something jump on my lap. I opened my eyes and saw Lady's tongue reaching for my face. Laughing, I hugged her to me and after licking my face and hands she curled up on my lap and went to sleep. She was warm and I felt the love emitting from her. I again closed my eyes and was dimly aware when she jumped down. Then back to sleep. I heard the back door open and opened my eyes. I saw that Tracy had opened the door to let Lady out. Soon I heard the back door open again but I didn't even bother to look. I knew Tracy had let her back in.

When I heard the crunch of tires on gravel I opened my eyes and looked at the clock. It was just a little after five thirty and I knew it was Paul coming home from work. I wanted to jump up and run to the door to meet him but I just didn't have the energy. I just sat there watching the door and soon I saw it open and he came in.

For a moment he stood there and looked at me, concern on his face. Then he asked, "Are you okay, Squirt?"

"I'm not sick," I said. "I'm just so very, very tired."

"You're probably low on iron. You haven't had a physical for over a year now. Tomorrow you should call Dr. Stringer and set up an appointment to get a physical."

"I will," I promised and held my arms open as he came toward me. He hugged me and kissed me and then stepped back.

"You don't seem to have a temperature. What did you do today?"

"Nothing, much. Just let Lady out and then let her in. Let her out and then let her in."

"Lady?"

"Yes, that's what I named the stray poodle."

"Shouldn't have named her, Squirt. I placed the ad in the paper this morning and they'll start running it in the morning. As well behaved and as good a dog as she is, she belongs to someone and they'll soon come and get her."

"I know, but until they do I have to call her something besides 'stray dog'," I said. But even as I said it I knew they wouldn't. I had never seen her anywhere in Stillwater. No, someone was passing through, they stopped at the lake, she had jumped out, and when they left, they had left without her. Lady was mine and she was here to stay.

I wasn't hungry at the dinner table but nevertheless I took a small bit of meatloaf, green beans, and scalloped potatoes. I picked at my food while Tracy and Paul ate and talked. I only said something when they asked me a question. I went to bed early and surprisingly enough fell right to sleep.

The next morning I awoke before Paul and I awoke to a beautiful day. The morning was calm and the sun was shining brightly. I could hear the birds singing in the tree tops. I eased out of bed so as not to wake Paul. His alarm would go off soon enough and then he would get up. I went to the window where I could see the redbud and saw it was in full and glorious bloom. I quietly dressed, put on a sweater and walked to the kitchen where Tracy was drinking coffee. I grabbed a cup, filled it and pulling my sweater close, I stepped outside. I looked at the redbud trees in the back and stepped back inside. "When is your first class, Tracy?"

"Ten o'clock, why?"

"You've got time; you simply have to come outside. You simply have to see this."

She got up, brought her coffee and came outside with me. "See, the whole world in pink with redbud blossoms. Sniff the air, you can even smell them. Isn't it glorious?"

"Yes, they are. You seem to be feeling much better today."

"Oh, I am. A day like today makes me want to burst with happiness." I heard lady scratching on the door so I went to it and let her out. She reared up and put her front feet on my knees. I picked her up and she began to lick my face and I laughed. Soon she was squirming to be put back down so I did. She went to take care of business and then wanted back in so I let her in. Tracy and I went to the chairs and sat down. We sat on the porch drinking coffee and tasted the morning.

Soon Paul joined us and Tracy went in to cook our breakfast. "You seem to be feeling better today than you were yesterday, Squirt."

"I am, Paul, I'm feeling much, much better. Isn't it a fabulous day?"

"Yes, but you had still better call Dr. Stringer and make an appointment for your hundred thousand mile check up."

"I will," I promised, but I thought, maybe I will and then maybe I won't.

Tracy came to the door and told us breakfast was ready. Paul, being always the gentleman, stood aside and let me enter first. The kitchen and dining room were warm so I stripped off my sweater and started to put it into the cupboard.

"Sharon, what are you doing?" Tracy asked.

"I don't need a sweater in here it's so warm. I'm just taking it off and putting it up."

"The sweater certainly doesn't go in the cupboard. Let me have it and I'll go hang it on the coat tree."

It was then I realized what I was doing and I was embarrassed. But I laughed nonetheless. "What was I thinking?" I said. "No, I'll hang it up and then watch out. Don't get between me and the table because I'm ravenous."

Tracy waited until I was back and sitting at the table before she joked, "Paul, you and I are going to have to keep an eye on that girl when spring is in full flow. You and I both know how she gets each spring."

"I'll try to behave, but spring is such a splendid time of the year," I said.

"According to you, so is summer, fall and winter," Paul said. "But I wouldn't have you any other way."

Chapter 8

I WAS HAPPY. I WAS NO LONGER AFRAID. *He, She, Them*, had given me their best shot and I had survived. I didn't phone Dr. Stringer for an appointment and no one came for Lady. Saturday finally came and after begging, wheedling and coaxing, I got Paul to go to the lake with me. Of course Boomer went to protect us from vicious squirrels and Lady followed us a short distance, but then she had to go racing back to her pups. I watched her until she was out of sight and then laughing, I joined Paul. Soon I heard her barking at the door and then it grew silent. I knew that Tracy had let her in.

It was such a wonderful, glorious day down by the lake and Paul was with me. Boomer was ahead of us doing his job of protecting us. He swept the ground from the lake into the trees, his mangled tail held high. "With Boomer out before us we have to be safe," I said to Paul.

"I'm sure," Paul laughed. "A great and noble beast that Boomer. But then we would be safe here even without Boomer."

"Uh-oh," I said when I saw Boomer suddenly freeze and glare at a small bush. "Boomer has spotted something dangerous."

Suddenly a squirrel burst from the brush and Boomer started after it. The squirrel passed up several perfectly good climbing trees before he went up one. "That squirrel is playing with Boomer, Paul."

"Why do you say that?"

"Didn't you see it? He ran by several good trees before it climbed one."

"That doesn't mean he was playing with Boomer, not according to what I've read or heard. It seems that when a young squirrel first comes down from a tree and starts exploring the world, if something frightens it, it runs up the nearest tree. Whatever has frightened it goes on by and the young squirrel is safe. It gives credit of its safety to that particular tree. Then again something frightens it and it goes to the same tree and climbs it. Again it is safe. Time after time when the squirrel becomes frightened, it runs to that particular tree. The world of squirrels is a very dangerous world. Next to rabbits, they are a carnivore's favorite food so there is a lot out there to frighten the squirrel. The tree becomes its safe tree. Every time the squirrel gets frightened, it runs to that particular tree and it is safe. No other tree will do because it knows it will be safe in its 'safe tree'."

"Is that true?"

"According to what I read or heard, it is."

"I'll have to remember that. I didn't know squirrels were that smart?"

"It's not always smart for the squirrel. If it is on one side of a street and its 'safe tree' is on the other and a coming car frightens it, the squirrel will dash across in front of the car going to its tree. Sometimes the squirrel doesn't make it and you see a dead squirrel on the pavement."

"Poor squirrel," I said.

We had walked down by the fountain and suddenly I felt frightened. I was a squirrel and I was a long way from my safe tree. "Are you about ready to go back?" I asked Paul, clutching his arm.

"Sure, but we haven't walked all that far. You're not getting sick on me, are you?"

"No, no, I'm just suddenly tired. Like a squirrel, I want to go to my 'safe tree'."

Paul looked at me for a long while but I smiled at him, hiding the fear I felt. We turned and started walking up the lakeshore. The blooming redbuds, which had been so gorgeous walking down, suddenly looked gray. The sky was gray and so was the water in the lake. The sun was still shining but the world had changed. It was no longer golden, it was gray. Paul said something to me but I didn't understand it. "What?" I asked.

"I asked if you made an appointment to see Dr. Stringer."

"No, but I'll call him as soon as we get back to the house."

"You can call him but he won't answer. Today is Saturday, remember?"

"I'll call him Monday then," I said. But I said it just to make Paul happy. I said it to make him feel better. I had no right to ruin his weekend. Deep down, I knew I wouldn't call on Monday. I knew I wouldn't ever call Dr. Stringer unless I was sick.

By the time we got to the house, I was more than tired, I was exhausted. A north wind had picked up and it had blown away all of my energy. "You had better go inside and lay down. You don't look good, Squirt, your face is gray."

"I think I'd rather go into the living room, sit in the recliner, get my feet up, and recline it back as far as it will go."

"Have at it, Squirt," he laughed.

A cup of coffee would taste good, I thought as I went from the patio into the kitchen. I poured myself a cup and went to the living room. I set the coffee on the table to the right of my recliner and sat down. I reclined the chair as far back as it would go and brought the foot rest up. When I was comfortable I looked up at the ceiling. The gray tile of the ceiling. I had the most terrible feeling, the feeling of impending doom. Not just for me, but for everything I loved; my whole world. I closed my eyes and kept them shut so I wouldn't have to look at it when it happened.

I felt something jump on my lap and I jumped. I opened my eyes and looked. A strange poodle was sitting on my lap, her paws on my chest and she reached up and licked my face. I laughed at the friendly little dog. Who was she and where had she come from. I saw from her tits that she had puppies somewhere and that she had just nursed them. She dropped her front paws from my chest to my lap, curled up and occasionally licked my hand. Yes, she was friendly and I wouldn't mind keeping her, but if I did, what would I name her. Lady came to mind, but I already had a poodle named Lady.

With a start I looked at her more closely. Why, this was Lady on my lap. Now I remembered her. She had three puppies in a cardboard box back in the spare bedroom. I suddenly grabbed her with both arms and hugged her tightly. It was then the tears came.

"Sharon, your lunch is ready," Tracy said.

"I'm not hungry."

"What's wrong, Sharon? You're crying."

"Nothing," I said reaching for a Kleenex, wiping my eyes and blowing my nose.

"I'd better go get Paul," Tracy said and left.

"Squirt, you have to eat. You've lost weight."

"I'm just too tired to eat."

"Maybe if you eat you will get your strength back. Tracy has fried us a big platter of shrimp."

Darn that Paul anyway, he knew shrimp was my favorite. He was trying to tempt me into eating. If I had been less tired or more hungry, it would have worked. "Paul, you and Tracy go ahead and eat. If I get hungry I'll come in and eat." I closed my eyes and felt him go away. I could hear Paul and Tracy talking as they ate lunch and I missed the companionship more than I missed the food. Lady got down from my lap and left, and then I was all alone in my recliner in the living room. I heard Tracy laugh and a fit of jealousy ran through me. Paul was supposed to make me laugh, not her. But then it passed quickly. What difference did it make? I didn't really care.

I must have gone to sleep but awoke when I felt someone take my hand. I opened my eyes and saw Paul had brought a kitchen chair into the living room and was sitting facing me holding my hand with a look of concern on his face.

"Are you sure you're okay, Squirt?"

"I'm okay, Paul. Just tired."

"But that's not like you. You might be small but you're vigorous. You've always had more energy, pep, and get up and go than ten other people combined."

"That was when I was younger; I've gotten a little older if you haven't noticed."

"Yes, haven't we all? Don't worry about calling Dr. Stringer and making an appointment."

"Good. I'm glad you realize that I don't need to see a doctor. I'm glad you realize that I'm not sick."

"Nothing of the kind, Squirt. I'm calling from the office Monday morning and setting up an appointment for you."

Oh, darn! I thought closing my eyes. There is no way out of this one. I could soon look forward to being poked, needles stuck in my arm, and all kinds of messy things. But then Paul was only doing it because he loved me and with that thought I was bathed with warmth. I opened my eyes again and looked at him, "Paul, tell me the story about the squirrel."

"The story about the squirrel?"

"Yes, the one you told me this morning about the squirrel and his safe tree. But stop before the last part where he runs across the street in front of the car."

"Oh, that," he laughed. "When a squirrel first comes down to explore his world and he gets frightened, he runs up the nearest tree…"

On and on his deep voice rumbled and I closed my eyes and it relaxed me and made me feel all fuzzy and warm inside. Then his voice stopped and I opened my eyes and looked at him.

"This is my safe tree," I said first patting the chair and then his hand. "Here in this comfortable chair and you holding my hand, I'm all warm and safe." He looked me in the eyes and smiled at me. The concern was gone and his eyes reflected love.

Suddenly I felt not only loved and safe, but I also felt happy. I looked through the window into the back yard and saw the afternoon sun was shining brightly and the wind had died down. The world was golden again. I was no longer tired. I was bursting with energy. I couldn't believe from the way I felt now that I had been as tired as I had been just before lunch. Paul turned loose of my hand, stood and took the chair back to the kitchen. I dropped the footrest and stood. I started to the spare bedroom to check on Lady and her pups but Lady met me in the hallway and wanted out. I took her to the porch door opened it and stepped outside. She followed me. It was so nice and calm on the porch that I found a chair and sat down. The world was so beautiful and such a wonderful place to be. The rest of Saturday was wonderful. A golden, warm, fuzzy day.

Sunday passed in a golden glow and being with Paul made it all so wonderful. But Monday, I awoke tired. I looked at the clock and saw it was already a little after eight. Paul had already gone to work so I just lay there resting.

Tracy came in and said, "Sharon, I have to go to class pretty soon and I need to fix your breakfast. What would you like?"

"I'm not hungry, Tracy. Go on to class. I'm going to lay here and rest for a while. If I decide to eat later, I'll just have a bowl of cereal or something."

"Are you sure?"

"Yes, I'm sure."

"Are you sick or something?"

"No, I'm not sick, Tracy. I'm just tired and sleepy. Go to class. Get, get, get."

She left then, but I didn't hear the latch click and knew she hadn't closed the door tightly behind her. But what difference did it make. I tried to go back to sleep but I wasn't sleepy so I lay on my back, stared at the ceiling and rested.

Perhaps a half an hour passed when from the corner of my eye I saw the bedroom door begin to open. *It will soon be over, He, She, It or them are coming in to get me,* I thought. I felt my heart began to hammer in my chest. The door eased open a little more. *At last I will see who He, She, It is. I will soon know who has been putting me through all of this.* The door opened even more and I held my breath. There was no one in the house but me. *Or there wasn't supposed to be.*

I let my breath explode out with laughter when Lady jumped onto the bed, came bouncing across the bed and started licking my face. I grabbed her in my arms and held her, laughing. "You scared the daylights out of me, Lady. You frightened me when you opened the door and came in." She wiggled loose, sat down beside me and began to whine. "What's wrong? What do you want? Oh, I know, I bet you're ready for your milk."

Lady jumped down when I rolled out of bed. I put on my robe. She followed me to the kitchen where I got down a bowl and poured it half full of milk. She stood on her hind legs and jumped around and then followed me to her room where I put the bowl on the floor. After dancing around some more in her way of saying thank you, she put her head in the bowl and began to lap. I picked up her puppies one at a time and began to admire them.

The first one I picked up looked just like lady, the same brown and white markings. However when I examined it more closely, I saw it was a male. I sat down on the floor still holding it and placed it in the lap of my robe. Lady gave me a quick glance and then went back to lapping her milk.

The second puppy I picked up was a female and it was marked like Lady except backwards. Where Lady was white, it was brown and where she was brown, it was white. I put it, too, in the lap of my robe and picked up the third puppy. It had but a few brown spots on it, so faint you could hardly see them and they were on her belly. The rest of her was almost solid white. "You're going to have a hard time keeping your coat clean," I said.

Lady drank all of the milk she wanted and was sniffing at her puppies in my lap. I put them back in the box and she jumped into the box with them. I got to my feet and left. I was feeling much better and wasn't tired at all. All I needed was to get up and stir around. I went back to the bedroom, showered and put on clean clothes. When I was dressed, I went to the kitchen for a cup of coffee with the intention of going outside and enjoying this beautiful day. I poured my coffee, took one sip, and the telephone rang.

"Phillips residence," I answered.

"It is?" came Paul's booming voice over the telephone. "Are you up, Squirt?"

"Of course I am," I said, glancing at the clock. My but it was just a little after eleven. "I've been up for hours." If I lied just a little he'd never know the difference.

"Have Tracy fix me one of those wonderful sandwiches she makes. I'll be home for lunch."

"You're coming home for lunch?"

"Yep, I'm taking the afternoon off."

"Just a minute Paul, let me look outside and see if the sky is actually falling. I can't believe you're really taking the afternoon off."

"Well, I am, we're going to see Dr. Stringer. I've made you a one thirty appointment and I'm taking you."

"I really don't want to go, Paul."

"You're going. You might wear the pants around the house most of the time, but I wear the bigger ones and you're going."

When Paul talked like that there was no arguing with him. I could keep the appointment with Dr. Stringer calmly or he could take me to see him with me scratching, biting, and fighting, but I would go. I could choose and I chose the former. "I'm ready, Paul. I've already showered and dressed. See you at noon."

Tracy got home shortly after twelve and said as she put up her books, "I'm serving turkey sandwiches for lunch. Are you ready to eat yet?"

"Make me one and cut it in half. Give the other half to Paul along with a whole one."

Chapter 9

AT ONE TWENTY-FIVE WE were sitting in Dr. Stringer's waiting room. It was full, but people were still coming in. One thirty came and went with occasionally a nurse stepping to the door with a file folder in her hand and calling someone. Whomever she called would get up and follow her back. From time to time people came from the same door and went out. The nurse came again to the door and I looked at her expectantly but she did not call the name of Sharon Phillips. By two o'clock I was seething with anger, here it was a beautiful day outside and I was stuck in a doctor's waiting room.

At two fifteen I stood and took Paul's arm and tried to get him to his feet. "Come on, Paul, let's go. It is evident the doctor is not going to see me today. Let's go home. There is nothing wrong with me anyway and it's beautiful outside. I'm just wasting my time here."

"Patience, Squirt, patience. Dr. Stringer said he might have to work you in. He'll get to you sooner or later."

He tugged on my hand and I sat down. Again I looked out through a window at the beautiful outdoors, blinked my eyes, and looked again. It was no longer beautiful; the world had turned gray in the blink of an eye. I suddenly realized I was tired, so very, very tired. I had a feeling of hopelessness. I had a feeling that my time on this earth had passed. I had done my job and there was nothing else to do. But I didn't care. Didn't care about anything. I didn't care whether I lived or died. Death might be better than living. If I were dead I would have no fear, no pain, no anything.

"Sharon Phillips," I heard the voice, I heard it well, but she had to say my name twice before I looked up. The nurse was standing in the door looking around. Paul stood and pulled me to my feet.

We followed her to a waiting room where the smell of antiseptic was strong. She stood me on the scales, wrote down my weight and then said "Have a seat." When I was sitting she took my blood pressure and counted my pulse rate. Then she left with, "The doctor will be with you soon," placing my file folder in a pocket beside the door. Sure he will, I thought. Paul and I were in the room alone and waiting. Strange to say, I no longer minded waiting. Everyone had to be somewhere and I would feel as tired at home as I felt here. I sat in the chair waiting in apathy.

We had begun doctoring with Dr. Stringer some five years or so after we were married. He was an old man by now and I suspected he was considering retirement. If he did retire we would have to find another doctor, probably we would use whoever took his place as long as whoever took his place wasn't a snotty nosed kid right out of medical school. I liked to doctor with older doctors, ones who have a lot of experience behind them. New doctors, fresh out of medical school probably know more about the latest, up to date medical techniques than the older ones, but in my opinion, experience trumps knowledge every day of the week.

At last Dr. Stringer came in. Although I was expecting it, I was struck by the changes which had occurred since we started coming to him. He had grown bald on top with a fringe of curly gray hair ringing the side of his head. He had grown a small mustache and a goatee. "So you're in here for your ten thousand mile check up are you, Sharon," he said in friendly voice. He looked at my chart and continued, "I see you haven't been in here for a little over eighteen months and you have lost some weight. That's a little bit long."

"It wouldn't have been that long if I hadn't had to sit in the waiting room forever."

Dr. Stringer only laughed.

"Not ten thousand mile check up," Paul said. "Its hundred thousand mile check up from the way she travels."

"Do you have any aches or pains that give you concern, Sharon?"

"No. The only reason I'm in here is because Paul drug me."

"I see, get up here on the table and let me check you over. Paul should have brought you in sooner. People at your age should get a physical every year."

"What do you mean by people my age, Dr. Stringer? You are older than I am."

He laughed as he put the earpieces of his stethoscope in his ears. He listened to my heart and lungs then had me lay on my back and poked me here and there on my stomach. "You can sit up now," he said and then turned to Paul. "Do you have any concerns about your wife, Paul?"

"She is slowing down," Paul said. "Now I know that we all slow down eventually but hers has come the past few weeks. She has slowed down so much I can almost keep up with her," Paul laughed.

"Does she complain about being tired?"

"Yes. Some days she wakes up tired and is tired all day. Other days she is going at full speed and then almost keels over from exhaustion."

"Does she act like she is sad?"

"She does when she is tired. When she is tired she acts like she is sad, mad, or apathetic."

"Hey, guys," I said waving my hand. "I'm here. Why don't you ask me the questions?"

Dr. Stringer laughed, "Okay, Sharon. Have you lost interest in things that you used to enjoy?"

"Some, of course a woman 'my age' loses interest in some things she was interested in when she was younger."

"For example," Paul said, "A month or so back, when my alarm went off and I got up to go to work, she would already have been up, dressed and ready to hit the great outdoors. This morning when I got up she was still asleep."

"I see, what time did you get up this morning, Sharon."

"I have to admit I slept in this morning. I didn't get up until after nine and wouldn't have gotten up then if Lady hadn't insisted."

"Lady?"

"Yes, Lady is a stray poodle that followed me home from the lake and then proceeded to have a litter of puppies under our porch. Someone didn't close the bedroom door well and she came in and jumped in bed with me. She wanted her morning's milk. Ever since she had the puppies and is nursing, I give her a little milk each morning."

"So you got up and gave her, her milk. Did you stay up then?"

"Oh, yes. The day was so gorgeous I couldn't go back to bed."

"Yes," Dr. Stringer said, "It was a beautiful morning. Is it still a beautiful day?"

"No," I said and decided to be truthful with him. "While we were sitting in the waiting room, waiting forever to be called back," and I made my voice as stern as I could, "the day changed."

"Oh, how did it change?"

"It suddenly turned gray."

"Oh, come on, Sharon, I didn't keep you waiting that long. The sun hasn't gone down yet. It's still shining."

"I know, but the day turned gray and it still is."

"Are you tired now, Sharon?"

"I'm exhausted, Dr. Stringer."

"I see," he said. "I think I know what your problem is and it's not serious. Nevertheless I want to do blood work to rule out anything else. I'm sending you to the lab to draw blood and we will have the results Thursday so I want you to make an early morning appointment either Thursday or Friday, whenever they can fit you in."

"Okay," I said, but even as I said it I could hear the listlessness in my voice.

"You don't really care, do you, Sharon?"

"Not really," I answered truthfully.

Dr. Stringer sat back with his hand on his chin stroking his goatee. "I'm tempted to start you on medication now," he said but then shook his head. "No, let's see what the blood work results are. I'll see you Thursday or Friday. I'll send someone to take you back to the lab."

"Okay," I said, easing myself down from the examination table. I sat in a chair beside Paul and waited.

Finally a different nurse came in to get me and take me to the lab. "I'll wait for you in the waiting room, Squirt. While I'm out there I'll make you an appointment for Thursday morning, I hope."

"Okay," I said as I followed the nurse down the hallway.

In the lab they stuck a needle in my vein and began to take vial after vial of blood. When the girl reached for the third vile, I said, "Hey, you're going to drain me dry." The young girl taking the blood only laughed as she finished filling the vial.

At last they were through and I rolled down my sleeve and went to join Paul in the waiting room. He stood when I entered, took my hand and led me outside. "We have an appointment at nine Thursday morning," he said.

I thought about saying, **we**, are you going to get a physical too? But it didn't seem worth the effort and it wasn't that funny anyway.

Tuesday was a beautiful day and March was going out like a lamb. I couldn't remember how March came in though, looking at the day, it must have come in like a lion. I ate breakfast with Paul and clung to him as I kissed him goodbye. Also, when I kissed him goodbye, since Tracy was back in her room, I gave him something to think about all day and to look forward to when nighttime came. The day was so dazzling that I worked all day outside tilling the flowerbeds. I was still at it when Paul came home from work, took me into his arms and reminded me of the promise I had made that morning when he left for work.

Wednesday was gray and I would have stayed in bed all day if Lady hadn't gotten me up for her morning's milk. I played with the puppies just a little bit, but I didn't enjoy it as I usually did. I got myself a fresh cup of coffee and set it on the table by my recliner where I always set it. I sat in the recliner, put my feet up and reclined back. I lay there staring at the ceiling and walls, safe in my 'safe tree'. I reached over, picked up my cup and took a sip.

When Tracy came home, she tried to get me to eat lunch but I wasn't hungry. That evening I nibbled at my food to keep Paul off my back but I really wasn't hungry then either. After dinner I watched the colored lights as Paul watched television but after a short time of that, I grew sleepy so I went to bed. I didn't even awake when Paul came to bed but sometime during the night I woke up enough to tell that he was holding me, his hand cupped my breast. It felt so comfortable that I scooted my bottom into his midsection and went back to sleep feeling safe, feeling loved. Paul even loved me on my gray days when I was so unworthy of love.

Thursday morning when Paul awoke me and told me I had better get up and shower, I remembered my appointment with Dr. Stringer and looked out the window. The sun was shining and the lake was calm and blue. In the reflection of the lake I could see the puffball clouds as they moved lazily in the sky. A glorious day indeed.

I quickly rolled out of bed and all but ran to the shower. After I was showered and dried, I put on my tan outfit I had bought at Wal-Mart, but I couldn't remember when. It had been sometime after Christmas hadn't it? Or was it before Christmas that I had bought it? Oh, well, it didn't matter.

Dressed, I hurried to the kitchen, grabbed myself a cup of coffee and sat at the table with Paul as Tracy finished cooking our bacon, eggs, and hash-browns. "You seem to be in a good mood this morning, Squirt."

"I am. Isn't it a most stunning morning outside?"

"Yes, it is."

"It's too beautiful of a day to spend waiting in a doctor's waiting room. Let's just call and cancel the appointment."

"I don't think we'll have to spend too long this morning. You're Dr. Stringer's first patient."

"Good. I hate to waste a minute of this glorious day."

We were sitting in Dr. Stringer's waiting room at a quarter to nine; the first ones there. At nine o'clock the waiting room began to fill. Oh great, I thought sourly, I bet all of those people go in before I do and I sit here half the morning. I was pleasantly surprised when the nurse opened the door and called me in. I was even more surprised when she didn't take me to an examination room, but instead, took me to his office. I was flabbergasted when she opened the door for me, telling us to go on in, and I saw Dr. Stringer behind his desk waiting on us.

"Have a seat, Sharon, Paul," he said waving his hand and indicating two empty chairs in front of his desk. "I have the results of your blood work back."

"And?" Paul asked.

"It is as I thought; you're as healthy as a horse."

"See," I said, turning to Paul. "I told you so. There is nothing wrong with me."

"But I'm afraid there is. Tell me, how has life been, Sharon?"

"It had been okay," I answered.

"No, I need more than 'okay'. Tell me about your feelings. Have you had a short temper lately? Do you feel sad or angry when there is no reason to? Are you afraid of something?"

"She has..." Paul started to say but Dr. Stringer interrupted him.

"Let Sharon answer the questions, Paul. In fact, I probably should send her to a psychiatrist. Would you like for me to make an appointment for you, Sharon?"

"You mean you think I'm sick in the head?" I said, my voice rising in anger.

"She is the sanest person I know, Dr. Stringer," Paul said suddenly standing.

"My diagnosis is that she has a chemical imbalance. To make sure I need to talk with her some more. She needs help, I can do it or I can make an appointment for her with a psychiatrist. Which do you prefer, Sharon? You know me well, I have been your doctor for many years and I thought you might be more comfortable with me. However, I must add that a psychiatrist is better equipped to handle the problem. When we prescribe for you, we both will use the shotgun method of prescription, I mean by that, we'll try one medication and if it doesn't work, we will try another and keep trying until we find one that will work. A psychiatrist will do the same except have a better knowledge of which drugs to try first. Which will it be me or a psychiatrist?"

"I would rather you do it Dr. Stringer. I know you and I trust you," I answered.

"Okay Paul will you wait for us in the waiting room."

Paul hesitated for just a moment and then reluctantly left.

"Sharon, many people even people younger than us, often have a chemical imbalance. This brings on a state of what is known as 'clinical depression'. That is what I think is wrong with you."

"Depression! Why would I be depressed? I have everything. I have a wonderful husband whose only fault is that he spoils me rotten. I have two of the most wonderful and successful children in the world. I have a beautiful house with a great view of the lake; I can have anything I want Doctor. Let me change that, I have everything. Why in the world would I be depressed?"

"Sometimes, everything is not enough. How do you feel? Do you at times feel sad, frightened, have the feeling of impending doom? Do you ever feel like someone is out to get you?"

After a moment's hesitation I said, "Yes."

"Yes? What do you mean by 'yes'?"

"Yes, to all of the above," I answered.

"Okay, which feeling is the most prevalent? We'll start from there and work our way down."

"I don't just think someone is out to get me, I know they are." Then I unloaded on him, telling him about someone putting my things in strange places, like my sweater in the deep freezer, and all the other things that had happened. By the time I had finished, I was crying. I finished by saying, "I don't know who is doing it and I don't know why, but it upsets me so very, very much. It upsets me so much that a beautiful day becomes black and I feel so very tired. So very tired and sleepy. It makes me feel sad that someone would do this to me and it frightens me. Not knowing who it is and not knowing why, gives me a feeling that my world is ending."

"I see," Dr. Stringer said. "Unusual but understandable. Instead of prescribing you medication, I'm going to send home with you a two weeks sample. Take one capsule every morning. You will not notice any effect for five days to a week. I want to see you again in two weeks and if the medication works, I'll write you a prescription. If it doesn't work, then we'll try something else."

He got up and went to the door, called a nurse and talked to her. Then he went to, I suppose the waiting room, anyway Paul came back with him and sat beside me while Dr. Stringer sat behind his desk.

"What I'm going to do, Paul, is to give her a sample of an antidepressant drug. If it works, then I will prescribe it for her. If it doesn't, then we'll try another. There are hundreds of such drugs out there and what we have to do is find the silver bullet. She should come back in two weeks or bring her back sooner if you see no change in five days."

I went back much sooner than two weeks. Not because I had gray days, I didn't. After taking the medicine for five days, none of my days were gray, they were white. White and sterile. No, there were no gray days, no black days, but neither were there any beautiful, gorgeous, glorious, golden days. It was as if I had a chemical lobotomy. I missed my breath-taking days. Paul didn't have to make the appointment for me to see Dr. Stringer. I made it myself and Tuesday I went to see him alone.

Chapter 10

THE FOURTH OF JULY WAS a great and golden day. I was up before Paul, I had to be. Lady was scratching at the bedroom door and it was time for her and her almost grown pups to go outside.

I slipped on a robe, opened the door without letting any of the pups in to awaken Paul and took them to the porch door; an excited tumbling, jumping mass of puppies. I never realized before that three small puppies would fill such a large space. When I opened the door, Lady stood aside while the puppies went tumbling outside. Boomer was lying on the porch taking an early morning nap but the nap was soon interrupted when Doc, the pup who looked like his mother, attacked him with yelps and growls. Boomer stood, gave Doc a disgusted look, and walked away. Doc followed him a short way but then came running back to the porch, looked at his food bowl and then at me.

Miss Calico jumped down from the patio table and came sauntering over to Elvira, the pup with the reverse marking of her mother, and started rubbing up against her. Elvira immediately jumped on Miss Calico and took her to the floor. They wrestled around a bit and then Elvira decided to check out the food dishes which were, of course, empty.

Flake, the almost white pup and short for Snowflake, went straight to the food dishes. She was fatter than the others and a real glutton. "Everybody's hungry this morning," I said, throwing up my arms. "So what else is new?" I turned, went in to the utility room where I scooped up a coffee can of dog food to take outside. I stopped by the coffee pot in the kitchen and turned it on.

Then outside to feed the dogs. I dumped most of the dog food in the four small bowls on the porch, the rest I took into the yard, found Boomer's bowl and fed him. By the time I

84

was back on the porch, Miss Calico was letting me know in no uncertain terms that it was time for her breakfast. She emphasized the point by twining around my feet, between my legs and almost tripping me. Back inside, I got a can of cat food, opened it, put it on one of the old plates I kept in the cabinet just for Miss Calico, took it to the patio and put it on the table where the pups couldn't reach it. Miss Calico jumped onto the table, sniffed her breakfast, gave it her approval, and then began to eat, purring as she did. With the animals all fed it was now time for me.

Using the excuse that I might wake Paul if I went into the bedroom, showered and dressed, I went straight to the kitchen, poured myself a cup of coffee, slipped on a sweater over my robe, and went back out into the glorious day. I sat on the porch and watched the pups play. Lady came to me, I invited her up, and she jumped onto my lap.

The pups were playing in the yard, running to and fro. I couldn't figure out the rules to the game they were playing and I doubt that there were any rules. They hadn't outgrown their clumsy stage and it seemed to me that their game included a lot of tripping and falling down.

I know the Bible tells us that God created the world in six days and rested on the seventh, but I have a different theory. If God is almighty and all-powerful, why would he get tired and need to rest. No, I think on the evening of the sixth day He created the puppy. Then He got so busy watching the puppy running here and there and playing that He didn't create anything else. The world and everything in it, He created before He created the puppy.

Suddenly I heard Paul cursing inside the house. I quickly set my cup on the patio table, put Lady down, and went inside to see why Paul was upset. I could hear him mumbling in the living room so that was where I went. What I saw made me laugh.

Paul must have left a newspaper in reach of the pups. Sometime during the night, the pups had proceeded to rip the newspaper to shreds and scatter it from one end of the living room to the other. Even on the couch and chairs. Paul was down on his hands and knees picking up the small shreds of newspaper and putting them in a plastic trash can he pulled along beside him mumbling as he went.

My laugh made him realize I was there, "It's not funny, Squirt," he mumbled, looking over his left shoulder at me.

"Oh, come on, Paul. It's not the end of the world," I said, dropping down and starting to help him clean the mess.

"Those damn pups have to go. They are plenty old enough to give away."

"I want to keep one, so which one do I give away first, Doc?"

"No, if you have to keep one, keep Doc. He's the only male pup of the bunch."

"Then I'll give away Elvira first."

"All the pups love you, Squirt, but Elvira is the one who comes to me and jumps on my lap." Then he looked at me and grinned, "And not Snowflake. She's so aloof and haughty I doubt that anyone else would want her. I guess we'll just keep them all." Then he grew serious with a distant look in his eyes. "All but one."

"All but one? Why can't we keep them all?"

Paul let out a sigh and said, "Let's get this mess cleaned up, then I'll get a cup of coffee and tell you about it."

"Tell me now," I begged.

Paul sighed again as he turned and sat down and leaned against the couch. "You know I did run the ad in the 'Found Dog' column when Lady first joined us."

"I know, and nobody came to claim her. I didn't think they would because I had never seen her in Stillwater before. I knew she was from out of town and one of the people who camped on the lake had lost her."

"But someone did call, Squirt. A Peter Owens from Sand Springs came and he recognized Lady. But at the time he came, you were having one of your bad days and you were still in the bedroom asleep. Thank God those days are over. But anyway, when I explained to Peter how Lady seemed to help you and how much you loved her, he decided to let her stay with one condition. He wanted one of her pups."

"Which one did he want?"

"The pups weren't very old, they didn't even have their eyes open, and he decided to wait. I have his phone number and I suppose I should give him a call. Sharon, he is going to take one of the pups and the one you lose will be up to him. You haven't had a bout of depression in over two months so I think you can handle it now, don't you?"

"Of course. Dr. Stringer finally found a medication that works for me. My outlook on life is like it used to be, plus I don't eat all the time like I did with the previous medications. The only problem with what I'm taking now is that it seems to affect my short term memory. I can remember perfectly well what I did last week but I can't remember what I did yesterday." Then I laughed, "It gives me an excuse for misplacing things."

When the paper was picked up I went into our bedroom and showered. Since I knew it was going to be hot today I dressed in shorts and tank-top. I put on a sweater, went to the kitchen, grabbed a banana for breakfast and looked for my coffee cup. I couldn't find it anywhere, I stepped out on the patio where Paul was and saw my coffee cup on the table where I left it. Paul was reading the paper and only grunted when I laid the banana on the table, picked up my cup and went back in for a refill. Back outside, cup full, I sat at the table and looked out over the yard as I peeled the banana and began to eat.

The pups were scattered here and there asleep. They were stretched out as if a nap-attack had hit them in full stride and they had fallen to the ground. Their front feet were stretched out in front of them and their back feet were stretched out behind them. Their tails, which were usually curled so tight against their backs that it appeared they had no tail at all, lay straight on their hind legs. I chuckled just a bit and Paul folded his paper and took a sip of coffee. "Looks like the crowd is gathering," he said nodding towards the lake.

I looked across the lake at the park and saw it was beginning to fill. Actually, most of the camping spots made for RVs were already filled but as I looked I saw young people scurrying about setting up tents. Even though it was hot, I could see tendrils of smoke climbing through the trees from banked campfires.

"When I take a vacation this summer, would you like to do that?" Paul asked pointing to a young couple with a toddler busily setting up a tent. "You want to buy a tent and go tenting around Oklahoma?"

"Been there and done that," I said finishing my banana and placing the peel on the table before taking a sip of coffee.

"What do you want to do this vacation?"

"It's your vacation, Paul. You decide. Remember, I'm on vacation every day. Whatever you decide, I'll go along with it."

"What if we didn't do anything? What if we just stayed at home this year and I play a lot of golf?"

"Oh, no," I said. "You can play golf everyday and all day of your vacation if you want to but I want you to do it someplace else other than Stillwater. You know if we stay at home, they will be calling you from the office every day and every time they have a problem. That wouldn't be much of a vacation for you."

"You're right," Paul laughed. Then he was silent for a while before he spoke, "What if we went clear to Guthrie, rented a nice hotel room and I played some of those courses? That way some of my golf buddies could come down and play with me when they could work in the time."

"If you don't mind driving that far," I laughed. Guthrie was only a forty minute drive from Stillwater, if that far.

It was so quiet and peaceful outside. The south wind was light and only made small ripples on the lake. I looked down at the fountain and saw the water sparkling in the sunlight. There wasn't a cloud in the sky, not even a puffball. Suddenly I was too hot and I felt the sweat trickle down my back. "The day is going to be hot. I'm already getting hot and it's still morning."

"Why don't you take the sweater off, Squirt? I don't know why you put it on in the first place. After all, it is July."

"Oh, I think I will," I said standing and working the damp sweater off. I was a little embarrassed as I hung the sweater on the back of an empty chair to dry and air out. I didn't know why I put it on in the first place anyway and Paul had to remind me to take it off. It was the medication I was sure. But the medication I was on seemed to work otherwise for me.

"I called Peter while you were showering, Squirt."

"Who?"

"Peter Owens, the former owner of Lady I told you about the other morning."

"Oh, yes, now I remember. When is he coming over to get his pup? Which one do you think he will take? Probably Doc and it will be hard to say goodbye to Doc."

"That's the thing of it. He told me he had changed his mind."

"Oh, no! he wants Lady back and her pups."

"No. He now has another dog and he has decided to leave Lady and all of her pups here with you, if you don't mind."

"Too bad for you," I said reaching over and patting Paul on the knee. "Of course I don't mind."

"I know. I'm going to have to learn to live with those pups under my feet all the time," he said gruffly.

"And to put the newspaper out of reach when you are through with it," I laughed.

I was sitting there enjoying the day when the first firecracker went off. All it did for the pups was awake them. They looked around with curiosity. Lady sat up. Then a whole package of firecrackers went off and Lady came running to me and jumped into my lap without waiting for permission. All three pups went waddling down to the lake to see what was making such a delightful noise. Lady squeezed closer to me and I held her trembling body tight as fireworks began going off all over the place. So that's what I did for most of the day, hold Lady. When I set her down to go do something, she was always on my heels following me around. When I sat down, she was in my lap.

The kids came over that evening, Kris first with her husband of less than a month, JT. She was happy and JT doted on her. I had trouble remembering her wedding as I was in the process of changing antidepressant medications at the time. I was just getting off of one that put me in a dreamy state all the time and starting a new one. I couldn't remember much about the month that I took that particular medication and I was sad about it. Life is built on dreams and memories and there was a hole in my life I could never fill.

JT helped Paul put the hamburgers and hotdogs on, arguing about the best way to cook them. Then Chris showed up with a new girlfriend. To my and Kris's sorrow, he had dumped Tiffany a month or so back.

I didn't care that much for his new girlfriend, Lacy. Compared to Tiffany she was shallow. True, she was beautiful with her long blonde hair and her pouting lips. She was tall and slim with good legs and a flat stomach which was on display tonight as she wore shorts that were far too short and the tiniest little halter top. But as I looked at her I saw she was very narrow between her big blue eyes. Oh, well, it was up to him to choose his mate of the moment and then his life's mate, but if things started to get serious I sure hoped it would get serious between him and someone like

Tiffany or even Tiffany herself if she would take the rogue back.

It grew dark and we watched as people across the lake began to set off night-time fireworks. Roman candles shot their fireballs out over the lake to fall sizzling in the water. Bottle rockets streaked up and out over the lake. More spectacular fireworks were occurring to the west in plain sight at the OSU football stadium.

By the moonlight I could see the silhouette of the three pups as they sat at the edge of the yard and watched these new and exciting things while Lady lay shivering and trembling on my lap.

Chapter 11

IT WAS THE MONDAY MORNING before Thanksgiving and I bet too many people it was a dreary day. The sky was heavily overcast and from time to time it drizzled rain. But I had on my raincoat and laughed when I pulled into HomeLand Grocery's parking lot. I smiled to myself as I found a parking place without any trouble. It was a little before nine and that was the good thing about shopping early, before others filled the store. The shoppers who were now in the store had taken up the parking spaces closest to the door but I didn't mind. I'd have to walk a bit but it was such a splendid day. There were raindrops on the windshield and it began to rain heavily as I opened the door and got out. I laughed as I pulled the hood of the red raincoat over my head. I loved such days as this.

Inside the door I pulled the hood back and shook my head like a dog shakes water from its coat to straighten my hair as I grabbed a shopping cart and all but skipped when I started pushing it down the aisle. The smells in the store were so splendid and the smell of spices tickled my nose as I moved down the aisles. I grabbed a can of sage and kept on going. Tracy did most of our shopping except for the holiday shopping, and it had been so long since a holiday, I had forgotten how much fun it was.

To the meat counter first, I thought. I'd pick out a turkey and then get the other things we would need for Thanksgiving Day. When I looked over the birds carefully, the one I liked was a bit large but I put it in my cart anyway. Then my eyes caught the hams. Should I get one? There was such a beautiful spiral cut ham laying there and begging me to take it home. Nonsense, the turkey was more than the six of us could eat, but I picked up the ham anyway and put it in the cart. Then I pushed the cart away and started down the aisles. Frozen cranberries, a can of readymade cranberry sauce, olives both black and green stuffed with red pimentos, celery, different cans of spray on cheese to make celery sticks and anything else that looked good. Canned yams, two cans. I thought about buying some gravy mixes, but then I remembered that Kris would cook the main dishes such as the turkey and ham while the family trusted me with only the hors d'oeuvre. Sure, I could squeeze cheese into a celery stick and onto crackers without messing them up too bad.

When my cart was full, I quit and wheeled it to the checkout stand where a checker rang up the tab and a pimpled faced, tall bagboy bagged it and put it into a carryout cart. I paid with a credit card and then headed toward the door, the bagboy following. It had stopped raining for the time, and when I stepped out, to my amazement, the parking lot was almost full. I stood there looking for my car in confusion. Embarrassed I turned to the bagboy and said, "I forgot where I parked."

"What kind and color of a car do you drive, Ma'am."

"A red, Pontiac Vibe," I said. "I know I parked it close to the door."

"Then we're looking for a red one. Don't worry, Ma'am, we'll find it. You'd be surprised at the number of people who forget where they parked. No one has had to carry their groceries and walk home yet since I started working here."

He started out pushing the cart and going down the middle of the parking lot. I followed him and saw that he occasionally stood on tiptoe to look over the top of the parked cars. I could have stood on tiptoe all I wanted but I'd never be able to look over the top of cars without a ladder.

Suddenly he turned to the left, crossed three driving lanes and across the fourth I saw my car. "That's it," I said, spotting my car. He pushed the cart to the rear, I unlocked the hatchback and raised it, and he began to place the groceries in the back. I'm going to have to start concentrating on where I put things; I said to myself as he put the last bag in. This medication is making me so forgetful I'm going to have to be extra careful. "Thank you so very much," I said as I closed the lid. "Not only for bringing my groceries out but also for helping me find my car."

"Think nothing of it, Ma'am," he said as he turned the cart and headed back towards the store. Then he stopped and said to me over his shoulder, "I bet I help ten or fifteen people a day find where they parked their car. You're just the first one today," and then he waved and smiled at me with a friendly smile.

I was home by ten thirty, so after I had the groceries put away, I called Kris at work.

"I've been shopping for Thanksgiving dinner, Kris, and I bought a turkey. Are you going to cook the turkey this year?"

"No, I talked to JT about it and he informed me that I wasn't. He would. He plans to cook it like his momma did back on the farm plus what he has learned since."

"Tell him this one is already dead, the feathers pulled out, and butchered so that's one job he won't have to do. I didn't buy anything for dressing, you usually do that."

"I will again this year, or we will. Don't worry about it."

"There was such a beautiful spiral cut ham at the store and I had to buy it. This year we won't have to decide if we want to have turkey or ham, we'll have them both."

"How many are coming for dinner, Mom?"

"There will be just the five of us unless Chris brings his latest girlfriend and then there will be six."

"So you're not going to be feeding the 45th Division of the United States Army. It sounds like you have enough. I'm sure he has a girlfriend but I have no idea who it is. Better count on six. Chris changes girlfriends like most people change socks."

"You're right there," I laughed and then she interrupted, "I have to go now, Mom. My boss, JT, has just given me something to research and he wants it as soon as possible."

"Give him a hug for me, Kris."

"I will, Mom. Bye now."

When I got up Tuesday morning the rising sun was peeking through the broken cloud cover. There was little wind and only small ripples on the Boomer Lake. Dressed only in my robe, I let Lady and her pups out, though one could hardly call them pups now. They were almost adult and their clumsiness rarely showed. After turning on the coffee, I went out with them. Although their clumsiness of puppy-hood had all but disappeared, their playfulness had not. Each took their turn sitting on my lap but not for long. It usually ended up with two of the puppies ganging up together trying to pull the one on my lap off. When they did, it turned into a game of free-for-all. That's how it started this morning. Doc was the first one to eat his fill and when he did, he turned and came running to me. He jumped onto my lap and Elvira and Flake saw him. They, too, came running over and jumped up and tried to grab him while he sat there and barked at them. Their actions were so quick that I couldn't tell if they got hold of Doc and pulled him down or whether he jumped down and joined the fray. Whichever way it was, the wrestling-tumbling match was on. Snowflake soon separated herself from them and while Doc and Elvira were still playing, she jumped onto my lap. She then turned around and looked haughtily down at what was going on at my feet.

The back door opened and Paul came out carrying two cups of coffee. He had showered, shaved and dressed. He looked over at Lady and asked, "Can't you control your rambunctious children." She looked back at him as if to say, 'You know teenagers, there is nothing I can do'.

"Thank you," I said when he set my coffee in front of me.

He looked at me and asked, "Isn't that robe a little light to be sitting outside in?"

I looked at him and saw he had on a light jacket. "A little," I said shivering, "but I only planned to be out here a minute."

"Don't you catch a cold. Even with a jacket on it's too cool for me. I think I'll go back inside. It sounds like Tracy is starting to cook breakfast."

When he turned to go in, I set Flake down, picked up my coffee and followed him inside.

"When does your Thanksgiving vacation start?" I asked Tracy while we were eating breakfast.

"It started yesterday."

"What? And you're not in Tahlequah?"

"No, Pete is coming to Stillwater and spending Thanksgiving with me. He wants to look the campus over and see if he can find a job. I have about talked him into starting college."

"You say he is good with computers?" Paul asked.

"He's very good."

"If he wants a part-time job, send him to me out at the plant. I would like to hire a fulltime computer man, but so far I haven't found one with qualifications."

"Tracy, what are you and Pete going to do for Thanksgiving?" I asked.

"I don't know; go to a restaurant I suppose. Pete will be staying in the dorm with a friend of mine. His roommate has gone home for the holidays but my friend is like me. He has to stay at school and finish a term paper, too.

"Would you and Pete like to eat Thanksgiving dinner with us?"

"We wouldn't want to put you out."

"You won't. Only Kris, JT, Chris and his girlfriend of the moment will be here, two more will hardly be noticed. I bought a ham and a turkey to bake so there will be plenty."

"Thanks, I'd like to and I'm sure Pete would enjoy it, but I should ask him first. I'm sure he'll agree, money is pretty tight for both of us and it would save him laying out the money for a meal trying to impress me," Tracy said and laughed.

Wednesday morning I set the turkey out to thaw and finally after much anticipation, Thanksgiving Day came. I had already showered and dressed when Kris and JT arrived shortly after eight, each loaded with a box of goodies for dinner. They took them to the kitchen but I stayed in the living room. I knew what was coming next and it did. Sitting in the living room I could easily hear Kris and JT.

"Don't put it there, Kris, it's in my way…No not there either."

"Where do you want me to put the box, JT?"

"On the table, in the living room, just anywhere out of my way."

"Okay, it's on the table. Anything else I can help you with?"

"Yeah, get me out a roasting pan big enough for this bird."

I heard the sound of pans rattling and water running. Then Kris said, "Is this big enough?"

"Yeah, that'll do just fine."

"Anything else I can help you with, JT?"

"Yeah, you can get out of my kitchen."

"But I have to get the ham ready, JT."

"I'll take care of it. We have hours to do that after I get this bird on. Now out, out, out." And Kris came into the living room smiling. "Mom, I think I have a temperamental cook for a husband."

Paul came in then, shaved, dressed and ready for the day. "The women letting you do all the work, JT? Need any help?"

"No," JT said crossly.

Paul came to the living room smiling, "JT gets in a mood when he's cooking, doesn't he? Are you sure he knows what he's doing?"

Kris laughed, "I think he does. He cooked his way through school, both undergraduate and law school. He has worked at some of the finest restaurants. Each time he quit, they offered him a good salary if he would stay. But he didn't take it. He had always dreamed of becoming a trial lawyer."

"I didn't know that. I didn't know that you not only married a lawyer but a professional cook as well," I said. "You know whom your rogue brother is bringing to dinner, Kris?"

"I have no idea who his latest squeeze is, Mom."

We were soon to find out. JT had the turkey roasting and had started on other things when Chris came bursting through the door. He had Tiffany in tow. "You guys know Tiffany," he boomed with his usual exuberance. "Where's JT?"

"He's in the kitchen cooking dinner," I said.

"And you guys are just lazing around in here and not helping."

"You go help him, Bro," Kris said. "I'm sure he'd appreciate the help. We women are on strike."

"I'll just do that. Come on, Tiffany, let's go give JT a hand."

Tiffany looked at Kris and Kris shook her head, no. Then she looked at me and I also shook my head. "Go ahead, Chris, I'll join the women who are on strike." She turned loose of his hand and sat on the couch.

"Listen to what is coming next, Tiffany," I said to her in all but a whisper as Chris went barging into the kitchen.

"Out! Out! Out!" we heard JT yell.

"What are you fixing now, JT? Yams and marshmallows?"

"Out of my kitchen!"

"But you don't know what the hell you're doing."

I looked at Tiffany and saw her laughing as I heard the sound of scuffling coming from the kitchen. Suddenly Chris and JT both appeared in the living room. JT had caught Chris in a bear hug from the back and he brought him to the living room. He set him in the middle of the room and when Chris turned around he shook his finger at him and said, "Stay, Stay." Then JT turned around and headed back to the kitchen with Chris following him.

"That brother of yours is either hard headed or a slow learner, Kris," Tiffany said.

"Both," Kris answered. "But he eventually learns. Take you, for example. You're the first girl I've ever seen him go back to. It takes him a while but he eventually learns what's good for him."

"I agree with my daughter," I said. "Perhaps he will stay with you for a good while. You'd be good for him if you can handle it."

"I can handle it and I hope we stay together a good long while," Tiffany said as she held up her left hand. On her ring finger was an engagement ring.

"All Right!" Kris all but screamed as she stood and rushed to Tiffany and hugged her. I was next in line.

"When is the happy event going to take place?" I asked.

"Chris wanted the wedding to take place on New Year's Day but I've always dreamed of being a June bride, so we probably won't get married until next June."

"Stick with your guns, girl. He's always had his way with women and it is time for that to change," Kris said. "Although, you can't become a member of our family too soon as far as I'm concerned."

"Ditto that," I said.

It was a little after eleven when the doorbell rang and Paul went to answer it. Tracy came in leading a tall, wide young man with a freckled face and bright red hair.

"This is the Pete that I have been telling you about," Tracy said and then went ahead and introduced the rest of us to Pete.

He is an impressive young man, I thought, and Paul must have thought so also. Before dinner was served, Paul took him back to the den and closed the door. When the door opened and they came back out, Mercury Marine had a new employee starting in two weeks.

Surprisingly enough, dinner got served in spite of Chris, and after one bite I understood why all the restaurants wanted JT to stay.

That night when Paul and I were getting ready for bed, I looked at him and murmured, "Hasn't this been a most wonderful day. I can't think of a thing that would have made it better."

"Neither can I, Squirt. Neither can I."

Chapter 12

SEVERAL LARGE FLAKES OF SNOW DRIFTED from the gray sky as I got into my car at the HomeLand's parking lot. It was only three days until Christmas and perhaps we would have a white Christmas this year. It would be so delightful if we did. I couldn't remember the last time we had a white Christmas.

I had the back of the car full of groceries and this time I hadn't lost my car in the parking lot. I led the same bagboy right out the door and he followed me right to my car. Almost. Of course I had parked it near the store and in sight of the door, which helped a lot. Even though I had done this, when I exited the store I had to look twice at the red Vibe to make sure it was mine. Perhaps I should see Dr. Stringer since the antidepressant medication I was on often completely erased my short term memory. But I could function with it and I hated to go through a trial and error period of finding a new one that would work. Also, I loved my outlook on life. No more gray days and no more sterile white days either.

As I drove, white flakes began to come down faster and I turned on the windshield wipers and leaned forward to see where I was, and to see where I was going. Suddenly I realized that in my inattention I had missed my corner. Ah, well, I'd just take the roundabout way home. See some of Stillwater I hadn't seen in a while.

I slowed down and peered through the falling snow. I was going down a two lane street which was lined with trees with their bare branches. Behind me a car horn blared and I looked into the rearview mirror and saw five cars were impatiently following me. I needed to go faster or get off this street. It was much too busy.

I was going west and I took the next street north. There was no traffic on it and I could go as slowly as I wished. I looked out of both windows, looking for something I could recognize. Nothing. I had lived in Stillwater all of my life but I couldn't remember ever seeing any of these houses before.

Suddenly a car backed out in front of me and I jammed on the brakes. Fortunately, the street was not slick and I stopped in time. The car continued to back out and then head up the street. I had gotten a glimpse of the driver and saw it was an elderly gentleman. But since he left his driveway open, I took the opportunity to pull into it and park. I sat there for a moment shaking like a leaf. I was frightened and bewildered. Where was I and how was I going to get back home?

Finally I had myself under control and again I looked around. The flurry of snow had stopped and I could see the houses and buildings plainly for all the good it did me. I didn't remember seeing any of them before. I knew I had to be in Stillwater, I hadn't driven far enough to be anywhere else. But you couldn't have proved it by me. I didn't remember seeing one thing that I remembered looking at before. I might as well have been in a strange town or city, one I had never been in, in my life. What was I going to do?

I saw an elderly woman looking out the window at me, wondering who was coming to visit her, no doubt. I knew I had three options. Get out and visit her, whoever she was. Sit there and let her call the police. Or back out, go down to the road I had been on and drive around until I saw something I recognized. I chose the latter.

I started the engine and after looking carefully up and down the street, I backed out and started south. When I came to the street that I had turned off of, I recognized it and made a left turn. Horns blared and tires squealed and at that moment I realized I had run a stop sign. Again I was shaking but I was on the street heading east and it was too late to stop now so I kept on going. I watched the side streets carefully, looking for my corner, but if I passed it, I didn't recognize it. I kept driving slowly east much to the irritation of the drivers behind me. Everybody lived and hurried through life too fast anyway, they could just slow down for this once, and I felt my chin jut out.

Slowly I continued to drive looking for something, anything I could recognize. Suddenly I did. Southeast of me was Wal-Mart with its blue and gray sign. I stopped at the highway and when I saw a break in the traffic, I pulled out and went south a few blocks before turning left and pulling into the Wal-Mart parking lot. Surely as many times as I had been to Wal-Mart, I could find my way home from here. But I did park, turn off the key, and sit for a while. I needed to stop shaking and get myself under control.

At last I took a deep breath, started the motor and drove to an exit. When I found a hole in the traffic, I pulled into it and got in the left lane. Carefully I drove with cars passing me on the right and looked for the familiar corner. When I saw it and turned. Relief flooded over me. I was going home. I was as happy as if I had found the prize egg at an Easter egg hunt. Everything was familiar as I drove home.

I put my hand through the handles of the plastic bags and carried a load in. When I opened the door the good smell of Tracy cooking dinner assailed me and grew stronger as I carried the groceries into the kitchen.

"Just set them on the counter," Tracy said. "Is that all of them?"

"Good Lord, no. I have the whole back end of my car full. I went shopping for Christmas dinner. You and Pete are going to eat with us, aren't you?"

"No, we're going home as soon as Pete gets off work tomorrow."

"I don't know what we're having for dinner, but it sure smells good whatever you're fixing."

"Paul said something about wanting a leg of lamb," Tracy said as she followed me out to the car. "So the last time I was in Tahlequah I picked up some mutton."

At last we had the car empty, all of it setting on the counter and table. I started to put the groceries away but Tracy stopped me. "I'll do that, Sharon."

Tracy had taken her finals and had only the spring semester left to go before graduation. For once she didn't have to sit around with her nose in a book studying. So that evening after Pete got home, Pete took Tracy to see the Christmas play on the campus. Paul and I had the house to ourselves. I wondered if I should tell Paul about me getting lost on the way home today. It was so incredulous as to almost be unbelievable. No, I decided, if I were to tell him, he would become very concerned and there was no need for him to be. I was okay; it was just the antidepressant medication I was on. However there was a small nag worry in my mind.

As we were sitting and watching television, I turned to Paul and asked, "How is Pete working out?"

"Absolutely fantastic. Tracy is right, he can make a computer do anything except stand up and salute. He's starting school next semester and I believe he'll breeze through."

"Good," I said. "He and Tracy make such a nice couple."

"They do at that," Paul said.

We finished the show we were watching and Paul switched to CNN to watch Larry King Live. I wasn't much interested but I stayed and watched to be with Paul. After Larry King was over, we got up and went to the bedroom and to bed.

The next morning when I looked out the window, it was still snowing. We're going to have a white Christmas for sure, I thought with delight. I jumped out of bed and I was showered and dressed before Paul's alarm even went off. I smelled coffee brewing so I headed for the kitchen with

Lady and her offspring following me. They went to the door and I let them out and stepped outside with them and watch the snowflakes drifting down.

It was a cold, brisk day and the poodles enjoyed it as I stood there with Lady and we watched her offspring run and tumble in the snow. I laughed when Lady could no longer sit idly by and jumped off the porch to join them.

I heard the door to the house open and I turned, wondering if it was Paul. It wasn't, it was Tracy. She just stuck her head out and said, "Sharon, aren't you cold? You're dressed pretty light to be outside. Why don't you come back in?"

I turned toward her, my whole body shaking in rage. How dare her to tell me what to do. I'd put her in her place. It was then I realized that my body was shaking with cold, not anger. "You're right," I said. "It is a bit brisk out here." Meekly I went back into the kitchen where it was warm.

After breakfast, I walked Paul to the door and told him goodbye. Then I went back into the kitchen, sat at the table and Tracy, bless her heart, warmed up my coffee before she sat down at the table with me.

We chatted about inconsequential things until I said, "The tree is trimmed, presents are under the tree and we are ready for Christmas, except for one thing."

"What is that?" Tracy asked.

"I haven't gone Christmas shopping."

"Well, go girl, there isn't that much snow out there. Get in that red Vibe and make like old Santa Clause."

I sat there in silence, should I tell her about me getting lost yesterday? In truth I was scared to go. What if I should get lost and could never find my way home? "Tracy, I'm afraid to," I finally confessed.

She looked at me quizzically, "Afraid, I didn't know you were afraid of anything."

"I am now. I'm sure it is the antidepressant medication, but I got lost yesterday. Imagine that, me lost in Stillwater where I have lived practically all of my life. It's hard to believe, isn't it?"

She looked at me oddly so I continued, "I left HomeLand grocery going west and somehow I got distracted and missed my corner. The first thing I knew, I was in a part of Stillwater where I had never been before. Or it seemed like it. I didn't recognize anything. It was as if I were in a strange town where I had never been. I turned off at a side street, found a place to stop and parked the car for a while. I was bewildered and frightened. When I stopped shaking, I went back to the busy street and headed east. Again I didn't recognize my corner but I kept on driving. At last I saw a place that I recognized."

"What was it?"

"Wal-Mart," I laughed. "I can always recognize a Wal-Mart. So I drove into Wal-Mart's parking lot, turned around and drove right home. I can always find my way home from Wal-Mart."

Tracy sat in thoughtful silence and then she asked, "Have you told Paul about this?"

"No, and I don't intend to. Not until after Christmas, anyway. He'll insist on dragging me back to Dr. Stringer and Dr. Stringer will give me another antidepressant drug. Then I'll go through it all again. He'll try different medications and they will probably make me feel sad or frightened. I like the medicine I'm taking now, except for it making me forgetful.

"Maybe after Christmas I'll tell him, but not now. Christmas is such a magical time of the year. Christmas is the season for miracles, anything can happen. Great and wondrous things can come to you at Christmas time. It's at Christmas time when the greatest miracle of all happened, Christ, our Lord and Savior was born."

Again Tracy sat in silence for a while and then she laughed, "If you don't mind shopping with the hired help, go fire up that Vibe and I'll go shopping with you."

"Hired help!" I exploded. "Don't you ever refer to yourself as 'hired help'. You're part of the family." Then I realized that I wasn't joking, I was actually angry. I had no reason to hurt such a woman as Tracy. I loved her and I started to apologize but before I could, she said, "Thank you," and there were tears in her eyes.

I think she thought that my anger was mock anger, but it wasn't. Let her go ahead and think it was mock anger, it was better that way.

"Give me time to clean up the kitchen and we'll be on our way."

While she bustled around the kitchen, I let Lady and her brood in and then hustled up some snow-boots. I was ready to go by the time she had the kitchen cleaned and had just stepped back inside after starting the car.

"Aren't you going to wear a coat?" Tracy asked as she took her coat from the tree and put it on.

"Oh, Yes. I almost forgot."

"You'd remembered soon enough when you stepped outside," she laughed. "Want me to drive?"

I really would have preferred that she did, and I would have said yes if she hadn't previously referred to herself as 'hired help'. Let my 'hired help' drive me around town? Not on your life. "I'll drive," I said.

On the way downtown I asked, "Are you and Pete going to have Christmas dinner with us?"

She paused for a moment, looked at me strangely and then said, "No, we're going to Tahlequah to spend Christmas with our families. And that reminds me, can we take my car? We could take Pete's pickup but it's a gas guzzler and it doesn't do all that well if there is snow or ice on the road."

"Of, course. Like we told you when you came to work for us, it's your car to use as you wish. All you have to do is put gas in it."

I drove a little farther before I said, "It really isn't any of my business, but are you and that hunk, Pete, planning on getting married?"

"Yes," she answered and blushed. "He has asked me and I said 'yes'."

"Have you set the date yet?"

"Not for certain. I want to wait until after I graduate, but Pete, the romantic fool, wants us to get married on Valentine's Day. To be truthful, the idea appeals to me too. But I want to keep my job with you guys and it is so handy to stay with you that I think we have to be practical."

I didn't say anything more about it, but I had some ideas on the subject. For example, Mrs. Cummings, the widow woman who lived two houses down the street had turned her detached garage into a small rental which she rented to married college couples. If I wasn't mistaken, the young couple who lived there now had finished school this semester. I would check it out shortly. The second house down the street would be a handy place for Pete and Tracy to live.

We hit every gift store in Stillwater and some of them twice but when we left the first store and Tracy again asked to drive, I let her. When the back of my car was full, we went back home and I had Christmas presents for everyone. Now I had to only wrap them. It had been such a glorious day and I had rediscovered that Tracy was a most endearing friend to have.

By the time Paul came home from work, I had them all wrapped and under the tree.

As usual, after we were through with dinner, Paul and I went to the living room to watch television. We were into the middle of Larry King Live and Paul had muted it for a commercial break when I asked, "How is Pete working out at work?"

I noticed that Paul gave me an odd look before he told me.

Chapter 13

I AWOKE AND FELT THE WARMTH of Paul as he snuggled against my back. It felt as warm and familiar as it had for all these many years. I snuggled back into him with a feeling of pleasure and then my eyes opened. I looked out of the window and murmured softly, "Oh, no."

The sun was shining brightly and water was dripping from the roof in a steady stream. Already there were puddles where the snow had melted. If it had just remained cold for one more day. One more day and we would have had a white Christmas. But it was not to be.

I got quietly out of bed and slipped on a thin robe and house-shoes. Softly I opened the door and went to the kitchen where Tracy was making preparations to cook breakfast. "No white Christmas again this year," I said to her as I got down a mug and filled it with coffee.

"Doesn't look like it," she said looking up from her work. "Too Bad."

I looked at the door which led to the porch and there sat the four poodles waiting to go out. Carrying my cup, I went to the door and opened it. The four dogs went dashing out with such enthusiasm that I joined them. I laughed as I stood there, sipped coffee and watched them dash about in the disappearing snow.

Time must have flown by as I watched the dogs and before I knew it, I heard the door open and Paul was there, all shaved and dressed for work. "Better come in, Squirt," he said, "I know it looks warm but it's too cold for you to be standing out there in a thin robe and house-shoes."

"You have to go to work today? Tomorrow is Christmas."

"Just until noon. The plant closes down today at noon for Christmas."

"When does it open again?" I asked, walking by him and stepping inside.

"January the second," he answered.

"And I'll have you all to myself until then," I said, tiptoeing and giving him a kiss.

"Yes, poor you. I'll probably have to go down and check on things from time to time, but if you want to, you can go with me."

After breakfast and seeing Paul off, I let the poodles back in. I freshened my coffee, sat at the table and watched Tracy as she cleaned the kitchen. "Are you excited, Tracy? Are you excited about Christmas?"

"Very much so," she said as she put the last of the dishes in the washer and started it. She then took her coffee cup and sat down at the table across from me. "All there is to do now is wait. Wait until the dishes are washed, then put them up and wait some more for Pete to get off work."

"Then you two will be heading to Tahlequah?"

"You can bet on it. It will be nice to go home."

"Don't you have to pack before you go?"

"I packed last night. My backpack is in the car and I've filled the car with gas. All there is to do is to wait until Pete gets off of work at noon. Then we hit the open road."

We sat there in comfortable silence and then I said, "Tracy, the other day when I went grocery shopping, the strangest thing happened. Coming home, I got lost. Isn't that unbelievable. I have lived in Stillwater practically all of my life and have probably driven every street in town a hundred times and yet I got lost." Can you believe it?"

Trace gave me a very strange look, maybe she didn't believe me, but I went on.

"I left HomeLand grocery going west and somehow I got distracted and missed my corner. The first thing I knew, I was in a part of Stillwater where I had never been before. I didn't recognize anything. It was as if I were in a strange town where I had never been. I turned off at a side street, found a place to stop and parked the car for a while. When I had stopped shaking, I went back to the busy street and headed east. Again I didn't recognize my corner but I kept on driving. At last I saw a place that I recognized."

I waited for her to respond but she just sat there with an odd look on her face.

"Wal-Mart was the place I recognized" I laughed. "I can always recognize a Wal-Mart. So I drove into Wal-Mart's parking lot, turned around and drove right home. I can always find my way home from Wal-Mart."

There was a long silence with Tracy just sitting there staring at me before she said, "Does Paul know?"

"No, I haven't told him. Perhaps I will," I said. "Perhaps after Christmas I'll tell him. I already know what he will do. He'll drag me to see Dr. Stringer and he will give me a different antidepressant. I know that is what caused it, the medication I'm on now, but I don't want a different one. This one works. But Dr. Stringer will give me a different one. Maybe it will work and maybe it won't. Maybe the new medication will make me sad, angry, or frightened. I hate to go through all of that again when what I'm on now works so well, other than I tend to forget things."

"I still think you should tell Paul and tell him soon."

"I will," I said, but even as I said it, I knew deep down that I wouldn't.

I was in the spare bathroom giving the poodles a bath. They had been so muddy when they came in that I knew it wouldn't do. Every one of them had to shake on me when I took them out of the tub to dry them off, even Lady. I had almost as much water on me as they did.

The last one to get a bath had been Snowflake, and I was just drying her when I heard the front door open and I could recognize from his voice that it was Paul. But he had someone with him.

Hurriedly, I finished drying Flake, set her down, and went into the living room. I saw immediately that the person who was with him was Pete.

"Look what followed me home, Squirt," Paul said as he came across the room to gather me in his arms.

"I'm going to get your clothes all wet and dirty, Paul."

"Who cares? I won't be dressing up again to go to work for over a week."

"Ready to hit the road, Sport?" Pete asked.

"I've made us some sandwiches, Pete. Should we eat them here or eat them on the road?"

"Let's eat them on the road."

"What about your pickup. You want to swing by your apartment and drop it off?"

"Mr. Phillips said I could leave it here. All I have to do is put my duffel bag in the car and we are on our way."

"Sharon, I have a pot of stew on the stove simmering. It will be ready for your dinner," Tracy said as she set the bag of sandwiches down and put on her coat.

"What kind of stew? Beef, I hope," Paul asked.

"Yes, there's some beef in it, along with left over chicken, pork, and lamb. I'd say it's left over stew. I cleaned out the freezer and fridge to make it," Tracy laughed. Then she said on a more serious note, "If I find some good lamb while I'm in Tahlequah, do you want me to bring some back?"

"Please do," Paul said, reaching into his hip pocket and taking out his billfold. "Let me give you some money."

"I'll take care of it and you can repay me when I bring it back," Tracy said as she reached for the door. "Bye, now. And have a Merry Christmas."

"You too," Paul and I both said and then Paul added, "Drive carefully."

"We will," she said as she closed the door behind her.

Then Paul turned to me and said, "Why don't you change those clothes and then we'll sit down to eat. You're all wet and I'm afraid you will catch a cold."

"Okay," I said and turned and headed to the bedroom. I tossed the towel into the spare bedroom on my way. As soon as I put on dry clothes, I rejoined Paul in the living room and we went into the kitchen to eat.

"They make a nice couple," I said to Paul as we were eating.

"They sure do. I wonder if they will ever get married."

"Oh, yes. Tracy told me that Pete has asked her and she said yes."

"When, I wonder."

"According to Tracy, Pete wants to get married on Valentine's Day, but Tracy wants to wait until after she graduates. She didn't say so, but I think she feels obligated to live with us until after they graduate."

"That's nonsense. They could go ahead and get married and both of them live with us until Tracy graduates."

"Paul! Newlyweds like to live by themselves. Have you forgotten?"

"No," he said, grinning a wicked grin.

I laughed and said, "What I've been thinking is that Mrs. Cummings, two houses down, turned her garage into a small apartment for married couples. I think the couple who lived there graduated this past semester and they are now in the process of moving out. Couldn't Tracy and Pete live there and she could still work for us?"

"You have it all planned out, don't you, Squirt?"

"Well, no, I've just been thinking."

"How about their wedding, do you have it all planned?"

"Of course not, Paul. But it would be so handy if they could live down at Mrs. Cummings and she could still take care of the house for us."

"Sure. I don't know what she is charging for rent, but with Tracy and Pete both working part time, I'm sure they could swing it. After lunch I'll call her and find out if it will soon be vacant and how much rent she charges. If I think the kids can handle it, I'll rent it for them as a Christmas present and a wedding present."

"Now, who is meddling in their lives," I said, laughing.

"We both are," he grinned. "But renting it for them and paying the first month's rent is a good idea, don't you think?"

"Marvelous," I said. "How is Pete working out at Mercury Marine?"

Paul put down his uneaten sandwich and looked at me with concern. "Are you okay, Squirt?"

"Yes, I'm okay. Why do you ask?"

"This is the third day in a row that you have asked me that question and I wondered what was going on."

"I'm sorry, Paul. It's just the medication I'm on. It makes it hard for me to remember anything. I'm always losing my shoes, clothes and misplacing my coat." I thought seriously about telling him I had lost myself the other day, about getting lost coming home from grocery shopping, but I didn't. That would be all he needed to drag me to Dr. Stringer.

Paul didn't say anything for the rest of the day. But that evening while we were watching Larry King Live, he asked, "Do you suppose we should make an appointment for you with Dr. Stringer?"

"Why?" I asked startled. "I'm not sick or anything."

"About you forgetting about what you have already said, and forgetting where you put things."

"No, no, you'll just have to be patient with me. You, Tracy, and the kids will just have to be patient and remember that I lose things. Other than making me forgetful, the medication I'm on now is working. You can do that, can't you? You and the kids can be patient with me and help me find the things I lose? Pleeeese!"

"We can, Squirt," he said and then he was quiet. The commercial ended and Larry King came back but Paul didn't turn the sound back on. Finally he put both arms around me and hugged me. "It has been a hell of a ride, Squirt, but all too soon and it will be over."

"What do you mean?" I asked, apprehensively. I didn't like the sound of what he said.

"Let's face it, Squirt. I'm already fifty-three and you'll be fifty this February. Both of us have more life behind us than we do in front of us. I doubt that you'll live to be a hundred and I doubt that I'll live to be a hundred and three. This isn't leap year, is it?"

"No," I answered. Larry King was asking his guest a question but Paul still had it muted.

"Then we won't be having a wedding anniversary this year. I can't believe that we thought it would be cute to get married on a leap year and get married on February the twenty-ninth," he laughed.

"I still think it's cute."

"Anyway, this year we will have been married twenty-six years. We will probably celebrate our fiftieth anniversary and maybe our sixtieth if we're lucky, but I doubt if we'll both be around to celebrate our seventieth."

"You're talking so sad, Paul. It makes me wish we could live our life over again."

"What would you do different?" Paul asked.

"Nothing," I laughed.

"I would."

"What?" I asked.

"I'd look for you sooner and when I found you, we'd get married right away."

"That's sweet," I said. Larry King was over and we had missed hearing the last half of it, but I had enjoyed listening to Paul much more than I would have enjoyed listening to Larry King. The last thirty minutes had been one of those rare, golden moments in life. It seemed as if a miracle had happened and it wasn't even Christmas. Not yet.

I was up long before sunup Christmas day and as soon as I let Lady and her brood out, I turned on the lights on the tree. We had left the Christmas lights strung around the house on all night.

Paul had set up the coffee pot before he went to bed and I turned it on when I let the poodles out. As soon as the coffee was done, I poured me a cup, turned off the overhead lights in the house and found my way to the living room where the Christmas tree was and sat down. I sat there watching the tree lights blink off and on with a feeling of awe. I took a sip of coffee and found it was cold. The cup was still almost full. It seemed a shame to pour out a full cup of coffee so I stood went into the kitchen and put it in the microwave. As it was warming, I heard the poodles scratching at the door wanting in. When I opened the porch door, I saw the first red streaks of dawn and not a cloud in sight. Christmas was going to be a gorgeous day, even without any snow.

I was sitting in my chair, my cup of coffee on the right side of me so I could reach it handily and my lap was full of poodles when Paul came in and turned on the lights. "It looks like you've been up for hours," Paul said.

"I've been up for a while. You know I always get up early on Christmas. Turn off the lights and let's look at the tree."

"As soon as I get my coffee. You need yours freshened up?"

I took a sip and found it had cooled. "If you don't mind," I said, handing him the cup. "I don't know if I could ever get out from under these dogs."

"Have they been out yet?"

"Out and in," I laughed.

When Paul came back in with our coffee, he turned off the lights and joined me. We didn't speak but still we communicated. Together we shared the awe of one more Christmas.

Chapter 14

AT FIRST I THOUGHT BEING MARRIED and living in an apartment next door, would slow things down for Tracy, but it didn't slow her down one bit. It was the middle of March and when I got up before Paul, I slipped on a robe and went to let the poodles out. Tracy was already in the kitchen and coffee was made.

"How is the old married woman this morning?" I asked as I went to get a cup of freshly brewed coffee.

She looked at me and blushed, "Dreamy," she said with a small smile on her lips. "I can hardly believe that yesterday was our first anniversary."

"Anniversary?"

"Yes, yesterday we celebrated being married a month," and then she laughed. "It's a good thing I loaded down on classes the first part of college and only have to take a light load to graduate. Otherwise I wouldn't make it. It's difficult to concentrate on my studies as it is. All I want to do is stay at home and be an Indian maiden waiting for her brave to return from the hunt. See, Sharon, you're not the only one who has flights of fancy and I'm also getting very absent minded."

"Oh, Lord," I said, "with two of us in the same house, there is no telling what will happen."

I saw Paul off to work and then Tracy went to class with a promise that she would be home by eleven-thirty. It was Tuesday and, with her light load, she had only two classes, a nine o'clock and a ten o'clock. I thought about going for a walk down by the lake but somehow it didn't sound exciting.

When Tracy left to go to class I let the poodles in. Again I looked at the lake and thought about taking a walk but for some reason I wasn't in a hurry. I heard the mailman come and walked out to the mail box. It was full of advertisements, catalogues, and bills. It was that time of the month and bills were due. I separated the bills from the other mail as I walked to the house. I dropped the mail, other than the bills, on the dining room table to look at later and went on back to the den where I placed the bills on the stack of other bills which had come in earlier. I looked at the stack of bills and knew it was time to pay them. This was a job that had gradually migrated to me in the first two years of marriage. Paul thought that since I had a degree in education with emphasis on mathematics, I should be the one to take care of the household finances. I don't know why, balancing a check book and keeping the books straight only need the skill of addition and subtraction and I had never in my life used the quadratic formula or had to find the first derivative of a fourth degree equation. I even had a desk calculator to do my addition and subtraction.

True, I taught middle school math until the twins came along and then Paul insisted that I be a stay-at-home mom. "I'll make the money and you spend it," he often said joking. It sounded pretty good to me and I took charge of the household finances.

Now it was time for me to jump in and do my part of the bargain. I sat down at the desk, took a letter opener and opened the one on top of the pile. It was a bill for the Chase credit card company. I pulled the papers along with brochures advertising luggage and copper bottom stew pans at the lowest price ever, dumped brochures in the trash and looked at the bill. I looked at it and looked at it. The more I looked at it, the less I could make head or tails of it. How much did I owe? Why did they have to make things so complicated?

I set that bill aside along with the return envelope and opened another one. It was from the electric company. Thankfully it had no brochures in it, just a plain old bill with a return envelope. This should be simple enough. Again I looked at it and then looked at it again. How much did I owe? I couldn't tell and I was beginning to become frustrated. I sat back in the chair and closed my eyes. I felt tears running down my cheeks. It was the antidepressant medicine I was sure. Perhaps I should go back to Dr. Stringer. If I had forgotten how to pay the bills, what more would I forget? Then I remembered what an awful time I had when I first started taking the antidepressant medication. I didn't want to go through it again if there was some other way. If I could figure out a way to pay the bills this month, maybe I would get my memory back next month. Maybe next month I could do it with ease.

But I couldn't let this month go. If I did, Paul would find out about it and what explanation could I give him? Logically there were two things for certain; one, the bills had to be paid, and two, I didn't remember how to pay them. Logically it therefore followed that someone else would have to, this time.

Tracy came to mind, she would have to do it. It was also evident that I couldn't go to her and say, 'Tracy, I've forgotten how to pay the bills, will you do it for me?" That would mean a trip to Dr. Stringer for certain. I had to find another way; I had to trick her into doing it without her knowing why. But how could I do that? Of course if I couldn't write, I couldn't make out checks, could I? So the logical thing would to be to break my right hand. But that would hurt and just the thought of it sent shivers up my spine. Breaking my hand seemed like overkill. Perhaps I wouldn't have to break it, just injure my index finger or thumb. If that should happen I wouldn't be able to write, would I?

Then I remembered; a little over four years ago, I had been driving a stake in the ground and I hit my finger with the hammer. The skin hadn't been broken but the finger was bruised and swollen. Paul thought that perhaps it was broken so he had taken me to the doctor to have it x-rayed. It hadn't been but they put a finger guard on it so it wouldn't hurt should I bump it against something. If I remembered correctly, I still had the finger guard somewhere.

I left the den and went to the bedroom and my closet. I found the shoebox which had old shoestrings and other junk in it and I sat on the bed to go through it. Sure enough, I found the finger guard. I put the junk back into the shoebox and the shoebox in the closet and went back to the den. If Tracy was to pay the bills she would need some signed checks.

I got my checkbook and opened it. I looked at the blank checks and studied them with confusion. I had even forgotten how to write a check. Nevertheless, I remembered where they were to be signed. I opened all the bills and counted them. There were six of them. I signed six checks and then went back to the bedroom where I found a roll of tape in the medicine cabinet. I slipped the finger guard over my index finger and taped it in place. When I finished, I inspected it closely. Looked good to me. But how did I hurt it? I had to think of something. I left the bedroom, went back to the kitchen, stepped out on the patio and sat down. How did I hurt my finger? I had to think of something.

I laughed when I saw Elvira and Doc wrestling with each other. They were both making such ferocious growls as they snapped at each other and their teeth clicked on empty air. Snowflake was sitting to one side watching them with an aloof expression. Then, almost on cue, they both turned and attacked Snowflake.

I heard a car stop in the driveway and I looked at my watch. It was eleven thirty. Tracy was home from class. How did I hurt my finger? I had to come up with something and fast. And then I had it. I jumped up and all but ran to the den. Although Tracy and Pete lived in their own apartment close by, Tracy still had her room at our house and that is where she did most of her studying. When she came by with her arm loaded with books, she must have seen the light on in the den because she stuck her head in and said, "Hi." I was sitting here clumsily holding the pen and trying to write and I looked up at her.

She took two more steps down the hall as my heart fell, but then she came back still holding her books. "What in the world did you do to your finger?"

"It was an accident," I said, trying to smile sheepishly. "Elvira and Doc were in a mock battle and one of them must have bit the other too hard and a real fight broke out. When I reached down to separate them, one of them, either Doc or Elvira, chomped down on my finger. They hardly broke the skin but they bruised it and made it swell. Of course you know how a sore finger is. Every time you bump something, you bump it with the sore finger, so I put the finger guard on to keep from hurting it."

"You think I should look at it?"

"No, I have it taped up pretty good. The only real problem is I can't write and I have bills to pay today."

"They can wait until after lunch, can't they?"

"Of course, I just want them ready to go into the mail in the morning."

"Then I'll put up my books and get with it. Pete will be here soon and he'll be in a hurry so he can eat and go to work." She hurried down the hall and soon passed the den again as she went to the kitchen. I heard her in the kitchen bustling around and then I heard a vehicle park in the driveway and Pete come in.

Tracy and Pete ate with us most of the time with breakfast being the exception. Pete wasn't a big breakfast fan and he usually had a bowl of cereal in their apartment before he headed off to his morning classes. Being a first semester freshman, and needing to enroll in everything, he enrolled so that all of his classes were in the morning. He didn't even check the afternoon classes. In the afternoon he worked at Mercury Marine.

I stayed in the den long enough for Tracy to greet him with what I supposed was an affectionate hello and then I joined them. Tracy had a slight blush as she went back to the kitchen with a dreamy look in her eyes. Soon she called, "Sandwiches are made," and the three of us gathered around the table.

Pete ate quickly, Tracy saw him to the door and he was soon off to work. When Tracy and I had finished lunch, she cleaned up the kitchen and we went to the den. I handed her a signed check and the top bill. "How is it that you have checks already signed?" she asked, looking at me with curiosity filled eyes.

"That's the way I do it," I laughed. "I count the bills, sign the checks and then fill each check out for the amount."

"Do you want me to record the amount in the register?"

"That is almost asking too much, but if you don't mind, yes."

I watched as Tracy paid the bills. She was very efficient as she seemed to be with everything she did. When the checks were made out and stuffed into the addressed envelopes, I put on the return stickers and a stamp. I then took them to a clip mounted on the wall beside the door and clipped them on to take out the first thing the next morning. That is if I could remember it.

I heard Tracy start the sweeper and I went outside. It looked so beautiful down by the lake with the wild plum trees blooming, that I started down there, Boomer in front, making sure I was safe from squirrels and with the poodles following him. Of course, all of the dogs had to wade out in the lake where the water was the very best and then they had to come right up against me to shake. After that, down the lake we went.

Boomer took the lead sweeping the shoreline, the three young poodles following him and watching him closely. Boomer spotted a squirrel and took off after it, the three young poodles hot on his heels. Lady walked by my side in a dignified manner.

After a mile or so, I turned back and after walking a short distance I became worried. There were so many paths leading down to the lake and they suddenly looked the same. Which one led to my house? Could I recognize it when I came to it? I was confused and I was lost. Lost in practically my own back yard. Everything appeared strange even though I had walked this part of the lakeshore since the twins had been toddlers.

Onward I walked, stopping at each path and looking up it. They all seemed to be the right trail and yet at the same time, they all looked wrong. Soon I was all but running and the dogs, thinking it was a game, ran in front of me. Even Lady ran at my side. What if I didn't recognize the right path?

The solution to that was simple. Once I knew I had missed the trail to my house, I'd head back down the lake and go up every trail until I saw my house. Surely I'd recognize my house, wouldn't I? I tried to see a mental picture of my house in my mind and I couldn't. I had forgotten what our house looked like. It was then I felt the tears running down my cheeks.

It wasn't that I was concerned for my safety. I knew I'd get home eventually. If Paul came home from work before I got home, he'd set out looking for me and he would find me. But how would I explain it to him. How could I explain being lost this close to home? He would insist on taking me back to Dr. Stringer. Maybe he was right and maybe I should go see the doctor tomorrow. When I explained to him that though the medicine I was taking worked but gradually I was losing my memory, he'd try a different medication and I would have to go through that again. But it would be worth it if I could again remember things. Remember things again like I did before I started taking the drug. Yes, that's what I'd do. Tomorrow morning I would make an appointment with Dr. Stringer.

With that settled in my mind, I did break into a run and the dogs ran even faster, except for Lady, and she started lagging behind. I was in a hurry to get back home; that is if I could find home.

Suddenly Boomer turned to the left and started up a trail, the pups followed him and I followed the pups. It wasn't until I got to the porch that I realized that I lived here. At last I was home.

Chapter 15

I KISSED PAUL GOODBYE INSIDE THE house, grabbed the envelopes from their clip as he left for work and followed his car to the mailbox. I put the letters in, raised the flag and shut the lid. As I was walking back to the front door I noticed weeds were peeking through the black earth of the flower beds out front. Suddenly I had a project for the day; probably all of the flower beds needed tilling and weeded. But could I do it with the guard taped on my finger? What was wrong with my finger anyway?

When I was back inside, I went to the kitchen table and began to unwrap the tape. When the tape lay in a wad on the table, I gingerly pulled the finger guard off and looked at the finger. I bent it, squeezed it with my left hand; nothing hurt. Why did I have the finger all taped up, anyway? I tried to remember why the finger had been bandaged but I couldn't. There appeared to be nothing wrong with it.

I threw the tape in the trash and put the finger guard back into the shoebox which I was beginning to refer to as 'my junk box', and as I passed the utility room I found the one-handed, three tined rake, that I used to till the flower beds along with the small, garden trowel. I took them out front and began to work in the flower beds.

It was such a beautiful day without a cloud in the sky. The redbuds were almost ready to bloom and there was only a light breeze. The smell of spring was in the air and the birds were singing in the trees. A flight of geese went honking north and I stopped for a while to watch them. When they were out of sight and only their voices could be heard I went back to work. I looked around at the neighbor's yards on each side and I saw I was alone. I couldn't help it, I burst into song. Not the words, I didn't remember the words, but I hummed the tune at the top of my lungs as I worked in the rich, black earth.

It was midmorning when I heard a vehicle coming up the street and I turned around to watch. It was the mail carrier. He stopped at our box, took out the bills, and put new mail in. I stood, brushed off my hands and knees and went to get the mail.

There were the usual advertisements and box holders along with one envelope with a window in it, which I knew was a bill. I left my tools in the flower bed and took the mail inside. I lay most of it on the dining room table but took the bill on back to the den. There I sat down, opened the bill, saw it was from the TV cable company and I owed them fifty-seven dollars and thirty-six cents. Might as well get this taken care of, I thought, as I reached for the check book and made out the check. After recording the check in the register, I put the bill stub in the self-addressed envelope, sealed it, stamped it, and put a return address label on it. On my way back outside, I clipped the bill in the outgoing clip.

Outside I again went to work on the flower beds. I had just finished up the fourth one and had two more to go when Tracy pulled into the driveway. I knew it was after twelve and time for lunch.

"What are you doing, Sharon!" Tracy asked.

"Working in the flower beds. Spring will soon be here and I'll want to set out flowers."

"But you're working in your good clothes. Shouldn't you be wearing old jeans or something?"

I looked down to see what I was wearing and she was right. I was wearing the tan outfit that I had bought for dress up clothes. "You're right. I didn't pay any attention to what I had on. Spring time got a hold of me and I just had to start playing in the dirt. I'll change clothes after lunch before I go back to work."

"No need now," Tracy sighed as we walked together to the house. "You have already gotten those so dirty that I don't know if they'll ever come clean. I see you have taken the guard from your finger. Does it feel okay now? Is it sore or anything?"

By now we were in the house and Tracy put her books on a table by a chair. "My finger feels just fine, it isn't sore or anything."

"Want me to look at it?" Tracy asked as she headed to the kitchen to fix lunch.

"There's no need to. It feels fine. I can write with it without any trouble. One bill came in and I paid it. It's already in the outgoing mail."

"Good, did you call and make an appointment with Dr. Stringer?"

"No, why would I do that? I'm not sick. I feel absolutely glorious."

"I don't know why. You just told me yesterday afternoon to remind you to make an appointment with Dr. Stringer. You didn't tell me why and I just reminded you," Tracy laughed as she began to fry hamburger patties.

Pete came and soon we were eating hamburgers. A hot lunch tasted good for a change.

Pete left, Tracy started a load of laundry and I went outside to finish up the flower beds. By the time Paul got home for work, I had them ready to set out flowers.

The next morning as soon as Paul left, I got ready to go to town. It was Thursday and again Tracy only had a ten o'clock class and an eleven o'clock class. She was still at home when I headed towards the door with car keys in hand.

"Where you going, Sharon?" she asked.

"Spring is here. I'm going down to the Feeds & Seeds and buy flower sets."

"If it can wait until after lunch, I can go with you. All I plan on doing is cleaning house and it can wait."

"Why should you go? I have seen no interest from you in gardening."

"Sharon, with you on your medication, you forget where you're going and tend to get lost, remember?"

I stood in thought. What was she talking about? Me getting lost? Me getting lost in Stillwater? Ridiculous! I had lived here most all of my life. I knew every street, nook and cranny in this town. True, I was going to Feeds & Seeds, and I couldn't tell anyone how to get there, but I could drive right to it. "No, I don't remember," I said. "Me getting lost in Stillwater, that's a joke."

"Where are you going to get you plants?" Tracy asked.

"Feeds & Seeds, why?"

"So Paul and I know where to start looking for you if you're not home by dinner time."

She was beginning to irritate me with her implications about me getting lost in Stillwater, but I didn't say anything. I just went outside, got in the car and left.

At Feeds & Seeds I found that their greenhouse was full of starting plants. Since we had lots of shaded areas, I bought several flats of Impatiens and for the sunny areas, I bought Marigolds, Petunias, and Vincas. Then I threw in settings of any flowers that looked pretty.

I was soon home and by the time Paul got home, I had the front yard planted.

"This is latter March, Squirt," Paul said when he saw what I had done. "But it is March and we could get a freeze. What happens if it freezes?"

"If it's a light frost, it won't hurt them much; it would take a hard freeze to kill them. If that happens then I have to replant."

"I don't know, Squirt. You might be pushing it. It's not spring yet."

The next morning when I got up, I didn't shower and I put on the same clothes I had worn yesterday. Even though it was a dress outfit, the damage had been done and there was no use getting a different outfit dirty. I knew what I'd be doing today and that was outside working in the flowerbeds. As soon as I saw Paul off to work, I went outside and got with it.

It was the middle of the morning and I was busily setting out flower plants when I heard the back door open and I looked up to see a young man stepping out on the patio. There was something familiar about him otherwise I would have been frightened, as big and muscular as he was. He had made himself at home and had a cup of coffee in his hand. As he drew closer, my mind triggered a memory and I recognized him. It was my son, Chris, but my how he had grown. He was sure a big bruiser.

Laughing, I jumped to my feet and went to him. "Why aren't you at work?" I asked.

"We've started a new schedule, Mom. We're now open from six until nine. That's a long time for one druggist to count pills so this week Joe goes to work at six in the morning and stays until three and I go to work at noon. We're both there from twelve until three and that's the busiest time of the day."

"So you came to visit your old mom, huh? Why not Tiffany?"

"She's in class."

"So you come to visit me when there is nothing else to do," I said laughing. "That's okay; I'll visit with you whenever I get a chance. Let me get a cup of coffee and we'll sit on the patio.

Chris stayed on the patio while I went in to freshen my coffee. Chris had almost taken it all. When I emptied the pot, I set it in the sink and turned off the coffee maker.

"Isn't it a most beautiful day," I said as I sat down at the patio table with my son.

"To be truthful, I hadn't noticed, Mom," and then he smiled as he continued, "of course with you, everyday is a beautiful day."

I laughed as I said, "I suppose so," then I looked at his face and saw it was solemn and troubled. "What's bothering you?"

He was silent for a moment and then he said, "It's Tiffany."

"What's wrong with Tiffany?"

"Nothing. In fact that's the trouble. She is a fine, beautiful, intelligent young woman. She's fun to be with and I enjoy being around her. You could say she is my best friend."

"I think you're right, she is a fine, beautiful, and intelligent girl. If you enjoy being around her, what's the trouble?"

"Tiffany and I get along well but is that enough? Is friendship enough? Should there be more?"

It was my turn to be silent. I looked at Boomer. He had found a place in the sun on the porch and he was asleep. Occasionally I saw his back foot twitch and I knew he was running in his dreams. The four poodles were also asleep in the sun on the porch. Miss Calico was stretched out on the patio table and I reached over and rubbed her side which covered my hand with cat fur. I brushed my hands together to clear them of fur and as the fine hairs floated in the morning breeze I looked at Chris and asked, "Is there someone else you care for more than you do Tiffany?"

"No, no there isn't, but there are so many girls out there I'm not sure I can settle down with just Tiffany."

"Are you still friends with Lacy? I mean is she as good of a friend as Tiffany is?"

"Lord, no. Lacy really turned me on but when it came to conversation, she was a zero. All she wanted to talk about was a cute pair of shoes she had found, changing the color of her hair, or getting her nails done. We had absolutely nothing in common. Besides, she isn't even talking to me since we broke up."

"But Tiffany is different?"

"Yes, with her when she is around I just feel, oh I don't know, content, warm and fuzzy."

"But she doesn't, as you say, 'turn you on'?"

"I didn't say that. I don't know how many times I've asked, even begged, her to spend the night with me and even move in with me, but she won't. 'Only after we're married,' she says. She's kind of old-fashioned in that way."

"But Lacy spent the night with you?"

"Yes, she even lived with me for three weeks but we only had one thing in common and it wasn't conversation, if you know what I mean. I couldn't see myself spending my life with her. There are so many girls out there and some I haven't even met yet that I truthfully have trouble seeing myself spending my life with anyone yet."

Again I sit in silence before I said, "Chris, I'm going to level with you. You might not like what I'm going to say but I'm going to say it anyway for it's the truth as I see it. I've met so many mothers whose hopes were that their children would be popular with their peers. Now I know it's shallow of them in my way of thinking, but it's true.

"With you and Kris, just the opposite was true with me. Both of you were popular with your classmates. With you, it was almost too popular, especially with the females. I can remember times in high school when there would be two or three girls hanging around you at the same time."

"I know, Mom, I like the opposite sex. I can't deny that."

"I know, Chris, and I wouldn't have it any other way. But at the same time it worried me. Oh, not that you liked the opposite sex, but it seemed to me as if girls flocked to you. You could have had a date every night of the week with a different girl, had you wanted to. That was what worried me. I have been afraid you'd take women for granted and not treat them with respect. It was just too easy for you to set your eyes on one and gather her in.

"Now you are at the age when young people choose a mate and like the swans and geese, the human animal tends to mate for life, or that is their intention. Let me ask you a question, who is your best friend?"

Chris mulled the question over and then answered, "Tiffany."

"Do you think she will always be?"

"I can't see it any other way."

"Then you won't be making a mistake when you two get married. I'm not saying that after you're married and a good-looking woman walks by you won't look at her with a lustful eye. That's natural, but it's only lust. Lust is only temporary while love is forever. After you have lived long enough the lust will soon be a thing of the past but love will still be there. Should you go ahead and marry Tiffany, you'll even grow closer as time goes by. You might believe you love her as much as is possible now, but you just wait fifteen or twenty years and then you will begin to know what love is."

Chris looked at me intently and then stood as he said, "I have to go now, Mom."

"Why?"

"We've drunk up the last of the coffee." Then he walked to where I was sitting, picked me up and gave me a bone bruising hug. "Thanks, Mom," he said as he put me down.

Chapter 16

CHRIS AND TIFFANY HAD a beautiful wedding. Many of their cut flowers came from the flower beds in our yard. I made arrangements of irises, marigolds and other flowers I had planted. I was rather proud of the arrangements I made.

Chris selected JT as his best man and Tiffany's sister was the maid of honor. JT and Chris looked so handsome standing up there waiting and then the piano began the wedding march. We all craned our heads toward the back door.

Tiffany appeared on the arm of her father. She was so beautiful I couldn't help it, I cried. Just the thought that this beautiful woman would soon be part of our family almost burst my heart with happiness. We were very lucky indeed.

She came floating down the aisle and soon she was at Chris's side and they joined hands. A few minutes later and it was over. Tiffany Jackson was Tiffany Phillips and I was so very, very proud.

We held the reception at our house. Tracy had worked all morning on the hors d'oeuvre and had offered to cook the meal but I knew that would be going far beyond the call so we had the evening meal catered. After the meal was served, Chris and Tiffany left for Oklahoma City and the airport. They had a night flight for Jamaica.

When Chris and Tiffany left, it seemed as if the house wilted. We had bought the house when we found out I was pregnant. It was a good place to raise the children, but now the children were raised, the last one was mated and would soon be building a nest of his own. I felt an empathy with the house. The house had raised them well and so had I, if their judgment in mating was any factor. If I had been choosing a mate for Chris, I couldn't have chosen one better than

Tiffany. My children had all flown the nest and time was moving on. Slowly my world was passing.

When the last of the guests left, Paul and I sat outside and watched the fireflies twinkle down by the lake. I was in a reflective mood. I reached over, took his hand and said, "I know you can't stop it, Paul, but can't you slow it down a bit?"

"What? What are you talking about?"

"The world, don't you feel it? It's spinning too fast."

Paul sighed, "I know what you're talking about now, Squirt. I feel the same way. It seems like just a short time ago that you and I were married. No, I can't slow it down but at times like these I wish I could."

It was the middle of July and the day had been hot. Surprisingly, when Tracy finished cleaning up after dinner, she came out to join us. Pete was going to summer school and had gone home to study.

"Paul, Sharon," she said hesitantly, "You know Pete will be in school for the next three to three and a half years. Maybe four."

"I know," Paul said.

"I've put in applications at the Stillwater hospital, the hospital over at Perry, and down at Guthrie. It seems like my prospects are bleak. Anyway, I'm thinking of continuing my schooling and getting my masters in nursing. At least as much as I can of it until Pete graduates."

"Good," Paul said. "You can never have too much education."

"I don't know about that," Tracy laughed. "I think the reason I can't get a job here in Stillwater is that I'm overqualified. They want RN's that have gone through the eighteen month program. They don't have to pay them as much. I'm worried about even getting my masters because I'm afraid I'll price myself right out of a job. But I don't want to move to Oklahoma City or Tulsa and leave Pete alone here by himself. The thing of it is can I keep my job here with you guys?"

"What a question!" I exploded. "Of course you can. You can work for us as long as you want to. I keep telling you, you're family."

"No need to get mad, Sharon, but thank you."

I looked at Tracy and saw she had tears in her eyes. "Now don't start bawling on us, Tracy."

"I can't help it, Sharon. I'm just so happy. You guys are the best people in the world." and then she really broke down.

I jumped up and went to her and took her in my arms. Since she was sitting down, I could put my chin on the top of her head by tiptoeing.

Tracy went home and the mosquitoes soon drove Paul and me indoors. Together we sat on the couch and caught Larry King Live on the tube. When the show was over I stood and said, "I'm ready to go to bed."

"Go right ahead. I'm behind you."

I took just a few steps and suddenly the world started spinning and it spun too fast for me to keep my balance. The next thing I knew I was kissing the carpet.

"What's wrong!" Paul said rushing to me.

"I'm clumsy, Paul. Are you just now finding that out? I'm okay." The drop to the floor had straightened the world out and I stood and made my way to the bedroom.

It was the end of July before I lost my balance and fell again. Fortunately, I was down by the lake with the dogs and there was no one to see me. I just lay in the soft sand until I was ready, then I stood and went back to the house.

I went into the house, poured myself a glass of iced tea. I went to the living room, sat in my recliner and set the iced tea on a coaster on the table to my right. I took a sip and set it back down on the coaster. In the back I could hear the vacuum running as Tracy cleaned house.

All four poodles came to me and jumped onto my lap. I laughed and petted them and I heard the vacuum turn off. I knew then that Tracy was now dusting. The poodles jumped down from my lap and went to the door. Laughing, I got up and let them out. I watched them for a while but when I saw they weren't about to come back in, I went inside and to my recliner. I saw Tracy was now at the far end of the living room dusting and the lemon smell of Pledge filled the room. I sat down, kicked off my shoes, reclined back and reached for my tea. It wasn't there. Where had I put it?

"Tracy," I called, "do you know where I left my iced tea? I thought I had left it right here on the table," and I pointed to the spot where I had left it.

"You did," she laughed, "but I moved it to the left hand table when I dusted."

She moved my tea and she didn't put it back where it belonged! How dare her! White hot rage washed over me. "Tracy, you know that my coffee or tea, which ever I'm drinking goes here," and I pointed to the coaster on the right hand table. "My shoes, should I take them off, goes here," and I pointed to my shoes on the floor. "I think in the future, should you move something to dust or clean, that you put it back where it belongs."

"Yes, Ma'am," she said, hurt in her voice.

She should be hurt. She should learn to put things where they belong.

The room was silent as she finished dusting. Housework done, she went back to her room. Had I been too hard on her? Yes, I had been. Really what difference did it make? I had hurt her and there really was no reason to. I felt the tears run down my cheeks as I thought of what I had done.

I grabbed a Kleenex, wiped my face, then I let the foot rest down and sprang from my recliner. I went rushing down the hall. Her door was open and I went rushing in. She was typing on her laptop. I rushed in and threw my arms around

her. "I'm so sorry, Tracy. The temper fit I threw was completely uncalled for. Can you ever forgive me?"
"Of course, Sharon. I completely understand." Then she stood and hugged me. "Don't let it bother you at all."

It was early August afternoon and I was weeding the flower beds. I had avoided the marigolds because they were in the direct sunlight and it was hot. At last there was no putting it off so I knelt by the marigold beds. There were webs between the leaves and even between plants. Spider-mites, I thought. Spider-mites were a problem I fought every year. I stood and went to the utility room and found the shaker box of dust that I had used last summer to kill the spider-mites. It felt awfully light. I held it close to my ear and shook it. I could hear the rattle and knew there was some left, but was it enough? There wasn't. I hadn't gotten one bed completely dusted before I ran out.

I went in, grabbed my car keys and headed to the front door. I heard the vacuum running in the back of the house but I didn't bother to tell Tracy where I was going. I'd just be gone a minute.

The car was hot when I got in it so I started the engine, rolled down the windows and when I felt the cool blast of the air conditioner I rolled them back up and left.

At Feed & Seeds I quickly found what I was looking for, paid, and went out the door. I left Feeds and Seeds with a round box of dust that was guaranteed to kill spider-mites and head across the parking lot to my car. "Watch out spider-mites, here I come," I said as I got into the hot car and started it. I pulled out onto the street and headed home thinking how I would get after those mites. I'd teach those little buggers a lesson they wouldn't soon forget.

I turned a corner and looked out on the lawn of a house. I laughed, slowed down to watch as I saw a cat chasing a dog, either that, or a dog chasing a cat. I couldn't tell which. They were both the same size. There was a wooden lawn chair set up. Around and around the chair they went. Maybe they weren't chasing each other, maybe they were just running.

I went on down the street and when I came to an intersection, I turned. I looked at the houses as I drove slowly past. I hadn't been in this part of Stillwater in a long time. Where was I? Was I still in Stillwater?

Of course I was, but where? I drove a little farther and then turned left. I didn't recognize anything on this street. I passed a motorcycle shop and for the life of me I couldn't remember ever seeing a motorcycle shop in Stillwater before.

But the town was growing and new businesses were coming in all the time. By now I was sweating even though the Vibe's air conditioner was blowing full blast. I turned left on the next street determined on following it until I recognized something.

The street began to have potholes, then it turned to dirt and then it ended altogether. Only a dirt path led on down to a creek. I knew it was a creek because there was a solid bank of trees. I backed up to a place to turn around and headed back. I looked for a shade to park under. I was beginning to get panicky. I was lost, now what did I do?

I found a shady spot, parked under it and began to breathe deeply. I was shaking like a leaf and I knew I had to get myself under control. I couldn't think. My mind was foggy with fear. I was lost! I was lost! I was lost! My every being screamed at me. I closed my eyes and made my mind blank.

It seemed I vaguely remembered being lost before. Think! Think! When I was lost before what did I do then? Again I tried to remember and then it came to me. I had driven to Wal-Mart and then had gone home. I could always find my way home from Wal-Mart. But where was Wal-Mart? Was it west of me or was it east of me? Had I crossed Highway 177? I couldn't remember. It didn't make any difference; surely I could find Highway 177.

It was getting hot in the car and I felt sweat running down between my shoulder blades. I had calmed down somewhat so I started the car. My, but the cold air on me felt good. I drove to the next east-west bound street and turned right. I looked at the street signs and saw I was on Fifteenth Avenue. If I followed it west, I would find Highway 177 and then I could find Wal-Mart. A few blocks farther and the road curved to the south.

I stopped and turned around. I was thankful I was in a small car, one I could turn around about anywhere. If one had to get lost, the Pontiac Vibe was the car to get lost in. At Fifteenth Avenue I turned left and started going west. I had gone but a short distance and the road ended. The road was paved and well maintained, but all at once, it just ended. Again I turned around, fighting panic.

When I realized I was running back and forth on Fifteenth Avenue, I pulled to the curb, rolled down the windows and parked. I was so lost I didn't know where I was lost from and there was only one thing left to do. I hated to do it and I knew what would come next, but it was the only thing I could do. I reached into the console between the seats and took out the cell phone. I couldn't remember many things but I remembered my own telephone number and I called home.

It cheered me when I heard, "Phillips residence, Tracy speaking."

"Tracy, this is me, Sharon."

"Yes?"

"Well, I hesitate to mention it, but I'm lost. I need some help finding my way home."

"Where are you? I'll come and get you and you can follow me home."

"That's just the point, Tracy. I don't know where I am," I laughed. And then I realized that my laugh sounded hysterical.

"Calm down, Sharon. Look at a street sign and tell me what street you're on."

"Just a minute," I said as I started the car and drove slowly to the corner. I looked at the street sign and said, "I'm on Fifteenth Avenue and 433 Road."

"My, but you are away off course. Just stay there and I'll be there in about twenty minutes."

"Are you sure you can find me?"

"I'm sure. I'll be there shortly," and she hung up.

I eagerly watched for her with anticipation and also with worry. What if she couldn't find me? I was in near panic when I saw her car coming down 433 Road. She turned the corner, waved at me as she passed and in the rear view mirror I saw her turn into a driveway, back out and pull up behind me to park. She got out and came to me.

"Are you alright?" she asked.

"Just fine, other than being a little lost."

"Do you want to leave your car here and ride home with me?"

"Nonsense, just drive home slowly and I'll follow you."

"Are you sure? You look like you're stressed out."

"I'm sure. I just want to get home. Get home before Paul does so I don't have to tell him."

"Okay," she said, and walked back to her car, got in, and soon she was in front of me. I followed her as she led me to Highway 177, past Wal-Mart and home.

"Where did you go, Sharon," she asked when we were in the house.

I thought and thought and then I had to tell her, "I don't remember. All I can remember is getting lost."

"I see," she said and looked at me thoughtfully. "Perhaps you would like to take a shower. How long did you sit in the car before you called me. It must have been a good while because your clothes are all sweaty."

"It seems like I sat in it forever."

"Well, go shower. A cool shower will make you feel better. Now this is a nurse talking," Tracy laughed. "Listen to your nurse."

I did and she was right. I felt much better after I showered and dressed. True, I was exhausted, but I felt good. I went into the living room, sat in a recliner and lifted the foot rest. I'd had enough heat for this day. I didn't want to go back outside.

Lady and the pups must have felt the same way because they were in the house where it was cool. When they saw me sit down they came running and I soon had a lap full of poodles. I heard Tracy in the kitchen cooking dinner but she soon came into the living room and asked, "Do you want anything to drink, Sharon? I have just made a pitcher of iced tea."

"A tall glass of iced tea does sound good," I said, reaching for the handle to lower the footrest.

"Keep your seat," Tracy said hastily, "Don't go scattering those dogs all over the house. I'll bring it to you."

She headed for the kitchen and soon she was back with a glass for me and a glass for herself. She handed me my glass and then sat on the couch facing me. She looked at me and I could see worry and apprehension in her face. "We need to talk, Sharon."

"What about?"

"About today and other things. Paul must be told."

"No! no," I said and I felt tears flooding my eyes. "If Paul knows, he'll drag me to the doctor and the doctor will start trying other medications, trying to find something that will work."

"Probably so, but that's what should happen. That's what you should do. Are you going to tell him or am I."

I thought it over before I said, "You. Go ahead and tell him. It will be easier that way."

Chapter 17

"SHARON NEEDS AN APPOINTMENT," Tracy said that evening. We had finished eating and Pete had gone home leaving Tracy at our house to clean up. She sat down at the table between Paul and me. "She needs an appointment as soon as she can get one."

Paul didn't say anything for a while, just looked at her quizzically. "What does she need an appointment for?"

"She needs an appointment with a doctor. I had to go get her today. She was lost and I had to find her and have her follow me home."

"Is that true, Squirt?" he asked, concern in his voice.

"Partly," I mumbled. I didn't like this conversation. I didn't like it one bit.

"Partly true? Sharon, what part isn't true?" Tracy asked.

"I could have found my own way home once we went by Wal-Mart," I answered brightly.

"Where did you go, Squirt. How come you got lost?"

I sat there quietly trying to think. Where had I gone? Why had I gone? I couldn't remember. I sat there and sat there trying to think.

"Sharon?" Tracy questioned.

It was then I burst into tears. "I can't remember," I sobbed. "I went somewhere for something and it was important but I can't remember what for or why. It's the medication I'm on."

Paul stood, reached for a box of Kleenex and set them in front of me. Then he scooted a chair beside mine, sat back down, and took me in his arms. "It's okay, Squirt," he said, patting my back as I buried my head in his chest. "It's okay; we'll make an appointment with Dr. Stringer for you. I bet he'll know just what to do. Soon you'll be as good as new."

"You're probably right, Paul," Tracy said, "but it might be something else besides her medication. I've been researching problems like hers since it first started.

"The research started out as a research paper I had to do but the more I got into it, the more interested I became. I read books and I spent hours on the internet. Sharon's actions and her behavior fit the profile. All but one. The one thing that puzzles me is, she is so young."

"Thank you, Tracy," I said brightly, looking up at her, wiping my eyes and blowing my nose.

"You probably don't know it," she continued all but ignoring me, "but this isn't the first time she has been lost in Stillwater."

"It isn't?" Paul said and then looked at me.

"No, it all started just before Thanksgiving. Luckily she found her way home then," Tracy said.

"Why didn't I know about it?" Paul asked a tinge of anger in his voice.

"Because Sharon didn't tell you. She told me and asked me to promise not to tell you. At the time she told me I also thought it was just the medication she was on. But since I've done the research and have observed her, I wonder."

"What else could it be, Tracy?"

"I'm just a nurse, remember. I don't do diagnoses. That's what a doctor is for. But let me ask you something. The past few months, have you noticed her asking the same question over and over again?"

"Well, yes I have."

"Be sure you mention that to the doctor when you take her. Also, have you noticed her telling the same story over and over?"

"Yes, I have. But I thought it was just because we were getting older. I probably do the same thing."

"I'm sure you do, at times," Tracy smiled, "but be sure you mention it to the doctor."

Paul sat there in silence before he asked, "Tracy, is there anything else I should mention to Dr. Stringer?"

"Well, yes, there is. Sorry Sharon, I should have told you, but you have been the subject of the research paper I had to write. I turned in the paper but I kept on researching and keeping a log on you. I'll print it out for you to take with you tonight, Paul. You can take it with you when you get an appointment."

Paul sat there silently and then he asked Tracy, "You are a genuine, graduated, registered nurse, aren't you."

"Well, yes. I have everything but a job."

"You've got one now, if you want it."

Tracy looked at him startled, "I do?"

"Yes. The job may not last for long, but if you want it, I'm hiring you as a nurse to take care of Sharon until this is over and we find her problem. I'll increase your pay to a nurse's pay."

"I could never do that, Paul. You folks have been too good to Pete and me. Oh, I'll look after her and give her all the help I can, but I can't take an increase in pay unless a doctor prescribes a private nurse for her. I'm not sure that will happen. Actually I don't think he will. But if that should happen, then I'm applying for the job now."

"It's yours," Paul said, reaching over and shaking her hand. Then he turned to me and asked, "Squirt, how about Tracy going with us to the doctor's appointment? Would you like that?"

"I don't care, it doesn't make any difference to me," and it didn't. In fact it would be a relief to have Tracy along. It would be a relief to have her there to answer Dr. Stringer's questions instead of me. Besides, if Dr. Stringer asked me a question and I didn't remember, Tracy would.

"Do you want me to call in the morning and set up the appointment, Paul?" Tracy asked.

"That's asking too much of you, Tracy."

"I don't mind, I really don't. I suspect I'll be doing it many times in my career if I ever find a job."

"Go ahead then. Call me at the office and let me know what time the appointment is."

"Why?"

"So I'll know what time to take her."

"If I'm going then why don't I just take her? No use of you having to take off work when I can do it. After all, you did offer to hire me as her nurse. A private nurse does things like that."

Paul laughed a strained laugh, "Okay, I'll leave it in your hands if that's okay with you, Squirt?"

"It's okay with me," I said. And it was. I didn't really care about it. If there was some way out of going I would have taken it, but there wasn't. Paul and Tracy continued to discuss it but I let my mind wander. It was their idea, not mine, so let them work it out. Suddenly I remembered. "Spider mites!" I said.

"What?" Paul asked.

"Spider mites, spider mites are into the marigolds again this year. That's where I went when I got lost. I used up the last of the spider mite powder and I went to Feeds & Seeds to get some more. I was on my way home when I became lost. I just now remembered. See I do remember things," I said feeling victorious. "Do I still have to go to see Dr. Stringer?"

"I think she should," Tracy said.

"Yes, Squirt. You haven't seen him for over a year. Tracy will take you."

Ah, shoot, I thought. I'd have to think of something else. Again the talk between Paul and Tracy droned on and on. I pretended they were talking about someone else besides me. It was boring.

"I'm going to bed, then. I'll leave it up to you guys to discuss what's good for me as it seems I have nothing to say in the matter."

They didn't try to stop me and I hurried to the bedroom as fast as I could. I quickly undressed, let my clothes lay where they fell, put on my pajamas and crawled into bed. Everything that could go wrong that day, had, and I felt as if the situation had spiraled out of my control. I wanted to get to sleep as fast as I could before anything else could go wrong.

The next morning the sky was gray and as I looked out the window, I saw a splattering of rain drops. I looked at Paul's side of the bed and saw he was gone. I faintly remembered a small kiss on the cheek and a whispered goodbye. It had been Paul and he had already gone to work. I felt sadness. I hadn't awakened when he came to bed last night and was still asleep when he went to work. I hadn't told him goodnight and I hadn't told him goodbye. My world was passing and an important part of it I had missed today.

I stretched, got out of bed and slipped on my robe. I went to the kitchen and Tracy wasn't there. Neither were the poodles. I poured a cup of coffee, went to the patio door and looked out. The poodles were sitting on the porch watching it rain and sitting in *my* chair was Tracy. She was just sitting there where I usually sat as if she could take my place. Resentment flared but then I laughed at myself. Tracy was so good to me. I don't know what I'd have done without her yesterday. I slid the door open and stepped out.

"Good morning, Sharon. Boy, you must have been tired. You almost slept the clock around."

"You forgot something, Tracy," I said, still feeling a small twinge of resentment.

"What?"

"Since you are now my nurse, you are supposed to ask, 'How are *we* this morning."

I looked at her and saw that I had said the wrong thing and I was immediately sorry. "I'm sorry, Tracy. I didn't mean anything by it." I picked *another* chair and sat down.

"Even though I got a good night sleep, I'm still grouchy this morning."

"A rainy day grouch, huh?"

"No, I just don't want to go to that, that, *damn* doctor."

"I've met Dr. Stringer in my practice nursing and he seems to be a nice man."

"Oh, not just Dr. Stringer, I don't want to go to any doctor. The less I see of doctors, the better I like it."

"But this is necessary, Sharon. Maybe by catching something early we can head off something that would otherwise become serious."

"I know. I know I should go, but it doesn't mean I have to like it, does it?" and I smiled.

"Your appointment is at three fifteen."

"You did it again, Tracy," I said in mock anger. "I was just getting in a better mood and you had to go and ruin it."

Tracy was as bad as Paul. The appointment was at three fifteen but she had to have me in the waiting room at a quarter to three. I could have easily told her that we would be lucky to get in before four o'clock. Anyway, that was usually what happened. But not this day. Surprise, surprise, we got in early. It was a little after three when the nurse called me back to an examination room and there Tracy and I waited.

"Where's Paul?" Dr. Stringer asked when he came in.

"He's at work, I suppose," I answered. "Dr. Stringer, this is Tracy. She is a recent OSU graduate with a BS in nursing. She has kept house and cooked for us since she was a freshman at college."

"What's the problem, Sharon?" he asked. He asked me but he was looking at Tracy.

"Sharon has lived in Stillwater practically all of her life and yet, yesterday afternoon, she got lost." Tracy answered. "Could it be her antidepressant medication?"

"That doesn't sound good. Jump upon this table and let me check you out."

I did as he asked and he began to poke, prod, and feel.

"You can sit up now," he said when he was through. "Let me listen to your heart and lungs."

"You know as well as I do, Dr. Stringer, that I don't have one."

"Have a what?"

"A heart, Doctor. I don't have a heart."

"Same old Sharon," he said smiling. "Now take a deep breath and hold it."

When he was through, he sat down on a stool and studied me thoughtfully. He gave me his doctor's look and said, "Sharon, I'm going to send you to a neurologist in Oklahoma City. I know when the problem is beyond this old country doctor's diagnosis. There is a new neurologist that just moved to the city, a Dr. Nickelous. From all the reports I get, he's a good one and has all kinds of blue ribbon pedigrees. I'll make an appointment for you and try to get you in as soon as I can. You can take her home, Tracy; I'll call you as soon as I get the appointment."

"Okay," I said, and jumped from the table to the floor. Tracy and I headed for the door. Suddenly the world spun and the next thing I knew, I was sitting on my butt on the floor.

Both Tracy and Dr. Stringer rushed to me. "What's wrong, Sharon," Dr. Stringer asked as he and Tracy reached down to help me up.

"My butt hurts," I answered. "But other than that, I'm okay." I was back on my feet again but Dr. Stringer had me by one arm and Tracy had me by the other. The world had stopped spinning so I shook them off. "I'm okay," and I again started for the door.

"Does this happen frequently, Tracy?"

"If it had, I would have mentioned it, Doctor," Tracy answered. Aha, I thought. See she doesn't know everything about me.

"What about it, Sharon? Do you frequently become off balance and fall?"

"First time, Doctor," I said cheerfully. But I could tell by the expression that he didn't believe me. I never had been able to lie worth a damn.

"I have a half a mind to put you in the hospital," Dr. Stringer said.

"NO!" I said emphatically. "No hospital. Why would you put me in a hospital anyway?"

"For observation," he answered.

"By the nurses? By nurses with only eighteen months of training? Why would you do that when I have a fully, qualified, four year graduate nurse with me at my own house?"

"You're right," Dr. Stringer said, and then he turned to Tracy. "Keep a log, Tracy."

"Yes, Doctor, but I have already started one. Here it is if you like," and she offered him pages of paper stapled together.

"Thanks, Tracy," he said taking the paper. "I'll look at it and see what I can find out."

It was hot and sticky as we walked to the car. The rain had stopped, the sun was out and the pavement was steaming. Hotter still inside the car. It felt like we were in a sauna. But Tracy seemed excited. "What are you so excited about?" I asked once the air conditioner kicked in and the car had cooled down.

"You're my first real patient, Sharon, and I'm your own private nurse."

"I doubt that I'll be your last one," I said cheerfully. Her mood was infectious.

"I should hope not and I also hope the job is a short time."

"Paul must increase your pay to that of a registered, private nurse since that is what you are now."

"He doesn't need to do that. It won't be any more work than what I have been doing." She drove a short distance farther and we had passed Wal-Mart before she asked, "Do you resent me taking over, Sharon. I mean do you resent me stepping in and telling you what you should do?"

I only thought about it for a second before I answered, "Lord, no, Tracy. The truth of the matter is I'm relieved. I'm in your hands and I don't have to make the decisions, not me anymore but you. Believe it or not, I think I'm in very capable hands."

"Stop it, Sharon," she said turning loose of the steering-wheel with one hand and wiping her eyes. "You're going to make me cry."

We had no more than gotten home when the telephone rang and I picked it up. "Is Tracy there?" I recognized Dr. Stringer's voice.

"Yes, she is."

"Let me speak to her, Sharon."

"Tracy," I called, "it's Dr. Stringer and he wants to speak to you." I held the phone to my ear until I heard her pick up the kitchen phone and then I hung up. I went to the door and the poodles wanted in. I let them in and went back to the living room where I sat down in a recliner. Soon I had a lap full of poodles. I could hear Tracy talking in the kitchen and then I heard her hang up.

She came into the living room and said, "You have an appointment with Dr. Nickelous in Oklahoma City at ten o'clock next Tuesday, but first I have to take you to the hospital tomorrow at three…"

"No, I'm not going to the hospital."

"You don't have to stay, Sharon. I'm just taking you there to get a PET-scan."

"Oh, that's different."

Chapter 18

"ARE YOU SURE I SHOULDN'T take time off work and go with you and Sharon, Tracy?" Paul asked the next morning at the breakfast table.

"No need, Paul. All we'll be doing is sitting and waiting for them to do the PET-scan. It really isn't that much, I promise."

"Okay, but you are sure taking on extra duties without the extra pay."

"Let's not get into that again," Tracy said, standing up and collecting our breakfast plates. She began to rinse them in the sink while I walked Paul to the door.

After seeing Paul off, I went back through the kitchen, freshened up my coffee and stepped outside. It was a beautiful day and it hadn't started getting hot yet. The morning air smelled as if it had been washed clean by yesterday's rain. There was very little wind and as I looked at the lake I saw only small ripples. Tracy stepped outside and sat on the patio with me.

"It's still cool, Sharon, what are you planning to do?"

"I should really dust the marigolds for spider-mites after all I went through to get the dust," I laughed. "But somehow I'm just not interested. I think I might go down to the lake. It will be cooler down there longer than it will be up here."

"Mind if I go with you?" she asked.

"I'd be delighted. But surely you have something else planned."

"I do. I still have to make the bed and vacuum the house, but I can take care of that after it grows hot. I can get a small start on the washing while you get dressed."

"Dressed?" I looked down and saw I still had on my pajamas, robe, and house shoes. I jumped to my feet and headed to the door. "It won't take me but a minute. If you're going to start something, you'd better hurry. Watch out lake, here we come!"

I quickly dressed and sure enough, when I passed the laundry room, I heard the rumble of the washing machine. Tracy was outside waiting on me, and so were the four poodles and Boomer.

I have no idea how the dogs knew we were going to the lake, but they somehow knew. As soon as I stepped out onto the porch, Boomer began to whine and wag his mangled tail while the poodles began yapping. "Come on boys and girls," I laughed, "Lake, here we come."

Of course when we got to the lake, all of the dogs jumped in and began swimming. When they came out, they came to Tracy and me and shook. I laughed and put my hands up which did very little to keep me dry. Then we started down the lakeshore with Boomer out in front in his usual position while the poodles stayed between us and him.

I hadn't been to the lake for a while. Anymore it frightened me to be at the lake by myself. What if I got lost like the last time except this time the dogs didn't turn up the right path to home? I felt safe and reassured to have Tracy at my side.

We had gone but a short distance when I saw two old lawn chairs with aluminum frames and tattered backing folded and leaning against a tree. I stopped and looked at them.

Tracy noticed and laughed, "Those belong to Pete and me. We spend a lot of evenings down here on the lakeshore. Money is tight for us right now and we're saving as much as we can to pay Pete's tuition. Sitting by the lake and watching the ducks and geese feed in the evening doesn't cost anything. Sometimes Pete even fishes, but he hasn't caught anything so far."

"Tracy, there are many more important things than money. You and Pete have your youth, your health, and your future before you. That's something money can't replace."

"I know, Sharon, but sometimes I wish we also had money." Then she laughed, "I guess I want it all."

"You have it all," I said reaching up and patting her on the back.

I was having such a wonderful time with Tracy as we walked by the lake that I hated for it to end. But then it started growing hot and we turned around to head back. Yes, I hated for it to end but it had grown so hot and sticky by the time we got back to the trail that even the dogs were drooping. As we approached the house I heard the deep rumble of the air conditioner.

When we got back to the yard, Boomer found himself a shady spot, dug himself a bed in the damp earth and lay down to take a nap. But not the poodles, they followed me into the house where it was cool. As Tracy became busy doing laundry and vacuuming the house, I sat in a recliner and leaned back. The poodles spread out in various spots in the living room and stretched out on their backs on the cool carpet, all four feet in the air. I glanced at the clock and saw it was ten forty-five. Just a few hours until Tracy would be taking me down town for a PET-scan. I dreaded it, saw no reason for it, and I willed time to slow down. But it didn't, the second hand on the clock kept going around and around. I wondered if the PET-scan would hurt.

At a quarter to two that afternoon, Tracy had me go and take a shower. When my shower was over, I took as long as I could to dress but it didn't make a lot of difference. By two fifteen we were in the car and heading downtown.

When they called me back for my PET-scan, they had me do some calisthenics and asked me all kinds of stupid questions, like what was my name, where did I live, who was the president and who was the president before him. Then they asked me questions that were really none of their business, like how old I was, how much I weighed, and how tall I was. Then they did the PET-scan and it didn't hurt at all. All that worry and dread had been for nothing.

"I think I'm in the mood to burn some steaks," Paul said Friday just as Tracy started to leave, "You and Pete have any plans for tomorrow evening?"

"I don't and I'm sure Pete doesn't."

"I'll give the kids a call and why don't you and Pete come over?"

"Okay," Tracy said, "If Pete has any previous plans I'm sure he'll change them when he finds out we're invited over for steaks. What do you want me to fix?"

"Nothing."

"What if I come over Saturday afternoon and whip up a devil food cake?"

"You talked me into it," Paul laughed. "That was sure hard to do."

"I'll have to make it over here; the oven in our apartment isn't worth a flip."

So it was set. Paul called the kids and Kris promised to bring JT over at four-thirty. Chris said he and Tiffany would be over at the same time. I was excited. Our kids were coming over and Tracy and Pete would be here too. I was so excited that I went out before bed time and dusted the marigolds.

Saturday was a beautiful, golden day. Surprisingly it was cool with the temperature climbing only up into the mid-nineties. In the early afternoon, and when Paul left to go get the steaks, I showered. Then, instead of putting on sweats, I carefully selected a chick outfit. I even wore sandals and put on makeup. I was sitting on the porch with Miss. Calico on my lap and it seemed as if I was matching her purr for purr, or felt like it. My whole body was tingling.

Tracy was in the kitchen and had potatoes in the oven while she stirred up a cake when Kris and JT came. I heard them come in and shoved Miss Calico off my lap stood and brushed the cat-hair away. JT came out first and I saw he was beaming as I went to him and hugged him. "You sure look proud of yourself and happy," I said.

"I am," he said. "I've just taken care of a problem."

"A problem? What problem is that?"

"Every since Kris and I started seeing each other I have wondered what I should call you. Should I call you Sharon, should I call you Mrs. Phillips, or should I call you Ma?"

"So you have finally decided. Which name did you decide on," I laughed as I sat down.

"Neither one," he beamed. "Now I'll call you Grandma."

I didn't say anything, I sat there stunned.

"Didn't you hear what I said?" JT asked.

"Yes, you mean I'm going to a grandmother? You mean Kris is pregnant?"

"Yes!" he said, standing there and beaming at me as if his shirt was going to pop its buttons.

"All right!" I yelled as I jumped up and ran into his arms. This time he not only hugged me but he picked me up and whirled me around. Darned if he wasn't getting just like Chris.

Kris came out then, tall slim and beautiful. She looked at us and her blue eyes sparkled. "You must have told her, huh, JT."

"Yes," he said, sitting me down.

I ran to Kris and threw my arms around her, "Congratulations, you two." Then I took her hand and led her to a chair near mine. We sat down with me still holding her hand. "When is the baby due?"

"Sometime early February," she said laughing.

"Maybe, just maybe, I'll get a birthday present."

"Could be," she said standing. "I'll join you after I get a salad made. Tracy shouldn't have to do all of the work."

I listened as Tracy and Kris chatted in the kitchen as they worked. Paul soon came out with a bottle of wine and glasses. The three of us poured a glass and Paul raised his glass and said, "To the new member of our family."

A baby, I thought, soon there will be a baby in my house again. I would soon be a grandma. This was such a wonderful day. The day belonged in the top ten days of my life. Soon there would be a baby on my lap and my arms hungered to hold it.

Chris and Tiffany came and then Pete wandered over. Soon Paul was lighting the broiler and brought the steaks out. I watched him as he worked and I could tell by the small smile on his face that he was as happy as I was. I tried to imagine what he would be like as a grandpa.

Suddenly I became envious of JT and Kris. I was happy for them but yet at the same time envious. Paul and I had worked and worked hard for what we had. And we had a lot. We had a nice house with a view of the lake, we had two wonderful children, and we had all of the creature comforts a person could ask for. But I remembered with fondness our struggles to get what we had. I remembered clipping coupons to take to the store and I remembered looking at the price of every item I bought. I remembered discussing how we could afford a new dryer when the old one wore out. How we would try to figure out what corners we could cut.

I listened to the steaks sizzle as the daylight faded and I tried to remember the last time I clipped a coupon or looked at the price before I bought something. I thought about how Kris and JT, Chris and Tiffany, Tracy and Pete were all doing as we had done. My heart went out to them and I wished to help them but I knew the best help I could give would be no help at all. Let them meet and conquer the challenges of life.

Yes, Paul and I had it all now. We had everything. Everything except the challenges of life before us. Everything but our future before us. I knew as I sat there and watched the fireflies blink, that slowly, my world was passing. Let me start all over again, I cried deep within myself.

Chapter 19

WEST TO I-35 AND THEN SOUTH. We left early, much too early to my way of thinking. We were on the road shortly after sunup and it was a beautiful day. A much too pretty of a day to be going to a doctor's appointment.

The previous rain had greened up the grass, the dark green of juniper spotted the sides of the red hills and the rim of the canyons. If I hadn't been going to a doctor's appointment it would have been a beautiful drive.

Before we left, Paul had asked Tracy, "Do you know where this Dr. Nickelous has his office?"

"Yes, it's down by the Baptist Hospital. When we get to Oklahoma City, I'll tell you how to get there."

"I've got a better idea. Since you know where we are going, I'll just let you drive, if you don't mind. Does traffic bother you?"

"No," she laughed. "I know it sounds strange coming from a girl raised in Tahlequah, but I love the hustle and bustle of city life."

Paul tossed her the keys and we both got into the back seat. As we sped down I-35 Paul looked at me and grinned, "Do you think we're asking too much of Tracy? Asking her to be our maid, nurse, and now a chauffeur?"

I saw Tracy glance at us in the mirror and saw her lips bend into a smile. "She can handle it," I said. "Tracy is a girl of many talents."

The Cimarron River had a full stream of red water in it when we crossed. The rain we had last week was still flowing down. My, I thought, this is unusual. I had seldom seen that much water in the Cimarron in August.

We passed Guthrie and then drove on. As we got closer to Oklahoma City, for some reason my mind flashed back to somewhere around forty years ago and I remembered the first time I had ever been in Oklahoma City.

I was ten years old and we had gone to visit Aunt Thelma. It was close to a three hour drive and I had napped on the way but when we got in sight of the tall buildings I was wide awake. "It will be a long time before we come to the city again, Sharon. So you had better make the best of it," Dad said. "What do you want to do while we are here?"

"See that tall building down there?" I said without a moment's hesitation pointing.

"Yes, what about it?"

"I want to get in an elevator and ride it clear to the top. When I get to the top, I want to go to a window and look out."

Dad laughed, "I'm sure that can be arranged. Your Aunt Thelma works in a building like that. I'm sure there will be no problem in getting you an elevator ride."

When Aunt Thelma heard what I wanted to do she laughed. "Come on, Sharon," she said the next morning. We left mom and dad at her house and she took me downtown in her car, a much newer and fancier one than the car we had.

She took me to the building where she worked. It wasn't the tallest building, perhaps, but it was tall enough. I remember it had thirty-two floors and we rode clear to the top floor and when the elevator door opened, I ran to a window and looked out. I could see the whole world spread out below me. I looked with openmouthed astonishment. Then we got back into the elevator and went down.

"Now what shall we do?" she asked. "We have the morning to ourselves."

"Can we ride the elevator again?"

"Of course," she laughed.

On the fourth trip to the top she gave me instructions on how to operate the elevator and on the fifth trip she had me do it by myself. Satisfied that I knew how, when we went up the next time we stopped on the nineteenth floor. "Come into my office, Sharon. See where I work. I followed her as she led me to her office. It was the grandest thing I had ever seen.

"I want to work in a place like this when I grow up, Aunt Thelma."

"Make good grades in school and you can," she said. "You are a smart girl and you can be anything and do anything you want. Are you tired of riding the elevator?"

"Not really," I answered.

"I have work I need to finish up before Monday. You know where the elevator is, don't you?"

"Yes."

"Well, hurry up, girl. Get on and start riding it. When you get tired, come back to the office and tell me. Don't leave the building; you're too young to be wandering around the streets of downtown Oklahoma City."

"I won't," I promised and made a dash to the elevator. Up and down I went. I gave that elevator one good workout. At times when I was on the top floor, I would stand at the window and stare out at the world below me. I was on my way back down when the elevator stopped on the nineteenth floor and Aunt Thelma got on. "I'm hungry," she said, "let's go have lunch."

It was one of the grandest times I ever had in my life. I not only learned how to operate the elevator but also learned that the world was big and wide. Before, my world had consisted of cows, pigs, chickens and weeding the garden patch but now my world had grown so much bigger and full of possibilities. I don't know why I could remember my first trip to Oklahoma City just like it happened yesterday. I could remember it even better. I remembered very little of what happened yesterday.

When we passed Edmond, the traffic had begun to pick up. Then in the smoky haze I saw the skyline of Oklahoma

City and the tall buildings and imagined I could recognize the building whose elevator I had almost worn out.

The traffic became very heavy and I glanced at Tracy. The traffic really didn't seem to bother her and she handled the car with the utmost confidence. A few miles on and she left I-35 and started west down I-44. She exited on a four lane road and the Baptist Hospital came into view. She left I-44 and soon she stopped and parked in a parking lot. "There it is," she said pointing to a brick building, four or five stories tall.

We got out and followed her as she made her way to the front door. Inside she led us to an elevator and we took it up. When we stopped and the doors opened I saw they opened into a lobby. The lobby was huge with padded chairs along three walls. Strangely enough, there were only a few people in it. But maybe there were more than there appeared to be. The lobby was so big that perhaps the few people there would have overfilled Dr. Stringer's office back in Stillwater.

The check in counter took up one side of the room. Behind the counter there were six receptionists, all busy checking patients in or working before a computer screen.

"Paul, Sharon, if you want to have a seat, I'll check us in," Tracy said. Paul and I found two chairs together back in the corner as Tracy went to the counter. I looked at the clock on the opposite wall and saw it was nine-thirty. Both Tracy and Paul had the same bad habit, get Sharon to the waiting room thirty minutes before the time of her appointment. That way I could wait thirty minutes before it was time for me to be there and then wait forty-five minutes to an hour for the doctor to get around to me. It seemed as if there should be more to life than waiting.

Tracy soon joined us with a clip board in hand and began efficiently to fill it out. When the front page was filled, she turned it over and started on the back. Then she began to ask,

"Sharon have you ever had---," and I think she named every disease and malady that could happen to mankind.

Then she started on the third page. When she was through, she handed me the clipboard and pen and said, "Sign here, here, and here."

When I had signed, she took the clipboard back to the desk and turned it in. I turned to Paul and saw his eyes were glued to the muted television as he read the news that scrolled along the bottom of CNN.

Tracy rejoined us and as she did she whispered, "It is good for me to do this, you know."

"How can that be? How can there be anything good about sitting in a doctor's waiting room?"

"Because someday I'll be on the other side of the counter, so to speak. Even when I'm there, I'll know what it is like to be sitting on this side."

Shortly after ten, a woman stepped in and called my name. All three of us stood and followed her. She led us down a corridor to a set of scales. I stepped on them and she wrote down my weight. Then she took my height. Then we followed her to an examination room. There she took my vitals and left saying, "Dr. Nickelous will be with you shortly." She shut the door behind her.

Yeah, shortly, I thought, maybe in an hour or two. "That is how they keep the waiting room so empty," I said to Paul and Tracy. "They bring you back here to wait."

"Don't be so impatient, Squirt. We haven't been here more than five minutes and you're already complaining."

Paul had no more than spoken when the door opened and a kid walked in. He was tall, almost as tall as Paul, but he had narrow shoulders I suspected would be wider when he grew up. He had dark hair cut in a buzz cut and was cleanly shaven, that is if he even shaved yet. He had on a white coat with brown slacks, the white coat, I suspected he wore to make him look like a doctor. "Looks like the whole family came in," he said with an engaging smile. "Are you Sharon Phillips," he said looking at me with his hand out.

"I've been told that's what my name is," I said shaking his hand. "This is Paul, my husband and this is Tracy, my private nurse." I could see that introducing Tracy as my 'private nurse' set him back on his heels.

"Private nurse?" he asked with a frown.

"I lived with them, cooked, and kept house while I attended OSU," Tracy said with a small laugh. "I graduated this spring with a degree in nursing. Sharon is just trying to make me feel important."

"I see," Dr. Nickelous said sitting on a stool. "What seems to be your problem, Sharon?"

"I don't have a problem," I answered, "they do. They keep running me to a doctor, running to get tests, and then the doctor prescribes medicine. If it weren't for them, I wouldn't be here."

"I see your doctor in Stillwater is Dr. Stringer. He sent me a preliminary diagnosis and in most cases the family doctor is right ninety percent of the time. But in your case I question it. You're so young."

"Thank you, Doctor," I said glowing at him.

"I also see," he said looking at a chart in his hand, "That he prescribed antidepressant medication a little over a year ago. How is it working?"

"Great, after we got the right one. It works great other than it seems to affect my short term memory."

"In what way?"

"If I may interject, Doctor," Tracy said, "Dr. Stringer asked me to keep a log. I have it here if you would like to see it."

"Yes," he said and took several sheets of paper from her. Then he sat silently as he read. When he finished the last page, he looked at me asked, "How long have you lived in Stillwater?"

"Practically all of my adult life. I went to school at OSU, Paul got a job at Mercury Marine, we bought a house and we raised our family there."

"You moved into your house right out of college?

"No, we moved into it two years later."

"I see you have found yourself lost in Stillwater at least two times in the past year. Has there been other times you got lost and didn't tell anyone?"

"No, just the two times. See, that's what I get from going to the doctor and taking medication."

"How about around your house. Have you ever found yourself lost in your own backyard?"

"No," I answered.

"Sharon?" Paul said giving me the look.

Why couldn't I lie like other people? I broke down and started crying. It was embarrassing but I couldn't help it. "Yes," I sobbed. "Several times I have been down walking by the lake and suddenly I didn't know my way home."

"Sharon was your mother or father, your grandmother or grandfather ever diagnosed with Alzheimer's?"

"Grandma was, but it was after she had grown old."

"I see. How old was she?"

"She must have been in her seventies. Do you think that is what is wrong with me?"

"I'm sorry, Sharon, but there are indicators that point in that direction. We need to run a few tests to confirm it. Can we begin tomorrow? Can you be here at eight o'clock in the morning?"

"We can be here," Paul said.

"But Paul, we'll have to leave Stillwater really early."

"Then we'll leave Stillwater early," Paul said.

I looked at Paul's face and saw from his expression that he was stricken. Just one look was all it took and then I really broke down. I knew how he must feel, or I know how I would feel if they suspected he had Alzheimer's.

"Sharon, Sharon," Dr. Nickelous said, standing up and coming to me and patting me on the shoulder. "Medications have improved since your grandmother's time. There is a lot we can do for Alzheimer's. It's not the end of the world."

"It's the end of my world," I said.

"And mine," Paul mumbled.

Chapter 20

THE SUN CAME UP WHEN we drove past Edmond on our way back to Oklahoma City. There were a few thin clouds on the eastern horizon and the sun painted them with a red, yellow, and blue brush. Paul was driving while Tracy and I sat in the back; today he was our chauffer. Paul had been to Dr. Nickelous' office once and once Paul had been someplace he could always go there again. I could count on one hand the times since we had been married that he had been lost and I could do it without using my thumb or little finger.

Like most men, he never stopped to ask directions, but he had the uncanny ability to look at a map and relate the symbols to the landscape around him. If there was a hill, he could recognize the hill on the map and if he was coming up on a road, he could see it on a map. No, Paul never got lost, only bewildered a few times.

Traffic picked up, people leaving early for work but Paul maneuvered the car through the holes and passed as many cars as passed us. I saw him glance at his watch for the umpteenth time and glance in the mirror at me. "If the traffic gets any worse, we're going to be late, Squirt. We should have left earlier."

I glanced at my watch and said, "No we won't. I'm to be there at eight and we'll get there just before eight. That's when my appointment is and that's when we'll get there."

"But I think we should arrive at least thirty minutes early."

"I know you do," I laughed.

Like Tracy, he exited on I-44 and then exited onto the same four lane boulevard. At ten minutes to eight he parked in the parking lot of the medical building.

Tracy checked me in at the counter of Dr. Nickelous' office and we didn't even have time to sit down before my name was called. "See, this is the way it should be," I said, taking Paul's hand as we followed the nurse back. "Going to see the doctor is bad enough, there is no need to arrive thirty minutes early."

But I didn't even see the doctor. The nurse led us past the exam rooms, past his office, and back to a small waiting room. "You two can wait here," she said, "better make yourselves comfortable. Sharon will be in there a while."

I followed her on back and she opened a door to the right of the corridor and I followed her in. There was a large oak desk and behind it sat a small, blond headed man. He was middle aged, wore glasses and had a small mustache with a pointed goatee. It gave him a Colonel Sanders look. "This is Dr. Brooks," the nurse said and then left the room, leaving my file on his desk.

"You must be Sharon Phillips," he said, standing and shaking my hand. "Have a seat," he said, indicating a recliner by his desk. "If you're ready, let's get right on to it."

"This is the first time I've ever sat in a recliner in a medical office," I said sitting down.

"It's because you are going to be here a while. It may be two hours or more. Of course it could take less, it depends. Go ahead, recline back and put your feet up if it will make you more comfortable. I want you to relax and be comfortable."

I did as he said and then asked, "What now?"

"I'm going to ask you a few questions and then I'm going to give you a series of tests. Are you ready?"

"I guess so," I answered. A series of test? Ask me questions? "What do I do if I don't know the answers to your questions?"

"Just say so. There is no pass or fail, and you're not going to be graded A, B, or C. Just answer the questions if you can, okay?"

"Okay, but don't make the questions too hard."

"I won't," he laughed. "Now I'm going to name three objects. Horse, penny, flower. Now what three objects did I name?"

"Horse, Penny, flower."

"See, that wasn't so hard. What year is it?"

I told him.

Is it fall, winter, spring or summer?"

"It's summer. Anyone who has been outside knows that."

"It is hot out there. What month are we in?"

"August."

"Good. Now what day of the week is it?"

I had to think on that one. I had seen Dr. Nickelous yesterday or was it the day before yesterday. I wasn't for sure but I thought it was yesterday and my appointment had been Tuesday. That would make it what today? "Wednesday? I think."

"Yes, today is Wednesday. What is today's date?"

"August the....the... I have no idea. So I missed a question. Does that mean I fail?"

"Not at all. I told you at the beginning there was no pass or fail. Also when we started out I named the objects, you remember?

"Yes."

"What were they?"

"A horse, a flower, and a... a... a, I don't remember the third one."

"That's okay, Sharon. Now I want you to count backwards from one hundred by fives."

That was an easy one. "One hundred, ninety-five, ninety," and so I continued on until zero.

"Very good. Now spell a word for me. Spell WORLD."

"Oh, a spelling bee," I laughed. "W-O-R-L-D."

"Now spell world backwards.

I had to think on that one. "D-L-O-R-W. No that's not right, D-O-L...I can't. I never was very good at spelling."

"Neither am I," Dr. Brooks said smiling. Then he pointed at a clock on the wall and asked, "What is the name of that object?"

"Are you pointing to the clock?"

"Yes, I am. Now what is this?" and he pointed to a book on his desk.

"A book," I answered brightly.

"Good. Now at the beginning of the session, I named three common objects. What were they?

"A flower, and...I can't remember what the other two were."

"Do you know where you are now, Sharon?"

"In your office, at least I think it is your office."

"What state are we in?"

"Oklahoma."

"Good, what city."

"Oklahoma City."

"Good, now what is the address of this building?"

"I have no earthly idea," I said, feeling irritation creeping in. I tried to not let it show. "Yesterday Tracy drove us here and today Paul drove. Why would I need to know what the address is? Since they were driving and they knew how to get here, I had no need to know.

"I can see your point. If you weren't driving you need not know the address. Now I am going to give you a famous saying. Are you ready?"

"Yes."

"'I know not what others may say, but for me, give me liberty or give me death'. Now repeat it."

"Give me liberty or give me death," I answered, recognizing Patrick Henry's famous speech, but even as I repeated it to him I had a feeling that I had left something out.

"Now, Sharon, I'm going to give you instructions and I want you to follow them. Do exactly as I tell you. If you are not clear on what I ask you to do, say so before you start, okay?"

"Okay, Doctor."

"You need to sit up and put your feet down before you start." I did as he asked and then he continued, "See this stack of paper," and he eased it over to the edge of his desk and I nodded my head, yes. "I want you to take one sheet, fold it in half and then put it on the floor in front of you. Understand?"

"Yes, that should be easy enough."

"Then do it."

I reached over, took a sheet of paper and folded it in half length wise. Then I reached over and put it on his desk. Doctor Brooks just looked at it.

"The first part of the test is over, Sharon, but let's take a break before we continue the second half. I have soft drinks in the back, would you like one?" the doctor asked as he stood and headed for a door in the back of his office.

"I would, I didn't realize it until you asked, but I'm thirsty."

"What kind?"

"Do you have a flavored soda, like a grape or orange?"

"I'll see," he said, opening the door and stepping inside. "We have grape, orange, and strawberry," he called back. "Which do you want?"

"Strawberry," I answered. "A strawberry sounds good."

Soon he was back with a Pepsi and a strawberry. He set the Pepsi on his desk, twisted the top from the bottle of the strawberry and handed it to me. The lid made a *tink* as he threw it into the metal trashcan. It felt so cold in my hand and when I took a drink it made my teeth ached. "Ah," I said, "That tastes good. I can't remember the last time I had a strawberry soda."

"How have things been going in your life, Sharon?"

"Absolutely terrific. I just found out a short time ago that I'll be a grandmother pretty soon."

"First time?"

"Yes."

"How many children do you have?"

"Just two and they're twins."

"What are their names?"

"Chris, spelled with a C, and Kris, spelled with a K. It's Kris with a K that is going to give me a grandbaby. It is due on my birthday, or close to it. Wouldn't that be a grand birthday present?" And I put emphasis the grand part.

"Yes, it would. Do you have any hobbies?"

"Not unless you count gardening and taking care of five dogs and one calico cat. I used to like walking; walking by the lake that we live on, but I don't enjoy it so much anymore."

"Why?"

I was silent for a long while before I spoke. But there was no use keeping it from him, everyone else knew, and he was such a friendly and likeable guy. "I get frightened and I get lost when I walk down there. I'm afraid I might get lost and never find my way home."

It was his turn to be silent. But soon he tipped his Pepsi up, drained it and said, "Other than being afraid at times that you will get lost, how's life treating you otherwise? How are your days?"

"Wonderful," I said. "Wonderful and golden."

"So you are happy?"

"So very much so and why shouldn't I be? I have everything a woman could want. I have a fantastic house with a great view of the lake. My husband is wonderful and I have two great kids. My daughter is pregnant and I'll have a grandchild in February. And Tracy, we hired her when she started to college and she cooks and keeps house for us and she treats me like I was her mother. What more could I have?

Everything in my life has gone my way. I have been one lucky woman."

"I can see you are happy. Have you always been this happy?"

"Pretty much so. Oh, I have days when I'm gloomy and sad, but most of my days are happy ones, golden ones."

"Tell me about your family."

So I told him. I told him about Paul, my kids, Chris with a C, and Kris with a K, and he laughed at their names and that they were twins.

He laughed as he said, "A lot of couples name twins with names that sound alike, like Tilley and Tommy, or Tracy and Macy, but this is the first time I've heard of naming twins the same name. Who else is there in your family?"

"There is Boomer, he's our dog that came wandering in and stayed. Miss Calico, the ugliest cat in the world who also wandered in and stayed. She is so ugly and somebody has to love her so I do. Then sometime back, a pregnant poodle followed me home and stayed. Then she proceeded to have pups which I named Doc…I can't remember what the other two pups names are. But they're all part of my family now."

"Mother, Father?"

"They were both killed in a car wreck. They topped a hill and met a truck passing another truck. They were killed instantly."

"Any siblings?"

"No, I was an only child." It was then I became suspicious. While at first I thought Dr. Brooks and I were just two people taking a break from work, he was learning very much about me. Perhaps this wasn't a break after all.

"What about you, Doctor? Any children."

"Three," he said and then asked, "Are you ready to complete the test, Sharon? You can take your drink with you."

Without waiting for me to answer, he got up and headed towards a door and I followed him. "In here," he said, opening the door and standing aside for me to enter.

The room was bare. No picture, no clock, no decorations of any kind. The bare walls were painted a dark green. In the middle of the room set the only furniture, a table with pencils and copy paper on it. On each side of the table was a padded chair like in the waiting rooms.

"Have a seat," he said, indicating an empty chair. He went to the other side and sat down. "Now," he said, "I want you to draw the face of a clock and then put in the numbers where they belong from one to twelve. Then I want you to put on the hands and set them so the clock reads ten to eleven."

That should be easy enough, I thought as I picked up a pencil and a sheet of paper. I quickly drew a circle and was proud of it. The few years I taught math I had learned to draw an almost perfect circle on the blackboard without a compass or any other aids. When I had the circle drawn I picked up the paper and showed it to him proudly.

"Good, Sharon. Now put in the numbers."

So I started putting in the numbers. When I got to twelve I saw I had goofed. I was through with the numbers but I had placed them too close. I only had numbers on one side of the circle. "Oops, do I get a do-over?"

"Let me have that one and yes, you get a do-over," he chuckled.

Again I drew a circle and this time I spaced the numbers wider apart. But still there was a wide gap between the twelve and the one. And something was wrong. I looked at it and looked at it but I couldn't tell what it was. I had the one at the top of the clock, was that right? It didn't look right but Dr. Brooks said, "Now put in the time."

"What was the time again? I know you told me but I've forgotten."

"Ten to eleven," he answered.

Where were the hands at ten to eleven? I thought and thought but I couldn't remember so I just guessed. When the drawing was through, I looked at it and looked at it. Something was wrong, but I couldn't tell what it was.

"That is all of the test, Sharon," Dr. Brooks said, taking my clock drawing from me. "I'll take you back to the waiting room."

Tracy and Paul were waiting; Paul was watching television and Tracy was reading the Your Health magazine.

"I'm through," I said, "are you two ready to go."

"It's eleven thirty," Paul said, "I suggest we go have lunch and then come back."

"Come back? I'm through with the tests."

"You have an appointment with Dr. Nickelous at three," Tracy said.

As usual when Paul was in charge, we were back in Dr. Nickelous' waiting room at two thirty. There we waited. Three o'clock came and went and at three-thirty the nurse at last called me back. Instead of going to an examination room, she took us to his office.

There were three chairs setting on one side of his desk and we sat down. Dr. Nickelous soon came in with an armload of material and took his place across the desk from us. He sorted through the material and when he had it arranged to his satisfaction, he picked two sheets and turned them so we could see them.

"This is a PET-scan of a normal brain," he said, pointing with his pencil to one sheet, "And this is your PET-scan, Sharon. Notice the cloudy area in the cortex."

"I see it," Tracy said. "Do you see it, Paul, Sharon?"

"Yes," Paul answered.

I didn't say anything. That was a picture of my brain, my total being. My brain which made me what I am. I didn't want to look at it if something was wrong with it.

"Let me test our recently graduated nurse, if you don't mind. Do you know what it means, Tracy."

"Yes," she answered. I looked at her and saw dampness in her eyes.

"What does it mean?" I asked, growing irritated at these guessing games.

"Tell her, Tracy."

She looked at me with moist eyes and said, "It means you have an early stage of dementia, namely Alzheimer's."

"She is right," Dr. Nickelous said, "It is the first indicator, but to confirm it, there is another test called MMSE. It is a mental test and you took it this morning. A perfect score is thirty. You scored twenty-two. A score of twenty-two indicates the first stages of Alzheimer's. I'm sorry, Sharon."

I quickly looked at Paul and saw his face had turned gray. He was taking it harder than I was. I looked back at the Doctor and asked, "How long do I have?"

"If it were to go untreated, you would have somewhere around seven years."

"Seven years isn't very long, Doctor, but if that's all I have, then that's all I've got."

"Sharon, I said if it were to go untreated you'd have about seven years. Great strides have been made in treating Alzheimer's the past few years."

"You mean she can be cured?" Paul asked.

"No, there is no cure and we can't reverse it, but we can halt it or slow it down until it is all but stopped."

"How much can you slow it down?" Paul asked.

"Can't really tell. We've caught it in a very early stage. So far, members of the test group who are in the same stage as Sharon, are functioning almost as well as they were when we started the trial. There has been some loss of mental capacity in all of them but not as much as there would have been without the new medication. Should we try it, Sharon?"

"Of course," Paul said.

"Since she has a tendency to get lost, it would be good if she had a companion with her most of the time."

"Would you prescribe such? Especially if the companion had a degree in nursing."

"Yes, of course," the doctor said. He quickly pulled a prescription pad and wrote on it, then he tore it out and handed it to Paul.

Chapter 21

"YOU HEARD THE DOCTOR, Tracy," Paul said as he drove home from the city. "You now have a full time nursing job which means a raise in pay."

"I don't feel right about it, Paul. It doesn't feel right, me taking money from you guys after all you have done for me."

"Who said anything about taking money from us?" Paul laughed, glancing at us in the rearview mirror. "It's not us you'll be billing, it's the insurance company. You heard the doctor; he prescribed a full time nurse. It won't cost us a thing. Squirt, what do you think about hiring a new freshman to take Tracy's place with the cooking and housecleaning?"

"You mean all you want me to do is stay with Sharon? You want someone else to clean house and cook?"

"Why not, it won't cost us any more?"

"You know I can do both."

"I know." Paul said, "You have been doing that this summer. But you and I both know that the time will come when someone needs to be with Sharon twenty-four sevens. You can't handle it, Tracy. You will need some time off to spend with your new husband. Also look at it this way, without it costing us anymore we can help some other girl get a college education."

"I had never thought of it that way," Tracy said. "I'll have to clean out my room in your house but I don't need it anyway. Since Pete and I have been married all I've ever used it for is a quiet place to study and I won't be studying anymore."

Paul drove on and we had just gone by Guthrie when he said, "I thought you were going to work on your masters until Pete graduated."

"Not if I'm going to be Sharon's nurse."

"Why not?"

178

"I won't have the time."

"Nonsense, I bet you and the new girl we hire can work out a schedule so that you can take some graduate courses. Of course you probably won't be able to get your masters as fast, but what's the hurry? I hope you like Stillwater because you will probably be living here a good, long while."

"At least until Pete graduates," Tracy laughed.

"I suspect it will be much longer than that. I've talked to Pete and he likes his job at Mercury Marine and more important, Mercury Marine likes Pete. He may work for us for a good many years."

Tracy was silent until we exited I-35 and turned east on Highway 51 towards Stillwater. "That would be okay with me. I like Stillwater and I could live there the rest of my life."

"Tracy, do you know of a young girl who would like to go to OSU but can't afford to."

Tracy sat in thought until we were just west of Stillwater. "Cathy Fox," she blurted. "Cathy Fox. She lives just outside of Tahlequah."

"Cathy would like to go to college?"

"Not Cathy," Tracy laughed, "but her sister, Breanne. Most people call her Breezy. She graduated from high school this spring and was the valedictorian. She's smart and would like to continue her education and she wants to be a doctor, but her family came upon bad times and she doesn't have the money to start school."

"Is she a hard worker and dependable," Paul asked from the front seat.

"If she's anything like Cathy she is. Besides you would like her, Sharon."

"I would?" I said, startled that I was included in the conversation.

"Yes, she's not much bigger than you, if any, and you'll have a hard time keeping up with her. She's such a live wire." Then Tracy laughed, "At her high school graduation during rehearsals, or so I've heard, she was so small she had trouble looking over the podium to give her speech. Everyone was worried about it except, Breanne. When graduation came and it was time to give her speech, she carried a small stool out on the stage, set it behind the podium, stood on it and gave her speech. It caught the administration by surprise, but it worked."

"My kind of a girl," I laughed.

"If she can solve her problems like that," Paul chuckled, "Give her a call and invite her up."

"She doesn't have a car and I'll probably have to go get her," Tracy said. "Would you like to go with me to Tahlequah, Sharon?"

After only a moment's thought I said, "I'd love to. Would it be okay, Paul?"

"If that's what you want to do, Squirt, do it."

That night after Tracy had gone home, Paul and I were watching TV when I looked over at him and asked, "If Breanne passes my inspection, do you want to interview her?"

He put his arm around by shoulders, looked at me and said, "No, Squirt, if you like her, you hire her."

I was surprised when he looked at me. It looked like he had aged a good twenty years just today. He was taking my diagnosis very, very badly. My heart went out to him. "Paul," I said, laying my hand on his thigh, "I am sorry and I am sorrier for you than I am for me. You're the one that is going to suffer from me having Alzheimer, not me."

"How do you figure it, Squirt?"

"Me, I'll go on living as I always have except as times pass and I get worse, each day will be better than the day before. The day will be a new and exciting day with a whole new and exciting world waiting for me to explore. You see, I won't remember the day before and everything will be new. I'm sure some of my personality traits will change, but I hope I remain happy. Actually in one way I'm relieved that my problem has been diagnosed as Alzheimer's. Now if I forget something or lose something, I know it's the Alzheimer's and I'm not losing my mind. I hope you learn how to be happy along with me."

"You're not unhappy about you having Alzheimer's?"

"I'd prefer that I didn't, of course, but we always can't choose what is going to happen to us in our life. I can think of many things that could happen to me that would be much worse that Alzheimer's."

He sat looking at me, the television program ignored. "All of our life when we had money left over, we've put it in savings. We were saving it for a time we might need it. Perhaps now is the time. Perhaps now is the time to use it. Perhaps we should start enjoying life more and worry about saving money less."

"You're not going to spend us into the poorhouse are you?"

"No," he laughed as he turned the TV off.

The next morning I got up before Paul and was sitting at the breakfast table drinking coffee when Tracy said, "I called the Fox's last night and talked to Breanne. She is very interested but as I suspected, she doesn't have any way to get here."

"Did you mention that we would come down?"

"Yes, but I didn't set a day. I thought you should do that. Do you want to go tomorrow, tomorrow is Friday?"

When Paul came in for breakfast he said, "Tracy, I'm taking your car to work. If you ladies need to go somewhere you can take the Vibe." Tracy reached into her pocket and handed him the keys.

I wasn't particularly suspicious; Paul did that when he took her car in to get serviced.

After Paul left, I took my coffee to the living room to get out of her way. The morning was cool and the poodles were still outside. When Tracy had the kitchen taken care of she came to the living room and asked, "Would you like to go outside, Sharon, and maybe take a walk down by the lake?"

"That sounds fabulous," I said, jumping up.

"Let me go change clothes and when I come back, I'll start a load of laundry. I'll also wash what you have on if you'll bring them out after you change."

I was back in the bedroom changing when it sunk into me. Tracy was becoming more diplomatic and in reality she had suggested that perhaps pajamas were not acceptable attire to wear while walking by the lake. I slipped on a pair of yellow shorts with a short sleeved green shirt. When I went out to the porch, Tracy was waiting and so were the dogs. I looked at Tracy and saw she, too, was wearing shorts but she looked much better in them than I did. "You don't look much like a nurse dressed like that," I laughed.

"I have a white, starched uniform with a cap," she answered. "Would you like for me to wear that?"

"Lord, no. It's bad enough that I need a nurse. Besides Dr. Nickelous said I needed a nurse and a companion with me. You make a good companion but I won't know what kind of a nurse you are unless you have to give me a shot."

On the way to the lake, I checked the marigolds. The spider-mites were gone and the marigolds where showing life again. I even saw new buds that were almost ready to blossom.

Even though the breeze was blowing across the lake, it soon got hot and we went back to the house. I hated to leave, it was so beautiful but the heat drove us home. As we came into the yard, I heard the deep rumble of the air conditioner and looked forward to going inside. And so did the poodles. As I opened the door, they went scrambling in. When I sat in a recliner, for once the poodles didn't jump in my lap but stretched out on their bellies on the cool carpet and went to sleep.

Tracy went to the laundry room and soon I heard the dryer running. I heard her going from room to room gathering up the dirty clothes. Soon the washer was running again.

I saw her as she went to the kitchen and soon I heard her fixing lunch. It took her so long, much longer than it would take her to make a couple of sandwiches, and I went in to see what she was doing. She glanced up and smiled as she said, "It's so hot, and I thought I'd fix something different for lunch. Instead of sandwiches, I'm fixing a chef's salad."

"That sounds good," I said.

Pete no longer joined us for lunch; he had been working full time at Mercury Marine and took a lunch to the plant.

After lunch it was too hot to go outside so I went to the living room and picked up a magazine to read. I heard Tracy vacuuming in the back part of the house. I must have dozed because when I looked at the clock, it was almost four. It wouldn't be long until Paul came home from work.

When it was almost time for Paul to come home, I started listening for him. Listening for the sound of a motor and the sound of tires crunching on gravel. For some reason, this evening, I was especially anxious for him to come home. And then I heard it. I didn't hear a motor but I did hear the crunch of tires on gravel and I rushed to the door. I opened the door and stepped out in time to see Paul getting out of a car. It wasn't Tracy's car either. It was metallic gray and it was big. It was shiny and looked luxurious. Paul came to me grinning from ear to ear. "How do you like the looks of it?" he asked.

"It looks pretty," I said, "and it looks expensive. Is that ours?"

"No, it's yours. I have always wanted to present you with a Cadillac and I decided if I was ever going to do it, I'd better do it now."

"Hey, Tracy," I shouted, "Come and look at my new set of wheels."

With Paul pointing out the features, Tracy and I gave the new car a comprehensive examination. It had leather seats and the new car smell.

"Where's my car?" Tracy asked, "Did you trade it in on this one?"

"I was going to," Paul answered, "and give you the Vibe. But they wanted me to give it to them so I decided if I was going to give it away, I'd rather give it to you and Pete. I suspect since Sharon has a tendency to get lost, you will be driving her where ever she wants to go, but when you start doing your graduate work you'll need a car to drive. Your car is waiting for us to come and get it down on the car lot. I'll sign it over to you this evening."

"Can dinner hold for a while?" I asked. "Can I drive my new car down to the car lot so you can pick up yours, Tracy's?"

"Yes, it will hold," Tracy said laughing. "Just let me turn the fire out."

As we waited for her, I got in behind the wheel and Paul showed me which button to push to elevate the seat and to move the seat forward. I was ready when Tracy came out.

I started the car and backed it out. It was so quiet I couldn't hear the motor running. I put it into drive and we were on the road. The Cadillac rode like a dream and handled so easily. It seemed to just float along and I felt like the road was moving under me and the car was setting still. I couldn't believe it, I was driving a Cadillac and it was mine. I saw the highway before me and asked, "Should I turn north here? Isn't the car dealership north."

"Yes, it is, Squirt," Paul said from the back seat.

"The car drives like a dream," I said. "It almost drives itself," and I turned north. Horns blared and tires squealed, and I looked in the rearview mirror to see a pickup had turned sideways. I caught Paul's expression and it wasn't a pleasant one. I glanced at Tracy and saw her knuckles were white from gripping the chicken handle so tight.

"The car may all but drive its self, but it won't stop at stop signs without help," Paul said.

"Sorry," I said. "I forgot."

A short ways farther on, Paul directed me into a car lot and pointed where Tracy's car was. I drove to it and stopped.

"Let Tracy drive home, Squirt. She should get a turn at driving a new Cadillac."

While Tracy put the final touches to dinner, Paul and I sat in the living room. "Tracy and I are going to Tahlequah tomorrow," I said.

"Oh," was his only comment.

"Yes, we're going down to interview Breanne Fox. We might even bring her back."

"That would be nice," he said, but I could tell he was only listening to half of what I said. He was distracted.

"What's wrong, Paul? What's bothering you?"

He turned to me and looked me in the eyes. "I don't know how to say this, Squirt, but I don't think you should be driving anymore. I don't know what I'd do if something were to happen to you. If you need to go anywhere, get Tracy or the new girl to take you. One of them will be here all of the time."

"Okay," I said, and I was surprised when I saw the expression on his face. It was the expression of relief.

Chapter 22

IT SEEMED AS IF I WAS FLYING in an airplane with only the noise of the wind as the big car glided down the turnpike towards Tulsa. "Doesn't it drive great?" I said to Tracy as she passed a McDonalds seventeen miles east of Stillwater.

"It does," Tracy answered from behind the wheel, "But I bet it guzzles gas like it was going out of style."

"Probably so," I laughed, "But I understand the new Cadillacs get much better mileage than the old ones did. But you'd better keep one eye on the gas gauge anyway. It's so wonderful to be going someplace. I haven't been to Tahlequah in ages."

"Believe me, Sharon, it's just like it was. You won't find it any different. I don't think anything has changed for the past hundred years."

I grew silent and watched the landscape go quietly by. Mostly it was red hills and canyons covered with brown grass and dotted here and there with dark green juniper. The silence between us didn't bother me and I'm sure it didn't bother Tracy. That was the kind of relationship we had developed between us this past four years. If we had something to say, we said it but if we didn't, we kept quiet. We didn't feel the pressure to fill the silence with empty chatter.

The car rode so comfortably that before I knew it we crossed Keystone Lake and entered the outskirts of Tulsa. Then the traffic picked up and I kept quiet on purpose, letting Tracy navigate her way through Tulsa with complete concentration on her driving.

Once through Tulsa, we headed east on Highway 412 until we got to 69 and then turned south. "You seem to know this road," I said looking at Tracy.

"I should; how many hundreds of times have I driven it?"

We stopped and ate lunch at Wagoner and then headed east on highway 51. We drove along the south shore of Fort Gibson Lake and I looked at it in wonder. It seemed as if we were in a different world. The landscape had slowly become heavily timbered. Now the countryside was covered by large oaks with a few southern pines thrown in. We went through the small town of Hulbert and then we were in Tahlequah. After a brief stop to gas up, Tracy took the road north for a mile or so, turned down a dirt road to the east. She drove slowly reading the mailboxes as she went. "There it is," she said and turned up a tree lined driveway. We soon coasted into a clearing.

We left the motor running so the air conditioner would stay on and sat in the car looking. The barn was weathered red and behind the barn was a pole corral. A sorrel horse stood in the corral, his head lowered in the heat and looking as if he were asleep. Back in a meadow I saw a herd of cattle grazing.

In the middle of the clearing sat a small camping trailer and in its shade, lay a red hound sleeping through the heat. I was surprised that our driving in hadn't awakened him. "He must be a good watch dog," I said, pointing him out to Tracy. She only laughed.

A short way behind the camper, was a pickup camper except it wasn't on a pickup but on the ground. In fact I didn't see a car or a pickup anywhere around. To the north piled almost to the trees was a stack of burned timber, and to my right I saw the beginning construction of a house.

Straight ahead I saw two young boys working in a large garden. I pointed them out to Tracy and asked, "Isn't it awful hot to be working outside."

"It is," she said, "but if they want to eat, they have to do it. All of the Fox's are real workers. Shall we get out and see if we can find Breanne?"

"That's the reason we came down here," I said opening the door and stepping out in the heat. From the new construction site I heard the whine of an electric saw and then it stopped. Out of the maze of framing half-ran, half-walked, a small girl dressed in cutoff jeans with a carpenter's apron on. She scampered up a ladder, put the board in place and then began to nail it. I had never in my life seen someone swing a hammer so fast. It sounded like a machine gun.

"Hey, Breezy," Tracy shouted. "It looks like you're being a carpenter today."

At the sound of Tracy's voice, the red hound came to his feet and bolted to us barking. "Easy, Red," I said and put out my hand for him to sniff. After inspecting both Tracy and me, he yawned and went back to the shade.

"Tracy, is that you?" Breanne asked, holding her hand on her forehead to shade her eyes. She dropped her hammer in the loop on the carpenter's apron and then broke into a run as she came towards us.

"That girl never walks anywhere," Tracy said to me under her breath. "Breanne, this is Mrs. Phillips I was telling you about. She's the one that needs a house keeper and a cook at Stillwater, if you're interested."

"Of course I'm interested," she said shaking hands with me. For a scrawny little thing she had a strong handshake. "I'd do anything for a chance to go to school."

"Can you cook?" I asked.

"Of course I can cook. I can cook a possum and sweet potatoes that will melt in your mouth."

"Breezy," Tracy scolded.

"Sorry, Mrs. Phillips, I tend to joke around and sometimes too much. Yes, I can cook. With Mom, Dad, and Cathy all working, it's been up to me to put the meals on the table. They all eat it like it's good and there's seldom anything left."

I looked at her and I liked her. She appeared to be fun loving and to be earnest and serious at the same time. "Can you go back with us? Once we're there, we'll furnish you a car. All you have to do is keep gas in it."

"You mean I'm hired, Mrs. Phillips?"

"Call me Sharon," I said. "Yes, you're hired."

"Hot Dog!" she exclaimed. "I'm going to get to go to school. Yes, I can go back with you. Let me go pack. That won't take long since the fire."

She led us to the camper setting on the ground and then said, "I'd invite you in but we don't have air conditioning and you'd probably be more comfortable sitting in the shade. It gets mighty hot in here. This is where Cathy and I bunk, the boys sleep in the trailer with Mom and Dad."

Tracy and I found some rickety chairs under a large oak tree. It was evident the chairs were used a good bit. It seemed these people lived outside and only went inside to sleep. "Poor little girl," I said.

"Now don't you go feeling sorry for her," Tracy said. "She'll hate you for that."

In no time at all, Breanne was back out, a paper grocery sack in each hand. "How do you like my matching luggage?" she laughed.

"I have a twenty-five piece of luggage just like that at home," I laughed. "Is that all you have."

"All but what I have on," she said and I noticed she had changed to faded blue jeans and a yellow shirt. "I saved out my best clothes to wear back with you."

Tracy popped the trunk and Breanne put her clothes in. Then she asked, "Can I go tell the boys goodbye?"

"Of course, you can," I said, "But I failed to mention that you get every other weekend off and you can drive your car home to see your family."

"That's right generous of you, Mrs. Phillips, but the family is on hard times right now. I think that right now they would rather see the gas money than me."

When Tracy and I got in, we left the doors open and Tracy started the engine. I watched as Breanne walked to the garden patch and gave each boy a long hug. When the air conditioner started cooling we shut the doors. After Breanne got in I glanced back and saw her big blue eyes were moist.

"Tracy, when we get to Tahlequah, can we stop at Gene's Grocery? I need to tell Mom that I've left so she'll know that she has to fix supper when she gets home."

"Sure," Tracy said.

"See," Tracy said while we waited for Breanne to talk to her Mom, "The Fox's aren't poor, they just don't have any money."

Breanne was soon out and when she was in the car we headed for Stillwater.

"I'm to take your place, Tracy?" Breanne asked.

"Yes."

"What are you going to do? Did you find a job at the hospital?"

"No, Sharon needs a full time nurse and they have hired me."

"You do?" Breanne asked looking at me. "But you look so healthy."

"I am healthy," I said, "Except for one minor thing. I have been diagnosed with Alzheimer's."

"But you're so young."

"Thank you, Breanne, but it happens."

"What's it like? What's it like to have Alzheimer's?"

"Breezy!" Tracy scolded.

"Tracy, you know I'm going to study medicine. I'm going to be a doctor of some sort. I haven't decided yet. It would be good if I knew how people felt when something was wrong with them. She doesn't have to tell me if she doesn't want to."

"I don't mind," I said, "Anything to further science," and I laughed. "But I don't know if I can. Right now I'm in early, stage one. My short term memory? Forget it. But before you feel too sorry for me, let me tell you it has some advantages. Tracy and I came down this road this morning; now for most people like us, going back over it going home would be boring. But not for me. I can't remember coming down this road so everything is new."

"That's not so bad," Breanne said. "What else?"

"I put things down and forget where I put them. Or I put things in places they don't belong. That is where I'm asking for your help. If you see me start to put my shoes in the deepfreeze, stop me."

"At first it was frightening for her," Tracy said. "When she put her sweater in the deepfreeze and later found it, she thought someone was playing a dirty trick on her and wondered why someone would be so mean."

"I can't drive anymore," I said. "Paul, my husband, bought me this car just a short while back. I can't remember when. I got to drive it once. Tracy and Paul won't let me drive anymore."

"Why? What did you do?" Breanne asked.

"All I did was run a stop sign."

"Yeah," Tracy said dryly, "she ran the stop sign on the busiest highway in Stillwater. Almost caused a ten car pileup."

"The doctor recommended that someone be with me at all times and that's Tracy's job. She is to see that I take my medicine and she drives me wherever I need to go. You see, another problem is that I get lost. I've lived in Stillwater practically all of my life and yet, here lately, I've found myself getting lost. So even if I could drive and not be a hazard on the road, I'd need someone with me so I can find my way home."

We had driven a while in silence when Tracy asked, "Sharon, would you like to visit the OSU campus tomorrow?"

"Sure," I said, "I can't remember the last time I was on the OSU campus," and I chuckled at my wit.

"Then we'll go. I'll show Breezy around and help her get enrolled, you did bring tuition money, didn't you Breezy?"

"Not if it costs more than five dollars," she said, and then she laughed, "But I've already filled out scholarship papers and have my acceptance letter with me. I got one scholarship for tuition and one to pay for my books. I filled them out and sent them in sometime during June and hoped and prayed that something would happen and I'd get to go. And now my prayers have been answered."

"As soon as you have your schedule made out and approved," Tracy said, "I'll make mine out."

"I thought you had already graduated," Breanne said.

"I did, but Pete hasn't. I'm going to take a few hours here and there in graduate work while we're here. When I'm in class, I'll ask you to take care of Sharon. In turn, I'll help you with your housework whenever I can.

We drove through Tulsa and were out on the turnpike when I asked, "Breanne, do you have any objections to wearing hand-me-downs?"

"Shoot no. That's all I've worn since the fire. My whole wardrobe came from the Salvation Army. Why do you ask?"

"You and I are close to the same size except I'm a bit wider, but once I was as slender as you. I bet if you were to go up into the attic while it was cool in the morning, I just know there are clothes that would fit you. Some of them are probably out of style but clothes like I have on now, never go out of style."

"Are you sure you won't wear them again."

"Breanne, I've outgrown them."

"I don't know about you guys," Tracy said when we caught site of McDonalds setting on top of the hill, "But I'm hungry enough to eat at McDonalds."

"I am, too," Breanne said. "Of course, McDonalds is my favorite place to eat."

"You've brought me a soul mate, Tracy," I said. "Any time Tracy isn't going to be home for lunch, you and I will go to McDonalds, Breanne."

Tracy parked the car and we all went in. After using the washroom, we stood in line to order. While we were waiting, Breanne put her hand in her jeans pocket and pulled out a five dollar bill. "Put your money back," I said, "You're on the payroll as of now and we furnish you board and housing."

She gave me a shy look but she put her money back. We all ordered Big Macs and sat down to eat. "Everybody you meet claims they don't like to eat at McDonalds," Breanne said. "Why do you think that is? Why do they lie like that?"

"What makes you think they are lying," Tracy asked.

"If they're telling the truth, then where did all these people come from?" Breanne asked indicating the crowded dining room.

Paul was still up and watching television when we got home. I introduced Breanne to Paul and Tracy showed her to her old room.

I sat down beside Paul and he put his arm around my shoulders. "So you hired her?" he asked. "Do you think she can fill Tracy's shoes?"

"I don't know and I don't care. I have never met a young woman who wants to go to college as bad as she does." Then I told him the circumstances from which she came and how she was enrolling in premed.

"She has a long, tough road ahead of her, Squirt."

"She'll make it," I said, "But I must tell you she has an odd outlook on life and a weird since of humor."

"Oh, Lord," he said, "I've got another one in the house."

Chapter 23

I AWOKE TO A MOST BEAUTIFUL, golden day. I looked over at Paul and saw he was still sound asleep. I eased out of bed, slipped my feet into my house shoes, and eased out the door. I quickly shut the door when I heard the singing coming from the kitchen. Breezy must be in there and she had the radio on. The singing was beautiful but much too loud.

I saw the poodles were in the yard running around and checking things out while Breezy was at the kitchen counter working away. She wore cutoff jeans and a light blue blouse but was barefooted. And she didn't have the radio on; it was Breezy that was singing. "Good morning, Mrs. Phillips," she said smiling and stopped her singing while she was speaking.

"Morning Breanne, you have a beautiful voice. I see you're up and at it."

"Yes, I usually get up early. Coffee's made. What time do you wish breakfast to be served?"

"Oh, somewhere between seven and seven-fifteen. Paul leaves for work at a quarter till eight." I took down a cup and poured a cup of coffee. I took one sip and saw it was much, much too strong. I poured half of it down the sink and filled it back up with hot water.

"Coffee too strong?" Breanne asked.

"A little bit."

"How about Mr. Phillips, does he like his coffee weak like you do?"

"We both drink it the same," I answered.

"Then I'll fix it," she said, picking up the carafe, pouring half of it down the sink and then filling it again with hot water before she set it on the hotplate beneath the coffee maker.

"How do you drink your coffee," I asked, "strong like you made it this morning?"

"That's the way my family likes it, me, I don't drink it at all. I just wish they could make a coffee that tastes as good as it smells."

"It's still cool outside. If you don't mind, when Paul is ready, you can serve us on the patio. Tracy should be over pretty soon."

And she was. As soon as I sat down, I heard her come into the house. Soon she came out with my pills in a small paper pill cup in one hand and her coffee in the other.

"Here you go, Sharon," she said handing me the pills. I took them and then squashed the cup and put it in the pocket of my robe. "Isn't it a beautiful morning?" I said.

Before she could answer, Breanne again broke into song as she worked. Tracy looked at me and said, "I hope you don't mind singing. That girl sings all the time."

"She has a beautiful voice, and no I like to hear her sing. I just wish I could sing like that."

We chatted and soon Paul joined us. Breanne followed him out with place settings and went back in to bring out breakfast. When she returned she had a skillet with a large omelet on it, a platter of bacon and a platter of toast. She sat them on the patio table and then seated herself.

Paul helped himself to a large portion of the omelet, then bacon and toast. He looked at the omelet suspiciously and then took a bite. "Umm," he said, "This girl can cook. You're hired for life. This is the best omelet I've ever eaten. What did you season it with?"

"Squirrel brains. I knocked a squirrel out of a tree with a rock and used its brains to make the omelet."

"Breezy!" Tracy scolded.

At first Paul was startled and then he roared with laughter. He laughed so hard that he had tears in his eyes. Paul looked at me and said, "This is a big house but I don't know if it's big enough for both of you. With both of you here, I'll probably die but I'll die laughing." Then he looked back at Breanne, and asked in a serious voice, "Since you used the squirrel's brains in the omelet, how are you going to tan the hide?"

"What do you mean?" she asked puzzled.

"Haven't you heard the saying, 'A squirrel has exactly enough brains to tan its own hide'?"

She laughed, "I don't know. I suppose I'll just have to whittle me out a stretching board. If I make enough omelets I'll have plenty of hides to make me a squirrel skin coat for this winter."

When Paul was finished eating, I followed him in as he grabbed his briefcase and kissed him goodbye at the door. Then I got my coffee cup, refilled it and joined Tracy and Breanne on the patio. I was surprised to see Breanne had Snowflake on her lap. I was even more surprised to see that Snowflake had lost all of her dignity and haughtiness and was all but whimpering in pleasure as Breezy stroked her fur.

"This is sure a nice dog," Breezy said, "What is her name?"

"Snowflake," I answered. "Sometimes we call her Flake for short."

"And what's this one's name?" she asked as another poodle jumped on her lap."

"That's...That's..." and I looked to Tracy for help.

"Doc," Tracy answered.

"And this one?" she asked, pointing to the pup at her feet.

"Elvira," Tracy answered, "And that is their mother. Her name is Lady."

By then Breanne had a lapful of four poodles. "I hope it's okay for me to pet them? I really like dogs."

"Sure, but let me warn you, they can be a real pest at times. They can really get under your feet."

"I don't mind," she said, pushing the dogs off her lap and standing. She quickly gathered an armload of dishes and scampered into the kitchen. Just as quickly she was back and gathered the rest of the breakfast dishes. As she left Tracy shook her head, "As I said before, that girl never walks. She's always in a hurry."

Soon I heard her singing again and, by the sound of running water, I knew she was rinsing off the dishes before she put them in the dishwasher. Then I heard the dishwasher running and Breezy was back out. "Tracy, are you going to show me where to start on the house cleaning?"

"Why don't we hold off on the house cleaning," I said, "you can do that while it's hot this afternoon. While it's still cool why don't you go into the attic and see if there are any of my old clothes you can wear."

"Okay, how do I get up?"

I took her to the utility room and helped her pull down the trapdoor in the ceiling and unfold the stairs. She went scampering up. "Oh, my," I heard her say. "Are you sure I can have these nice clothes."

"You can have any or all of them," I answered, and then I left her and went to dress. When I was dressed and went back out of the bedroom, Breanne was just coming out of the utility room and her arms were loaded. I looked at what she had. "Bellbottoms," I said, "Surely you could find pants other than bellbottoms."

"What's wrong with bellbottoms?" she asked.

"Nothing, really. They have just been out of style for twenty or thirty years."

"Well, I tried them on and they fit me. I think they look good on me so maybe I'll just bring them back into style."

"Okay," I laughed. "You're perfectly old enough to know what you want to wear, but you should wash them first, and I showed her the laundry room.

When she had the clothes washing Tracy said, "While your clothes are washing, why don't Sharon and I show you the campus and how to get there.

"But shouldn't I do my chores first?" Breezy asked.

"You just got here last night, we can cut you a little slack today," I said. "Come on, let's go see where you are going to be practically living for the next four years. I went to the key board and took down the keys to the Vibe and handed them to Tracy.

"Let me get something out of the freezer for dinner so it can be thawing," Breanne said. "Is there anything special you'd like."

"I think there is a nice pork roast in the freezer," Tracy said. "Perhaps that is one thing you and Sharon should do today. Perhaps you should go grocery shopping."

"We'll do it," I said, as we walked to the vibe and got in.

First, Tracy drove us through the campus to show Breanne where all of the buildings were. Then she parked as close to the administration building as she could find a space and we got out and went in.

It brought back feelings of nostalgia to be on the campus again. I remembered so clearly going to school here and I remember the good times and the bad. I remembered meeting Paul here, though we had only a few classes together. At the time I met him, I thought I was so much in love. But now after living with him over half of my life, I now realized what a deep feeling love really is. He was now part of me and I was part of him. It was the case of two halves being much greater than the whole.

All of this I would one day forget. When I did, a good part of my life would be gone. I believe a life is made up from memories and made up of hopes for the future. My future was bleak and my memories would be taken from me, and then what would I become. I scolded myself. Sharon, there is no use thinking about it. Live each day as it comes and wring as much joy from it as you can.

"Sharon," Tracy said, "We've done all we can do here. Breezy has an adviser assigned to her and an appointment with her at two o'clock tomorrow. We're ready to go if you are."

"I'm ready," I said.

Tracy handed Breanne the car keys and said, "You drive us home, Breezy."

Breanne got in behind the wheel and said, "The seats too low. I can't see out very well."

"Reach over to the left side of your seat," I said. "Feel that handle?"

"Yes."

"Pump it up and down. It will raise your seat."

She went to work. "Neat," she said when she had it high enough. Then she reached down and scooted the seat forward. Only after she had the rearview mirrors adjusted, did she start the car, back out, and take off.

When we got home, Breanne parked, killed the engine, took the keys out and started to hand them to me. "No, keep them. This is your car to drive."

"My own car to drive while I go to college. It's a dream that's almost too good to be true."

"However, this afternoon you have to drive me to the grocery store, remember?"

"Tracy, can you go with us this first time?" Breanne asked. "I don't know where the grocery store is and I don't want the woman who gets lost all the time to show me," she grinned at me.

"Breanne!" Tracy scolded.

"That's okay, Tracy," I laughed. "We all must face the fact that I have Alzheimer's and I'm going to get worse. It's better if we meet the challenge head on. We can't hide it forever."

It had grown hot outside and the poodles wanted in. Three of them lay on the carpet at my feet while Snowflake followed Breezy around. While Tracy made the sandwiches for lunch, Breezy put her clothes in the dryer and then gathered up the other clothes and put them in to wash. Then we all three sat at the kitchen table to eat.

"You should make out a grocery list, Breanne," I said.

"Okay," she said, jumping up from the table and almost tripping over Snowflake as she rushed to get a pencil and paper. When she sat back down she asked, "What do you me want to put on it?"

"You're the cook," I laughed, "you decide what you need."

"I know we're about out of eggs. Tracy, what do you usually cook for them?"

"Just regular food. Check the kitchen and see what we need. Just make like you're cooking for your family at home."

When she was through eating, she began wandering around the kitchen checking what was in the pantry, cupboards, and freezer. She had quite a list when she was through.

As soon as the lunch dishes were through and Breanne had her clothes hung up and the dryer was running again, we left with Breezy driving. I sat in the backseat and Tracy gave directions. Before I knew it we were in HomeLand's parking lot.

"How big is my budget for groceries?" Breezy asked as we went into the store.

"As much as you need," I answered. "We might cut corners other places, but not on groceries."

It was fun grocery shopping with Tracy and Breezy. Especially Breezy. She put so much enthusiasm into it.

When the cart was full, we checked out and I paid with a credit card. The same redheaded box boy loaded our groceries on his carry out cart. I saw him eyeing Breanne but he spoke to me, "Do you remember where you parked your car, Mrs. Phillips?"

"Of course she does!" Breanne jumped to my defense. "If she doesn't, I do. I remember exactly where I parked it."

"You parked it? You're not big enough to drive."

"Well, I drove it anyway," she said haughtily and headed towards the door with him following her.

"You're new in town, aren't you?"

"Of course not. I've almost been here a whole day."

When the groceries were loaded, we got in, Breanne behind the wheel. "The nerve of him," she said as she looked over her left shoulder to back out. "He had no business making such a remark to you about you forgetting things like he did, Mrs. Phillips."

"I think he was speaking to you and not to me, Breanne. I think he was trying to flirt with you."

"Well it won't do him any good. I've given up on boys," she said as we left the parking lot.

"Given up?" I asked.

"Yeah, they all treat me like I'm their little sister or like I'm a china doll, frail and easy to break."

"That will change, Breanne. That will change, you just wait and see."

"Maybe, but I don't have time for them now anyway. I'll need to spend my spare time studying. It's going to take a lot of hard work for me to become a doctor."

Chapter 24

"SQUIRT, HAVE YOU MENTIONED to Kris or Chris about our visit to Dr. Nickelous or his diagnosis?"
"No, I haven't. Do you think we should?"
"Absolutely," and then he sat there in silence as we watched the sun set. "What if we have a cookout tomorrow and while they are all here together, we make the announcement?"
"Whatever," I said, "It doesn't make any difference to me. The only thing is I want you to tell them."
"Why?"
"It will sound like I'm whining if I tell them."
Paul stood and headed towards the door. "I'll call them and make sure they haven't any plans."
I stood and followed him. The house was quiet and Breezy was in her room studying. I'd have to say this for her, if her grades were not good enough to get her admitted to medical school, it wouldn't be for the lack of trying. She never went out and she spent all of her time taking care of the house or studying.
Tracy had worked her schedule around Breezy's and it seemed that one or the other was always in class. Paul went to the telephone and called Chris. I paid very little attention to the conversation and when he hung up I heard him call Kris. Then he called Tracy and Pete.
With the calls made he came to me and said, "Everyone is free tomorrow evening but there is only one hitch. Instead of steak, they want chicken. They claimed I hadn't barbecued chicken in years."
"I think we have a package of drumsticks, a package of thighs, and a package of chicken breasts in the freezer," I said.

"But they want it barbequed like I used to do it which means I have to marinate it all night and tomorrow. There isn't time to thaw frozen chicken and then marinate it. Do you suppose HomeLand is still open?"

"What time is it?"

Paul looked at his watch and then said, "A quarter till nine."

"Yes, they don't close until ten."

"Let's go then," he said.

How foolish, I thought as we pulled into the HomeLand parking lot. Here we made a trip down to the grocery store just to buy a few packages of chicken. But I didn't mention it to Paul. Instead I said, "Better pay attention where you park. Cars tend to get lost in the HomeLand parking lot."

"They tend to do that in a lot of places," he laughed as he got out and headed into the store.

With the chicken bought we headed home. But before we were out of the parking lot I undid my seat belt, scooted over next to him and snapped the lap belt. I placed my hand on this thigh and asked, "Does this bother your driving?"

"Well, yes," he answered. "It makes my mind wander and I think of other things rather than my driving, but I'm willing to take the chance if you are."

At home Paul got out a huge plastic bowl, washed the chicken and placed the pieces in the bowl. When he was done he started looking through the cabinets. "Where's the cooking sherry?"

"I don't know. I'm not sure we have any. Ask Breezy."

I heard him go down the hallway and knock before he went in. Soon he was back. "We don't have any," he said. "We don't have cooking wine of any kind. Guess I'll just have to use regular wine." He opened the doors above the built in pantry and started looking. "This ought to do," and he took down an unopened bottle of Concord grape wine. "But we'd better taste it first," and he took down two wine glasses and poured them half full. He took a sip and smacked his lips. "Yes, this will do right nicely. It would even be better if it were cold."

He covered the chicken completely, put the plastic lid on the bowl tightly and set it in the fridge along with what was left of the gallon of wine. We went into the living room and watched television until it was time to go to bed.

"Since you're doing the cooking, what do you want me to do?" Breezy asked the next afternoon as Paul began to get ready to barbeque the chicken.

"You're relegated to potato peeler and onion peeler," he said. "You're in for a real treat. Tonight we're going to have potatoes *'Au Paul'*."

When Paul got out the cutting board and started cutting the potatoes into small squares, I went out onto the porch. I was worried. Worried not about myself but about the kids. How would the kids take it when we told them? Would they treat me as they always had? Would they give more sympathy than I could handle. It is funny how people are. A broken leg or a broken arm is okay, but if something is wrong with the mind then it's a whole different story. People will talk for hours about an operation they had. An operation to make their bodies healthy, but if it is something to do with the brain, they keep mum and never say a word.

I hoped the kids didn't pity me. I could handle anything but that. I couldn't stand it if they tiptoed around in their conversation and was careful to never mention the problem I had. I thought I knew my kids and I didn't think they would, but one never really knows.

Miss Calico walked over and jumped on my lap. She snuggled down as I petted her. Through the kitchen window, I could hear Breezy and Paul talking as they worked. Soon Paul came out to the patio and lit the gas barbeque and then went back inside. Then he was back with a long tinfoil tube of potatoes. He placed them on the very top rack and closed the lid. "You ready for a glass of wine?" he asked.

"That would taste good. Isn't the afternoon lovely? I think the hot weather is over for this year."

"Don't kid yourself, we'll be having a few more hot spells before fall sets in," he said as he went back inside. He was soon back with two glasses of wine and Breezy following him with a bottle of Orange Crush. She had no more than sat down than Snowflake was at her feet whining to get on her lap. She set down her bottle, picked her up and Snowflake all but whimpered with pleasure.

"Squirt, it looks to me like you've lost one of your poodles."

"That's okay, I have three more," I said.

"Have you been out in the front yard today?" Paul asked.

"No I haven't, why?"

"The Bowers Real Estate company put a for sale sign on the Humboldt house this morning."

"I'm not surprised, he's been in the rest home the past five years or so. I guess none of his kids wanted to move into it."

"I know, and it's run down the past years, but I think I'll look into it Monday."

"What in the world for?"

"Investment. From the outside it looks like it has an excellent design and if the structure is sound, we might buy it. I think with a remodeling, it would make a beautiful place to live."

"Sounds like you might be taking on more work. I thought you had enough to do."

"I wouldn't be doing the work myself, I'd hire that done. The only thing I'd be doing would be overseeing it and make sure it was done properly.

Tracy and Pete came wandering in. "I could smell the cooking from our apartment," Tracy said. "After Pete got a whiff of it there was no holding him back."

Wine's in the fridge," Paul said. "We are serving the best. It's Concord grape and we opened a gallon of it. I know white wine is to be served with fowl but we didn't have any."

"Want a glass, Honey?" Pete asked.

"Thank you, but I don't think I should. If you find a Pepsi in there I'll have it."

Pete was back with his wine and Tracy's Pepsi when I heard the front door open and Chris's booming voice. "Where is everybody?" he called.

"Back here," Paul called.

Chris and Tiffany came out. Chris shook his father's hand and then he came to me. When I saw him coming I set down my wine glass. Chris plucked me out of my chair, lifted me into the air and whirled me around. He sat me down, shook Pete's hand, hugged Tracy and then looked at Breezy. "Who's this?" he boomed.

"I'm sorry," I said, "But you haven't been over to the house for a couple of weeks now. That is Breanne Fox, she is our new cook and housekeeper. She's a freshman in college."

"Housekeeper and cook? She doesn't look big enough for that."

"I'm plenty big enough," Breezy said, setting down her Orange Crush and standing up.

"You are?" Chris laughed, grabbing her around the waist, lifting her over his head and whirling her around twice before he set her down.

"I'll let you get by with it once," Breezy said, her chin out and her nose in the air. "But don't do it again. I'm sure your Mama taught you better. So don't do it again or…"

"Or what?" he said laughing and reaching for her again. As quick as a wink, she escaped and jumped from the porch into the yard.

She stood there in a boxer's stance shuffling her feet and clowning. "I'm warning you for the last time," she snorted through her nose, "don't do it again."

Laughing, Chris lunged off the porch after her and the dust flew. When it cleared, Chris was laying flat on his back with his head and shoulders on the ground and one leg up the tree. Breezy was standing up brushing the dirt off.

Tracy rushed to Chris, "Are you hurt?" she asked

"No, and I wouldn't admit it if I was." Then he tilted his head back and looked at Breanne, "How the hell did a little thing like you throw me like you did?"

"Easy," she said, walking to him and putting her hand out to help him up. "I'm sorry for throwing you so hard but the trick is to use someone's momentum against them and you came off the porch after me awfully fast."

"You put me down here, you can damn well help me up," he said grinning and taking her hand.

When Chris was standing on his feet, he brushed himself clean and then asked his father, "Where's the wine? I need some pain killer."

"In the fridge. There's a gallon of it except what I used to marinate the chicken."

"Want a glass, Tiffany?"

"Of course," she answered.

"What about you Little-Bit"

"Not for me, I'm too young to drink, but I'll have another Orange Crush."

When he came back out, he handed Tiffany her wine and Breezy her orange. "Thank you," Breezy said.

"Friends?" Chris asked, holding his glass up.

"We were never anything else," Breezy said, clinking the top of her bottle against Chris's glass. "We just had to get acquainted."

Paul put the chicken on and turned the heat down as low as it would go. The steady hum of conversation was around me like the gentle swells of the sea rolling upon the shore. I was happy, truly happy. Every time I thought of Breezy throwing Chris against the tree, I chuckled if only to myself. It served the big brute right. He had always had his way with girls but this time his way had turned out to be the wrong way. Served him right indeed. I hoped he treated Tiffany with respect. She deserved it and she was one of the best things that could have ever happened to him.

The door opened and a most stunning young woman stepped out onto the patio. She had a bowl of the most beautiful salad in her hand, but who was she. It seemed as if I should know her. Paul had just finished turning the chicken and he shut the lid and turned. He walked to the beautiful woman and hugged her. "It's about time you got here, Kris," he said.

Kris? I had a daughter named Kris. Then I looked at her more closely and recognized that this beautiful young creature was my daughter. How could I have forgotten her? I jumped to my feet and rushed to her. I threw my arms around her and hugged her tight. "Where's JT?" I asked.

"He's following me around someplace," she said. "Don't worry, he'll show up when it's time to eat."

I led her to Breanne and said, "Breanne, this is my daughter, Kris. Kris, meet Breanne, or as we sometimes call her, Breezy. She and your brother have just gotten acquainted."

"How was that," JT asked, stepping out onto the porch.

"See how little she is?" Chris asked pointing to her.

"Yeah."

"Well, treat that little thing with big respect. Otherwise she will do you like she did me."

"What did she do to you," JT asked.

"See that oak tree there," he said pointing. "Well, she threw my ass halfway up it."

"She's our new housekeeper and cook," I said.

"So, Tracy, you found a job as a nurse? Congratulations."

"Well, sort of."

"Sort of?" Kris asked. "Mom, Dad, what's going on around here?

"Squirt, this is probably as good a time as any to tell them, don't you think?"

"I was hoping we could wait until after dinner and not ruin it for them"

"Tell us," Kris said. "Don't hold off or I won't be able to eat a bite."

"Well, Kids," Paul said, "it's like this. Even though your mother is young, unfortunately she has Alzheimer's. Her doctor his written a prescription and she is to have someone with her all the time. That is Tracy's new job."

"How far along is it?" Kris asked.

"Early stage one," I answered.

"Then you can't hide your own Easter eggs yet?" Chris asked.

"No, but maybe next year," I laughed. Leave it to Chris. I wondered if he ever took anything seriously.

"That wasn't nice, Chris," Breezy said. "You shouldn't make fun of your Mamma."

"Have you started forgetting people, Mom?" Kris asked.

"Sometimes I do. I hope I don't hurt your feelings, but when you came in awhile ago; I had the hardest time recognizing who you were."

"Then just think of all the new people you're going to meet in the future," Kris said.

"Yeah," Chris chimed in, "Maybe this year you can buy your own Christmas present and then be surprised when you open it. I've even got a better idea. Buy yourself a good book and you'll be set for reading material the rest of your life."

"How do you figure that," I asked.

"Well, by the time you finish reading it, you will have forgotten it and you can read it over and over and over."

"You kids!" Breezy said standing and stomping her small foot. "It's not funny. How can you be joking about your mother's condition?"

"They're not making fun of her, Breezy," Tracy said, "Once you have been around them as long as I have, then you'll understand. When misfortune comes, they laugh in its face instead of cry."

"But you are right, Breezy, the conversation is getting rather gloomy. Would you liven things up and sing for us?"

"I don't have my guitar; it got burned in the fire."

"I've heard you singing as you worked and you have a beautiful, unique voice. Your voice is beautiful even without your guitar."

She walked out to the middle of the porch, turned to face us and cleared her voice. "I've grown up down by Tahlequah in a rich family. As I was growing up we kids had everything, everything but money. We learned to entertain ourselves. Every evening just at dark when supper and the chores were done, we'd gather and play music. Momma played the violin, Dad and me played the guitar, while Tommy and Joe, my youngest brothers played the banjo. Tommy played the five string banjo and Joe played the tenor banjo. Cathy, my one and oldest sister, played the tambourine and at times would sing with me.

"My first number is one I wrote last night; *"I loved you when I first met you and I'll love you from now on..."* and she continued to sing in her deep, rich voice. It was a song about two children falling in love their first day of school and began with *"I held you the first day of school when you cried as your mother walked away,"* and now though they were old and gray they were still very much in love.

I glanced around to see if the others were enjoying Breezy's singing as much as I was. I saw that all of their eyes were damp. Even Chris's eyes. I knew then that by the time Breanne graduated, my family would have her spoiled thoroughly rotten.

When she finished the song, everyone began to applaud but before the applause was through, she grinned an impish grin, raised her leg, slapped her thigh, clapped her hands and began to dance as she broke into *"Got a fishing line strung across the Louisiana River, gotta catch a big fish for us to eat...*"

For thirty minutes or more, Breezy sang and entertained us. Then the chicken was done and we heaped our plates high. Chris took the first bite, looked at the thigh he was eating and said, "I'll be damn, purple chicken. I've never eaten purple chicken before."

"Looks a lot like crow," Breezy said, "but tastes a lot better. Crow is kind of tough and stringy."

"Breezy!" Tracy scolded. "You've never eaten crow in your life."

"Tracy, if you don't quit butting in, I'll never build a reputation up here."

"Cooking sherry," Paul said. "We definitely need cooking sherry. Make sure you put cooking sherry on your grocery list, Breanne."

Chapter 25

THE REDBUD TREES WERE IN BLOOM and I could see them through the living room window. I could see pickups and vans sitting across the street at the old Humboldt house, remodeling, I supposed. Paul had thought about buying it and fixing it up. Had he? I couldn't remember. Perhaps he had and it was our house they were working on. I just wish I could remember.

But I could remember a spring day like this a long time ago. Back then I was a sophomore in high school at Canton. According to the administration and school board, each class was allowed to have one party a year. Spring came and we realized that we hadn't had our party. The class voted and we decided to have a weenie roast. More than a weenie roasts, actually. John Fillmore's dad had a team of mules and a wagon. Some of the boys helped throw some loose hay on the wagon and we had a hay ride to boot.

We left from the school house at six o'clock and I can still remember to this day the clopping of the mules as they took us down to the creek. All of us girls wore shorts and I wore red ones which were very, very tight. For most of us girls, we had just matured, achieved our wares so to speak, and were advertising them. My halter top, like the rest of the girls, was so tight that my nipples showed. Of course in those days, no one wore a bra.

When we got to the creek, we gathered dead falls and built a fire. This took longer than it should have because of the horseplay which ensued. Trina fell in the creek, or that's what Willard claimed, though she swore that he pushed her. At last we had willow sticks cut and whittled to a point and we were soon sitting around the fire roasting hotdogs. Nothing tastes as good as a hotdog roasted on a green willow sapling. But to be truthful, to fifteen and sixteen year olds, everything tastes good. I can still remember to this day how good the hotdogs tasted and the blackened, sticky marshmallows tasted even better.

But there were so many worlds to be seen and so much life to be explored that after eating we became restless. Soon we were back on the wagon with the mules clopping along. It was early yet so Mr. Fillmore was taking us over the dirt roads of the country side. The stars were out and a new moon was setting in the west. It was a most wonderful night except it had grown a little cool. Many of us had brought blankets and we were laughing and talking as we huddled under them. All except Bobby and Peggy Sue. They were in the back of the wagon, a blanket over them and very quiet.

We watched as Billy, always the cutup, eased back to them on his hands and knees. Quick as a wink he reached out and jerked the blanket off, laughing, and then he hastily covered them back up. His red face showing even in the darkness.

We all looked at Mrs. Miller, our sophomore sponsor, and she glanced from one of us to the other. "I didn't see anything, did you girls?"

"No, Ma'am," we answered.

"Bobby," Mr. Bell, our other sponsor said, "You come up and sit with me. Peggy Sue, you sit with Mrs. Miller."

Soon they were both sitting up front with the rest of us but the life seemed to have gone out of the party. Mr. Fillmore turned the wagon around and took us back to school.

"Sharon," Tracy suddenly said at my elbow bringing me back from yesteryear, "It's time for you to go in and take your shower."

"Are you sure," I asked, looking up at her. "I took one this morning when I got up, didn't I"

"I'm afraid not, Sharon, and you didn't take one yesterday either. You simply have to take one today. I've laid out your clothes on the bed."

I looked one more time at the crew working across the street and then went back to the bedroom where I showered and dressed. As I came out of the bedroom, Breezy come whipping by with a laundry basket. I was surprised that she was already home from class. "We'll have lunch as soon as I get a load of laundry going," she said and went running on by. Tracy was right. That girl never, ever walked.

After lunch, Tracy left for class and Breezy switched the laundry from the washer to the dryer. A whirlwind later, the house was vacuumed and dinner was on. I was sitting in the recliner resting. It seemed as if I was tired all of the time these days. "Want a glass of iced tea, Mrs. Phillips?" Breezy called from the kitchen.

"That would be nice."

"Keep your seat; I'll bring it to you."

I heard her hustling and bustling around the kitchen and then she came in. She set my glass of iced tea right on the coaster where it was supposed to go, bless her.

"Having one of those bad days?" she asked when she brought it to me.

"It's not one of my best ones." And then the silence built as she sat on the sofa. "I know what would make me feel better, if you have the time."

"What?" she asked.

"If you would sing for me, but only if you don't have to study or have something else to do."

"When you don't have time for music, then you don't have time for life," she said, jumping up and heading for her room. Soon she was back and she had a guitar strapped around her neck.

"You have a guitar!" I said in excitement.

"Yes, Chris gave it to me for Christmas. He said he was loaning it to me but loaning it to me for life. It's the best and most expensive guitar I ever had in my life. It's a Gibson."

I remembered when Chris was fifteen and he wanted to learn to play the guitar. I think he felt if he could play and sing he could impress even more women. I think he pictured himself on the high school stage playing and singing with girls swooning at his feet. Finally, Paul and I had bought the guitar and even provided guitar lessons.

Chris quickly learned to strike the pose, learned to make all the moves of an entertainer, but that was all. He was not musically inclined and gave up after a few short weeks.

Breezy fine tuned the instrument and said, "I have a gig this Friday and Saturday night at Eskimo Joe's. They claim they want me to play and sing rock so I have been busily writing some rock songs, but I know it's a waste of time. I'll give them a couple of rock songs then I'll hit them with a good old country western and when I do, the people will hit the floor dancing. I'll sing you a couple of rock songs I've written and then we'll get to the good stuff."

And she did and she was right. I didn't care much for her rock music or anyone else's for that matter. But she was as cute as a bug's ear as she danced, played and sung. Then she started singing country western and the music washed over me. I inhaled it, was bathed in it and it relaxed me. I closed my eyes and let the music flow over me like the warm surf of the sea.

The door bell rang and Kris stepped in. "Warming up for Friday and Saturday night, Breezy?" Kris asked.

"Kind of. Mrs. Phillips wanted to hear me sing so I took the opportunity to shape up my act, you know, decide what I was going to sing."

Kris had the baby in her arms all bundled up like they had been out in a blizzard instead of the springtime sunshine. She began to unwrap him, starting at his head. As soon as he saw me he started grinning and reaching for me. "There's Granny, Jared. See Granny?" which started him kicking and soon he had unwrapped himself.

Jared! That was what his name was. I had been trying to think of it ever since she brought him in.

"JT and I plan to be there," Kris said, "That is if we can find a babysitter," and she looked right at me as she handed me my grandson.

"That is one thing about grandchildren," I laughed, "It brings you closer to your children. They always need a babysitter."

"Would you, Mom?" Kris said. "That's great. We won't be out too late and we'll only go Friday night. I'm afraid Saturday night will be packed. Dad will not work late Friday night, will he? He'll be here."

"Of course," I answered.

"I hope so," Breezy said.

"Hope what?" Kris asked.

"I hope there is a big crowd, and I hope they leave big tips. It'll help my dad buy boards for the house."

"When do you think the house will be done," I asked.

"Oh, it will be done in time for the wedding," she said with all confidence in the world.

"You're getting married?" Kris asked in surprise.

"Not my wedding," she laughed. "It could never be done in time for that unless I get married when I'm very old. The wedding of my youngest grandchild."

The dryer buzzer sounded and quick as a wink, Breezy picked up the guitar and trotted down the hall to her room. Soon I heard her humming as she hung up and folded the clothes.

"Has she been home to Tahlequah since you brought her up here?" Kris asked.

"No, she claims her folks need the money more than they need to see her. By her request, we pay her in cash and she sends all but a small bit of it home."

"Well, if she fails in her medical career, she can always drop back on her music. JT and I went to the Cowboy Tavern a month or so back where she was singing and the crowd loved her. She's so cute up on the stage singing away."

"She's not going to fail in her medical career, Kris. Last semester she got a four point oh. She's smart. And not just smart in book sense either. If the book doesn't tell her how to do something, she can figure it out on her own."

Breezy came back through on her way to the kitchen to check on dinner. "Breezy, it's none of my business, but is Eskimo Joe paying you pretty good for Friday and Saturday night," I called.

"You bet. He's paying me seventy-five dollars a night and I'll almost make that much in tips. That'll buy a lot of boards."

"When are you going back to work, Kris?" I asked when Breezy went back to her room to study.

"I planned to go back in March, but I didn't. JT and I have been talking it over and we have about reached the conclusion that he needs a mother to look after his son more than he needs a legal research specialist. I may not go back to work until after the kids are grown."

"Kids?" I questioned.

"Yes, we plan on having a whole passel of them."

Tracy came in from class and Kris soon left. When Tracy came back from taking her books home she asked, "Sharon, have you been outside today."

"Yes," I answered. "I was out this morning. Or I think I was."

"I don't think so. I was with you all morning and I didn't take you out. Let's go outside, the fresh air will do you good and bring life to you. You'll need a light sweater; after all, it is only the middle of April."

There would have been a time when I would resented Tracy telling me what to do. But no longer. Instead, I felt relieved that I had someone like her to make decisions for me.

Outside, we walked around the yard and looked at the flower beds. They were in bad shape. Usually by this time of the year, I would have had them dug up and ready to plant or maybe they would even be planted. This spring I had done nothing. I had lost interest. I didn't really care. The only thing that looked good was the irises and they would take care of themselves.

"If you're going to have flowers this year, Sharon, it's time to get started."

"I don't know if I want to plant flowers this year."

"Come on, Sharon. You always grow the most beautiful flowers. If you need help preparing the beds, I'll help you."

"You will?"

"Yes, you noticed I said preparing the beds. You don't want me to be planting anything. I don't have a green thumb; in fact my thumb is black. Anything I plant wilts and dies. But we can get started on it the first thing in the morning."

"Let's get started now. Help me find the tools and we'll get as much done as we can before Paul comes home."

Chapter 26

IT WAS AS IF MY MIND KNEW that soon it would no longer function and it raced a million miles an hour trying to do those things which it soon would not be able to do. I lay in bed that Friday night listening to Paul's heavy breathing and afraid to move for fear I would awaken him.

I should have been tired and ready to go to sleep; This morning Tracy and I had finished cleaning the flowerbeds and had them ready to plant. Then when Tracy came home in the afternoon, we had gone straight to Feeds & Seeds where I bought tray after tray of seedlings and put them in the trunk of the Cadillac. What an indignity, I thought as I packed the trays in, what an indignity to use a Cadillac for a farm truck. "Sorry Mrs. Cadillac, we will treat you with the stateliness you deserve after this." Of course no one was in the parking lot so no one heard me. That was a good thing. If they had, they would have thought me crazy unless they knew me. If they knew me, they would have known Sharon was just being Sharon.

When we brought the plants home it was late so we only unloaded them and carried them to the back porch. By then Tracy had to go in and finish dinner as Breezy prepared herself for her first performance at Eskimo Joe's. Breezy was too excited to eat but she did sit at the table with us and toy with her food. Then she took her guitar and left.

Tracy cleaned up the kitchen and I was thinking seriously about going outside to start setting the plants out when Kris and JT came with my grandbaby.

It was joy, pure joy to watch our grandbaby wallowing on the floor. Knowing how new mothers are, I waited until JT and Kris left before I turned the poodles in on him. He was delighted and laughed as they licked his hands, face and legs. He became one of them, a puppy himself and squirmed himself into their pile before he went to sleep. And that was where he was; sleeping in a pile of poodles when I heard a car park outside and knew that Kris and JT, true to their word, had left Eskimo Joe's early.

Quick as a wink I jumped up, ran to the heap and snatched my grandbaby from the pile of puppies and by the time they came in, I was rocking him in my chair.

"Did Jared give you any trouble, Mom?" Kris asked.

"None whatsoever," I answered.

"I see you introduced him to the poodles. What did he think of them?"

"He liked them. He laughed as he sat on my lap and watched them bound around."

"I hope you didn't let them lick him all over."

"No, of course not. I wouldn't do a thing like that."

Kris looked at me skeptically; damn I wish I could lie. To quickly change the subject I asked, "How is Breezy doing?"

"She's wowing them, Mom. You wouldn't believe it; she is really wowing them. She is a natural entertainer. They have a microphone for her but she seldom uses it. Of course the crowd was still growing when we left and she had to use the microphone more and more as the din rose. But she seems to have a sixth sense of when to step up to the microphone and when to step away. That girl really has talent."

JT and Kris soon left and when they did, Paul and I went to bed and now here I was tossing and turning, or would be tossing and turning if it wasn't for the fear of waking Paul. Finally I couldn't take it anymore and I got up. I slipped on a light robe and padded to the kitchen. I opened the refrigerator, took one of Breanne's Orange Crush's and went to the living room. As soon as I sat in the recliner, four poodles jumped into my lap.

I must have dozed because it didn't seem that long until I heard Breezy pull in and park. Soon I heard her key in the door and she came in ever so quietly.

"How did the night go?" I asked.

She jumped and turned, "Oh, hi, Mrs. Phillips. Having trouble sleeping?"

"Yes and I don't know why. After everything I've done I should have been able to drop right off to sleep, but for some reason I couldn't."

"I know what you mean, Mrs. Phillips. I'm the same way. I'm tired but wired if you know what I mean. Any Orange Crush left."

"Plenty, get yourself one and if you're not too tired, you can tell me about your night."

She laid her guitar on the couch and went to the kitchen. I heard the refrigerator open and close and she was back. She sat on the couch, crossed her ankles and leaned back. "Oh-eeh tonight was fun. It was crowded by the time I was through and they didn't want me to leave. But the manager said that was all I was going to do and if they wanted to hear me again, come back tomorrow night.

"I told him I would stay a little longer but he said 'No, leave them hungry for more,' so I left. He wants me next weekend, too, but I told him I couldn't. I only got every other weekend off."

"Breezy, we could have worked something out. We could have given you next weekend off also."

"No, screw him. I felt I should follow his own advice and leave him hungry for more. I bet I made Eskimo Joe's five hundred dollars extra tonight and I bet I will double that tomorrow night. I told him that I could perform weekend after next. I didn't mention that it might cost him a bit more; I'll wait until sometime next week before I decide. I made a hundred fifty some dollars tonight, counting my tips. That'll buy a few boards. I need a couple of weeks to write some new songs anyway. I ran out of original material tonight as it was. I suspect tomorrow night I'll be giving them mostly requests."

We sat there in silence for a while and enjoyed our pop. "Are you ever going to take a weekend off and go home, Breezy?"

"Not as long as I can make two-fifty to three hundred dollars a weekend. It sure helps my family out. It helps them much more than seeing my smiling face."

"Don't you miss your family? Don't you want to see them?"

"Of course I do. I miss them more than anything in the world but think what I can do for them once I'm a surgeon and knocking down over a hundred thousand dollars a year. But that's a long time off," she said wistfully.

"I'm sure they miss you. You might be surprised at how much more they would rather see their daughter than see an envelope with a money order in it."

She sat there in lonely silence then giggled and said, "I got five proposals tonight."

"Proposals?"

"Yeah, marriage proposals. The ole boys had been drinking a bit too much. None of it was serious."

"You'd better watch it, Breanne. Some of them might be more serious than you think."

"No," she laughed. "They called me Little-Bit when they asked. That ornery Chris started it. He and Tiffany were in and he hollered to me and called me Little-Bit. They were just having fun."

"You still might be surprised," I said. "Some of them might be recognizing a good thing when they see it."

"If they were serious they wouldn't have called me Little-Bit but would have seen me as a woman." She finished her pop, stood and carried the empty bottle to a trash can where she dropped it in. "I still don't know if I can sleep just yet, but I'm going to my room. If I can't sleep, I'll write another song. I have a zillion ideas. Of course as much pop as I have had to drink, I'll probably spend a good part of the night in the bathroom sitting on the throne peeing. Are you going to be okay?"

"Sure," I laughed, "you go right ahead. I'll probably go back to bed myself shortly."

"Goodnight, then. I'll see you in the morning." She picked up her guitar and headed down the hallway to her room."

After she left, I sat in the recliner staring at the walls and feeling restless. Finally I shoved the poodles off my lap and stood. I walked to the back door and looked out. The moon was almost full and I could see the back yard clearly. I could see the fresh tilled flowerbeds and I could see the seedlings just setting there ready to be set out. The poodles had followed me to the door but when I opened the door they backed away. They were in the house for the night. I stepped outside.

The air was cool but not cold and I smelled the fresh smell of spring. I wasn't sleepy at all and I looked again at the seedlings. The planting trowel was laying on the porch right beside the flats. I walked over and picked up the trowel. Again I looked at the empty flowerbeds. This is crazy, I thought. Nobody plants flowers during the middle of the night. Besides, if I did, I'd get my pajamas dirty. But maybe there was still a way.

I looked through the trees at the only house to be seen. All I could see was the moonlight reflecting from its metal roof. The house was dark and no windows were lighted.

I stood there motionless and looked everywhere. No one was about at this time of the night. I slipped off my robe, folded it and put it in a chair. I listened but all I could hear was the call of the night birds down the lake a way. I slipped off my pajama top and after folding it, I placed it on the robe. Again I stood motionless and listened. I didn't hear anything and I didn't see anything only the moon shadows cast by the great oaks. I pulled the bottoms off and stepped out of them.

I picked them up and put them on top of everything. Again I stood motionless, naked in the moonlight. If someone were to see me I'd be committed for sure, but my pajamas would remain clean. Again I picked up the trowel, a flat of marigolds and headed for the nearest flower bed.

Digging in the soft, damp earth, setting the plants out and tamping the supple earth around them had a most relaxing and soothing feeling. I might not be able to remember people's names and I didn't remember how to make out checks to pay the bills, but by-golly I could still plant flowers. I could still make the world a more beautiful place.

When the first bed was planted I sat back on my heels and looked at it. Yes, when the flowers grew they would fill the bed and when the flowers bloomed, it would be beautiful. Another flat of flowers and to another bed I went. My knees were becoming raw and my thighs burned but over all, I felt good. And just to think, I had considered not planting the flowerbeds this year. "Thank you, Tracy," I murmured into the quiet night. "Thank you, thank you, and thank you." I owed Tracy so much. If not for her I would probably be spending my days in a special home drooling in front of a television all day. While we both claimed that she helped me live a normal life and still do all of the things I had always done, that wasn't exactly true. It was true I sat with her in the den and signed the checks; it was Tracy who paid the bills. If I forgot to eat, she reminded me. If I forgot to bathe, she reminded me. She gave me my medicine when it was time. My so called normal life depended entirely upon her.

The moon had set and the first red streaks of dawn were showing when I finished the last bed in the back yard. I wanted to water them but I knew if I turned on an outside faucet, they could hear the sound of running water in the house. Oh, well, the plants could go a few hours without being watered.

Back on the porch I brushed the dirt from my hands, knees, and feet and put my pajamas back on. I stacked the empty flats out of the way and went inside. I was tired and drowsy. I knew if I went to bed I'd wake Paul up and he liked to sleep in on Saturdays. Today was Saturday, wasn't it? I went to the living room, sat in my recliner and leaned it all of the way back. I was halfway asleep when I felt the first poodle jump into my lap and it was soon followed by the other three. I gathered them in my arms and with a thrill of happiness, drifted off to sleep.

Slowly the whiff of coffee drifted by and I knew someone was in the kitchen. But who? Was Tracy over here already? It couldn't be Breanne, this was her day off. The poodles were gone so I suspected that whoever it was had let them out.

I lowered my feet and brought the recliner to upright. I stood and wandered into the kitchen. It was Breezy and she was humming as she prepared breakfast.

She glanced over her shoulder and saw me. "Did you sleep in that recliner all night?"

"Pretty much so. Is the coffee ready?"

She looked at the carafe and said, "Yes, it's all dripped through."

I poured myself a cup and took it outside. Yes, all of the flowerbeds were planted and no, I hadn't dreamed it. Yet, now I was wide awake. I sat down in a chair at the patio table and Miss Calico jumped into my lap. The poodles were out running and scampering among the trees and the big dog was lying on the porch. He saw me, stood and wiggled his mangled tail before he walked over to me. He lay down at my side and went promptly back to sleep.

Life is good, I thought, life is golden. Then Paul came out to join me and life suddenly got better.

Chapter 27

THE CARDINALS WERE SINGING 'pretty-boy' in the evergreens as I set out flowers in the front yard. Tracy was watering the beds in the back and I hoped she wasn't drowning them. I sang with the cardinals as I worked. I had just set out the last plant when Tracy came dragging the hose around the corner of the house. "Talk about timing," I said as I sat on the front step and watched as she began to spray the freshly planted sets. "We make a good team."

"Yes, we do," she laughed and continued to spray the beds.

I looked at her; there was something different about her today. She seemed to walk more flatfooted and in a labored way. Then I recognized what it was and I laughed in delight. "Tracy!" I said, "You're pregnant."

She looked at me and frowned, "Well, yes, I am."

"When is the baby due?"

"Somewhere around the end of July or the first of August. Sometime during then."

"Why didn't you tell me sooner? There are secrets a woman can keep but there are others that are bound to come out. Being pregnant is one of the latter." I quickly stood, ran to her and took her in my arms. I hugged her tightly. "I'm so happy for you and Pete but why didn't you tell me before now?" I asked as I stepped back from her. I saw her lips were trembling and she had tears in her eyes.

"I did, Sharon. I told you and Paul as soon as I found out."

"You're about to drown those flowers," I said, and then I looked at her. It was easy to tell that it bothered her that I was losing my memory. Bothered her much more than it did me. So far the only downside of having Alzheimer's was that it made other people uncomfortable. "I bet I was happy and excited when you told me wasn't I?"

"Yes, you were," she said smiling.

"And now I'm happy and excited all over again. See, I got twice the delight out of it than I would otherwise have gotten. There are some things about this Alzheimer's that's not so bad."

Tracy lost control and would have drowned us both if I hadn't grabbed the hose. She stepped away and bent over laughing. "You're weird, Sharon," she said when she could speak again. "Only you could look at life that particular way."

After the flowerbeds were taken care of, we went inside. Breezy was busily fixing lunch. "I'll help Breezy while you go take a shower, Sharon."

"I took a shower this morning, didn't I?"

"No," she said shaking her head. "The last shower you took was Thursday morning. You've put in a lot of work since then."

"Okay, but don't you guys start eating without me. Where's Paul anyway?"

"He's across the street checking out the remodeling job. He'll be back in time for lunch."

It was such a beautiful day outside that the first thing I did before showering was to lay out the clothes I would wear. I got out a pair of green shorts and a yellow blouse. I'd spend the rest of the day looking like a dandelion.

I stripped down, showered, and dried off. As I dried my knees, I found they were sore. I moved to where the light was good and looked at them. They were raw, scratched in some places and stone bruised in others. It looked like I had been crawling on them in my shorts. I planted flowers this morning but I had worn long pants, hadn't I? I looked in the dirty clothes at what I had just taken off. Yes, I had worn jeans this morning. How had my knees gotten in such a shape? I didn't know. I couldn't remember, but something told me I had better not let anyone else see the shape my knees were in. I put away the green shorts and found a pair of green warm-up pants to take their place. I was still dressed like a dandelion.

It was such a beautiful day we had lunch on the patio. "Paul, Tracy told me you were across the street checking out the remodeling job. Is it coming along like you expected?"

"Better than I expected. The house will be ready for occupancy in thirty to forty days."

"I'm so anxious," Tracy said. "I can hardly wait."

She's anxious? I thought to myself as the conversation buzzed around me. What is she so anxious about? I listened carefully to the words they were speaking and yes, I could understand them as plain as day, yet I couldn't understand them at all. What they were saying didn't make any sense. I was in a foreign country where they still spoke English but somehow the words had different meanings. It struck me that I was sitting in the group having lunch, yet, I was alone.

"As soon as I get this mess cleaned up, I think I'll go take a nap," Breezy said.

"Go take your nap now, girl," Tracy said, "for someone who's on their day off, you've put in a lot of work today."

"Oh, I can help clean up."

"Scoot, go take your nap. I have to get dinner started and you've got another big night ahead of you. Now listen to your elders."

"I think she's trying to get rid of me," Breezy said as she went inside. "She must want to talk about me or talk about something that my tender ears are too young to hear."

I went in, found my recliner and leaned it back as far as it would go. I raised the foot rest and drifted off to sleep.

I didn't wake up until Tracy awoke me. "It's time for dinner, Sharon. As soon as you wash up we'll eat."

I stood still groggy from sleep and looked around. I could see from the shadows that it was evening. I heard Paul talking in the kitchen. He had come home and I had missed greeting him. My Hero, home from the wars and I had failed to welcome him. Then I remembered it was Saturday and I hadn't missed him coming home from work because he had never gone to work. I washed my hands and face and sat at the table. There was one missing. "Where's Breezy?" I asked.

"She has already gone," Tracy laughed. "Pete and I may sneak down to watch her for a moment. Cover charge is five dollars each but I think we can afford it just this once."

After dinner, Paul and I went outside and watched the sunset but soon after dark the mosquitoes drove us in. Paul and I were sitting on the couch with him watching television while I watched the colored lights. All at once the feeling came over me. I was lonesome and I wanted to see Mom and Dad. It seemed as if I hadn't seen them in years.

A commercial came on and Paul muted the television. I turned to him and asked, "Paul, next weekend, if you have nothing planned, can we drive over to Canton?"

"Canton? Sure, Squirt. Why do you want to go Canton?"

"We haven't seen Mom and Dad in the longest time. I would like to see them."

Paul froze. He sat there motionless without breathing. He picked up the remote and turned the television off. He rubbed his eyes and ran his fingers through his hair.

"What's wrong, Paul?"

"Tracy," he called, "Where are you now? Why aren't you here when I need you? I don't know what to do."

I sat back in alarm. Paul had never acted this way before. "What is wrong, Paul?" I asked again.

For an answer he took me in his arms and kissed me on the temple. "I love you, Squirt. I loved you when I first met you and I'll love you from now on. Nothing could ever change that. Are you sure you understand?"

"Of course, I do. You know I feel the same way about you."

"Sharon---your Mom and Dad are dead. They have been for close to twenty years."

"No!" I screamed, drawing back from him. "Why are you saying that when you know they are still alive?"

"I'm sorry, Squirt."

"It's not true! It's not true! It's not true---is it?"

"Yes, it's true," was all he said.

The tears came and I rushed into his arms. I buried my face in his chest and cried and cried and cried. Slowly I was able to get control of myself and when I did I asked, "How did it happen?"

"A car wreck or I should say a wreck between your mom and dad's car and an eighteen-wheeler. According to the report, your dad was driving and they were just topping a hill west of Canton on Highway 51 when two semis came over the hill side by side. Your dad tried to swerve and miss them but they were too close. The truck on the wrong side of the road caught him broadside and they both went into the ditch with the truck on top of them. The funeral was closed casket."

"What about the truck driver that killed them? Did he die too?"

"He didn't even get a scratch. The highway patrol and the county sheriff hauled him right off to jail."

"Good!" I said with seething anger. I hope he's still in jail. He deserves it."

"I agree with you. He deserved to be in jail, but that wasn't the reason they took him straight from the scene and locked him up. They did it for his own protection. Later they had his trial and he was sentenced to five years at McAlester."

"Then he's out by now?"

"Oh, sure. He's been out for years."

"You said they locked him up to start with for his own protection. Why did they need to do that?"

"Your mother and father were well known in Canton and they were well liked. There was a, I don't know how to describe it, a feeling in the community. I think that if they had not locked the driver up, the people might have administered their own form of justice.

"Even at their funeral, which they held at the community building so there would be room for the crowd, there was an underlying current; one of anger and tension. The reverend who preached their funeral kept mentioning how your mother and father were such forgiving people and how the Christian Faith is a forgiving religion. But I'm not for sure that the crowd listened much. The driver was locked up and they couldn't get to him and I believe that is the only thing that saved his butt."

"I still miss them," I said and as I spoke I felt the tears begin to flow.

He held me and patted me on the back until the crying stopped. Then he locked up and we went to bed. I dropped right off to sleep but awoke a short time later. I could hear the heavy breathing of Paul and the ticking of the clock. Try as I might, I couldn't get back to sleep. Finally I gave up, slipped out of bed, put on a robe and eased out the door. This is getting to be a habit, I thought to myself as I went to the kitchen, opened the fridge and got an Orange Crush. I went into the living room and had no more than sit down when I heard Breanne's key in the lock.

"Having trouble sleeping again, Mrs. Phillips?" Breezy asked as she came in.

"Yes, I don't know what's wrong with me," I said and then I amended it by saying, "Yes, I do. I have my days and nights mixed up. I stayed awake most of last night and then I slept all afternoon. Now I can't sleep tonight. How did it go tonight at Eskimo Joe's?"

"Just like last night only a lot more of it. Eskimo Joe had standing room only and some other things happened. Let me get myself an Orange Crush and I'll tell you about it. That is if you want to know."

"Of course, I do."

She laid the guitar on the couch and went to the kitchen. Soon she was back and sat on the couch facing me. "I get every other weekend off and I'm wondering if I could change that. I wonder if I could work every weekend and take an hour off every Saturday and an hour each Sunday? Of course I'd want to take the evening off every other weekend so I could do a gig at Eskimo Joe's."

"It would be okay with me," I said, "but it is something you'd have to work out with Tracy. What's the idea anyway?"

"It's like this; Eskimo Joe wants to sponsor me on a radio show at our local station. I'd have a thirty minute spot on Saturday afternoon and a thirty minute spot on Sunday morning. On Saturday, I'd do regular songs, you know, country western, some rock, but on Sunday, it would be mostly gospel. He'd pay me seventy-five dollars a show, not bad for thirty minutes of singing."

"Can you do that and still keep your grades up?"

"I'm pretty sure I can. I told the manager that I would consider it but it would have to be a week by week thing. If I saw it was taking too much time away from my studying, I'd have to quit. The extra money would sure help out at home but not near as much as I can help them once I become a surgeon."

"Breezy, do you send every spare nickel home to your family?"

"Pretty much, they need it."

"Don't you think you ought to start saving some to pay for your medical school? You know medical schooling doesn't come cheap"

"Oh, I'll borrow money when I start to medical school. The government has a program where you can borrow money to become a doctor and then once you start practicing, most of the loan is forgiven if you will practice your skills in an assigned area. You know places that need a doctor but can't afford one. That's kind of what I want to do with my life anyway."

Breezy tipped up her bottle and drained it. "I think I'll get to sleep easier tonight than I did last night," she said as she picked up the guitar and went to her room.

I sat for a while wide awake. Finally I stood and went outside. Again I tried to get the poodles to go with me but nothing doing. But the outside dog, the dog with the mangled tail, greeted me. There was just enough wind from the south that it plastered my pajamas to me and blew my robe open. I gathered the robe tight around me and made my way to a chair. The dog followed me and when I sat, he placed his head on my knee. I stroked it and scratched him between the ears. He soon lay down at my feet and went to sleep.

I looked down at the lake and the moonlit water rippled in the breeze. I sat there, looking at everything but seeing nothing. I sat there, the wind blowing in my hair. I grew drowsy with the first red streaks of dawn so I went inside and curled up in my recliner. When the fourth poodle jumped into my lap, I drifted off to sleep.

Chapter 28

SPRING DANCED IN, TOOK a bow and then said goodbye and it was followed on stage by the lazy days of summer. It surprised me when neither Breezy nor Tracy enrolled in summer school. I had them both under my feet and it was delightful.

It was one of those rare lazy mornings with the sun reflecting from the mirror like lake as Tracy, Breezy and I meandered along the shore. The big dog was leading, as usual, sweeping the shore line on the lookout for a dangerous squirrel. The poodles romped along the beach, sometimes in the water and sometimes rolling in the sand.

"What is today?" I asked to no one in particular.

"June the eleventh," Tracy answered. Breezy who generally chattered all the time was unusually silent.

We were across from the fountain when I stopped, found an old weather-beaten log and sat down. The girls sat down with me but the poodles continued to romp and play. The big dog spied a squirrel, chased it up its tree and sat at the roots while he looked up at it and occasionally whined. "Isn't this a grand day?" I asked.

"Yes, it is," Tracy said her hands clasped over her protruding stomach.

"Mrs. Phillips," Breezy blurted, "there was one thing we didn't discuss when I went to work."

"What was that?"

"Do I get any time off in the summer? I mean do I get like vacation time?"

"We didn't discuss it Breezy because most of the girls who have worked for us enrolled in summer classes. Do you want some time off?"

"If it's possible."

"You're finally going to go home and see your family? Good for you, I'm sure they would be glad to see you."

"Well, I want to do that too."

"That too? What else, Breezy?"

She turned, straddled the log and faced me. "Dr. Griffith, the head of the music department at OSU, heard me on the radio a while back. He must have liked what he heard. Then he came to Eskimo Joe's and watched me perform. Then a couple of months ago, he invited me to cut a demo using my original stuff. I did. We tried it with a backup band and then he had me to do the songs over with just me and my guitar. It turned out that just me and my guitar sounded best. Anyway, he thought so. Me, I couldn't tell much difference.

"To make a long story short, he asked if he could represent me as my agent. To me it didn't seem like it was anything serious so I said sure. He drew up a contract and I signed it. Then he duplicated the demo and sent it off to several recording companies."

I realized I had been holding my breath. I let it out, looked at her and asked, "And?"

"Well, as it turns out, he received replies from several of them. Anyway, Dr. Griffith is ready to set up an appointment for me at the RCA recording studios in Nashville. They want me to cut an album, test market it and see what it will do."

"Breezy!" Tracy exclaimed. "Why are we just finding out about this now? Why haven't you told us before?"

"Because, I didn't think anything would ever come from it. Anyway, they want me to come to Nashville but I didn't see how I could, then when I got to thinking about it, I thought that if I have vacation time, I'd give it a shot."

I looked at her through misty eyes. Just to think she had such a chance and was asking me for permission to take some time off. "What if I said you don't get vacation time?" I asked.

"Then I wouldn't go."

"Just that simple," I said. "You'd pass up an opportunity of a lifetime if I said, no."

"Of course. I'm up here to become a doctor and nothing else. Anything else I do is just a lark. You're giving me that chance to become a doctor and that is what is important. I will always be grateful to you and Paul."

"Oh, Breezy!" I said jumping up and giving her a hug. "Of course you can go. When will you be leaving?"

"I don't know. I'll give Dr. Griffith a call and let him know and then he will set up the appointment. Then all I'll have to do is figure a way to get there."

"To Nashville?" I asked.

"Yeah, to Tahlequah and then to Nashville."

"You could always hitchhike," I grinned at her, "or, you could drive the Vibe."

"The Vibe? I thought it was just for my use around Stillwater. You mean you'd let me drive the Vibe clear to Nashville?"

"Of course, it's your car to do with as you wish."

"Hot dog! Maybe Cathy can take a few days off and drive with me to Nashville. That sure would be fun."

"You just make sure you come back before the end of July," Tracy said. "Don't go and start having too much fun and forget to come home. We'll need you here when the baby comes."

"Probably won't be gone much over ten days," Breezy answered with a grin. "Doubt if this place would hold together if I'm gone much longer than that."

When we got back to the house, Breezy called Dr. Griffith and a short while later he called her back. I was sitting at the kitchen table and Tracy was making a salad for our lunch when Breezy joined us.

"Things are happening much faster than I thought they would," she said. "I need to be in Nashville by Tuesday of next week."

"You'll need to spend a few days with your folks," I said.

"Well, yes. Maybe I ought to leave tomorrow."

"After you call and let someone know in Tahlequah that you're on your way."

"I can do that. I'll drive to a payphone and call Cathy. She should be at work by now."

"Why don't you use the house phone?"

"Mrs. Phillips, its long distance and I don't want to run up your phone bill."

I was flabbergasted. Here was a girl so determined not to intrude and so determined not to be obligated that she was willing to drive to a public phone and make her call rather than making it here in our house. Make the call at our house so we wouldn't be charged thirty-five cents. "Breezy, sit down," I said. "We need to talk."

"Yes Ma'am," she said as she sat across the table from me.

"When we hired you, whether you like it or not, you became a member of our family. Every girl we've hired and helped through school has become a member of our family. Do you understand that?"

"Yes, Ma'am."

"Good. Now that we have that understood, you are more than welcome to use any and every facility we have in the house or around the house. That includes the telephone. I don't care if the call you are going to make is long distance or not, if you need to make the call, do it. Understand?"

"Yes, Ma'am, you are being very generous but I don't want to be beholden to anyone."

"I've noticed," I chuckled dryly. "And you won't be. It goes with you taking care of us."

"But what if I should run up a thousand dollar phone bill? How do you know I won't do that?"

"Breezy, if I thought you were that kind of girl, you would never have ridden back with us from Tahlequah. We would never trust you in our house with all of our things. You have access to things that are far more expensive than a thirty-five cent phone call. However, there are two things I want you to do for me."

"Yes, Ma'am, What are they? I'll get right on them."

"The first thing I want you to do is go out to the Vibe. In that box between the seats there is a cell phone. I want you to go get it, bring it in and make sure it's charged. Then I want you to go in to the phone in the living room where you can have privacy and call Cathy and tell her you are leaving in the morning. Then there is a third thing I want you to do. I want you to make sure you take the cell phone with you and call us every chance you get. Keep us in touch with what's going on. Share the happenings of your life with us."

"But won't that cost you a lot of money?"

"Not a penny more than what the cell phone is costing us already. Not unless you talk over five hundred minutes. Now let's see, that would be around eight hours and twenty minutes. I doubt that you will have that much to say."

"Thank you, Mrs. Phillips. Thank you so very much." Then she stood and ran to the front door and out. In a jiffy she was back with the cell phone and charger. She quickly had the cell phone setting on a kitchen counter charging. "I'm going to go call Cathy now," She said as she dashed to the living room.

We sat at the table and waited for her. She talked longer than I thought she would but after a while she came in and sat down.

"Well," I said, "Is your sister going to be able to take some time off and go with you?"

"No, but Dad is."

"Your father?" Tracy asked in amazement. "I didn't think he ever took time off from work."

"He doesn't have much choice of whether to take time off or not," Breezy said. "He cut his hand with a power saw day before yesterday and he almost lost some fingers, but they were able to save them. Cathy said that she has to work extra now to take up the slack until the compensation insurance came through so she said she would talk him into going with me. I don't think it will take much talking. He's always been the one to push us kids in the musical direction and I bet even with his bandaged hand he packs up as soon as he finds he has a chance to go to Nashville. For him, it will be a thrill of a lifetime."

After lunch I took a nap and was disturbed only slightly as Breezy packed and carried her stuff out to the car in plastic grocery sacks. If that girl gets much into traveling, I thought groggily, I'm going to have to buy her a set of luggage.

That night when Paul and I went to bed, I went right to sleep. A dreamless sleep which lasted until shortly after midnight and then I awoke and started thinking of Breezy. She was awfully young and awfully small to be making the trip to Tahlequah by herself. So many things could happen to a little girl like her.

I could hear Paul's heavy breathing and knew he was asleep. At last I gave up, slipped out of bed, put on my robe and went to the living room. I wandered the living room, the kitchen and then stepped outside.

The night was warm and a southerly breeze whispered in the oak trees and the moon was hidden behind the clouds. The dampness from the freshly watered lawn hung in the air. I tried to remember if I had watered the lawn or not and I couldn't remember that I had. Of course that didn't mean anything, perhaps I had, or Tracy, or Breezy, or perhaps even Paul had when he came home from work.

I stumbled around in the darkness until I found a chair and sat down. I was tired, God, I was tired. I felt a movement by my leg and looked down. The big dog had come to join me and he laid his head on my thigh. I reached down and petted him.

"Breezy will be leaving in the morning, Dog," I said as I began to scratch him between the ears. "I know she is old enough to be out on her own but she seems awfully young to me. Of course once she reaches Tahlequah, she will have her father with her from there to Nashville and back. But she is awfully young and awfully little."

"You were once that young and that small, Half-Pint."

I jumped and turned toward the voice. I wasn't alone. I could just make out his silhouette in the light reflecting on the water from across the lake. Only one person in my life had ever called me Half-Pint. "Daddy!" I exclaimed. "I'm surprised to see you. How long have you been here and how long can you stay. I have missed you so much."

"I have been here forever and ever and I will be here always," he laughed and he laughed as only my Dad could laugh.

"If you have been here why haven't I known about it?"

"You've known."

I was silent for a moment and then said, "Yes, I've known. But still, I have missed you."

"I know. One day we'll be together forever and ever. Breezy will do okay just as you have done okay. But it is still hard to let go. It is still hard to see one so small and so young head out on their own. Believe me, I know."

"I suppose you do," I laughed, "But was I ever that young?"

"You know the answer to that," he laughed. "Now it is time for you to go to bed and get some sleep."

"But Daddy, I don't want to sleep when I can visit with you," and I heard the whine in my voice. It was as if I were a little girl. "Besides, why do I need to go to bed? Why can't I sleep out here?"

"There is no reason why you can't sleep out here if you want to. Don't worry about visiting me. We will have many more visits in the days to come."

"Well, next time bring Mom with you. I miss her, too."

"I will," he laughed. "Now get comfortable, close your eyes and I'll tuck you in for the night. Don't worry, I'll watch over you and keep you safe."

I leaned back in the chair, brought my feet up and tucked them under me. I closed my eyes and his fingers were like the breeze as he tucked my robe around me. Then I felt him no more and I drifted off into a sound but happy sleep.

"Sharon," the voice came from a far distance. "Sharon," and this time it was closer. I opened my eyes and the sun was shining so brightly into my eyes that I quickly closed them again. I rubbed my eyes with my fists and then opened them again. Tracy was standing there and, bless her heart; she had a cup of coffee in her hand.

"Tracy, you're a lifesaver," I said as she handed me the cup. "Is Breezy up yet?"

"She's up and gone," Tracy laughed. "I think she was more anxious to go home than she let on."

"I suspect you're right," I laughed. "I know I would be if I were in her shoes, wouldn't you?"

"Yes, she's been up here close to ten months and she hasn't seen her family. Imagine that, and the Fox's are a close family. Coming up here was her first time away from home. I just hope she doesn't get a speeding ticket heading back to Tahlequah."

"I just hope she doesn't drive faster than she can handle the Vibe. But Tracy, just imagine the thrill she must be feeling. Not only is she taking her first long road trip, not only is she going home, but she is also going on to Nashville to cut a record."

"I know," Tracy said. "What a thrill it must be for her but even if she cuts a CD and it sells a million copies, it won't change Breezy in any way. That is another thing about the Fox's, they don't lay much stock to money. Money is the least important thing in their lives. The most important thing in their lives right now is to get themselves a house built so they can all live under one roof again."

"That's how it should be," I said.

"Did you sleep out here by yourself all night?"

"No, I had company."

"Company?" then she looked at the dog sleeping at my feet. "Yeah," she laughed. "I guess you did."

Chapter 29

I SPENT THE MORNING weeding the flowerbeds. The weeds had about taken over and by the time I was through with the front yard, sweat was running from me in rivers.

I had just finished the last bed in front when Tracy came out. "Sharon?" she asked, "are you about ready for lunch?"

"Is it lunch time already?" I asked, looking at the sun. "Yes I suppose it is." I stood up, took off my gloves and picked up the small flowerbed rake and planting shovel. "Just let me go put these up."

"Are you through for the day?"

"Yes, it's getting too hot."

"Then why don't we hold off lunch until you shower and change clothes?"

I looked down at my knees and feet. They were truly dirty and I knew that I would have to be careful when I went inside or we'd be able to plant flowers in the living room and kitchen. But Tracy, she was becoming one shower happy person. It seemed as if she was always asking me to go shower. But there was no use fussing with her. No use mentioning that probably all I needed to do was change clothes for after all, I had showered this morning. Hadn't I? But if I mentioned it to her she would argue that I hadn't and to be truthful, I really couldn't remember. "Okay," I laughed as I headed toward the front door.

Inside I went back to the utility room and put the gloves and tools up. Then I headed on back to our bedroom. Usually I lay out the clothes I'm going to wear before I bathe but one look at my hands told me that today I would wait. I stripped, got the water just right and then stepped in. When I was clean I stepped back out and dried. I went to the closet, got a pair of green shorts and a yellow blouse. After putting on my underclothes I stepped into the shorts, buttoned them and saw immediately that they were too big. I stepped to the bathroom scales. Ninety-two pounds and that was partially dressed. I was losing weight. I found a belt in the closet, put it through the loops and cinched it tight. The green shorts puckered around the waistline. Then I put on the blouse and went barefoot to the kitchen.

"What happened to your knees?" Tracy asked.

I looked down and saw they were scabbed and scratched here and there. "I don't know, I've been spending too much time on my knees taking care of the flowers, I guess."

"Well, they are sure a sight."

After lunch I went to the recliner in the living room, sat down and reclined it back. I could hear the sound of the washer running as I closed my eyes. In the back of the house I could hear the whine of the vacuum cleaner as Tracy cleaned house. But I was tired and sleepy and knew those homey sounds would not keep me awake. I had just closed my eyes when the phone rang. I sat up and reached for the receiver. "Phillips residence," I said.

"Hi, Mrs. Phillips, it's me, Breezy. Guess what?"

"Where are you Breezy? Not driving I hope."

"No," she laughed, "I'm home and guess what?"

"I don't have to guess, I know. You drove too fast."

"No, no I didn't. Not much anyway. The boys and I are helping Dad and we're running wires and tying wires everywhere. Dad, since he has his left hand practically in a cast, can hardly do anything except supervise and tell us what we're to do next. Dad says that if we keep working like we have been working, we'll have electricity in our new house before he and I head to Nashville."

"You mean the house is about done?"

"Gosh, no. but the roof is on, the walls are sheeted, and the windows are framed. Soon as the wiring is done and we turn on the electricity, we can move in."

"Won't you need windows to do that?"

"No, we'll just nail some screen wire over the window holes and that'll keep the bugs out."

"What if it rains and blows. Won't that get you wet if you don't have any windows?"

"Well shucks, if that happens, we'll just move to the other side of the house and if the rain is blowing in on our beds, we'll just move our beds. It's not like our house is all cluttered up with furniture. Actually, we have very little furniture left after the fire. Is Tracy handy?"

"She just turned the sweeper off down the hall."

"Is it okay if I talk to her?"

"Tracy," I yelled, "Breezy is on the phone and she wants to talk to you." I waited until I saw Tracy go by to the kitchen and I hung up when she picked up. I could hear Tracy laugh as she talked to Breanne and after a while she hung up. Well, there went a chunk of the eight hours and twenty minutes I thought to myself. But suddenly I wasn't sleepy anymore. I felt full of energy and ready to go. I went to the bedroom and changed out of the shorts into work jeans. I noticed they also fit loosely and I had to use a belt to keep them up.

"Are you going outside and work in this heat?" Tracy asked as I started out the back door with gloves and tools in hand.

"Yeah," I laughed, "I feel rip, roaring and ready to go."

"Make sure you don't get too hot," Tracy said with concern.

"Don't worry about it, I won't. I'll work mostly in the shade."

During the middle of the afternoon Tracy called, "Time for a coffee break," as she stepped out onto the patio with two ice filled glasses and a pitcher of tea.

We sat and chatted and told each other what Breezy had told us then I started getting impatient. There was work to be done and here I was sitting around. When I finished my second glass of iced tea, I set the glass on the patio table, stood and went back to work.

By the time Paul came home from work, I had the flowerbeds weeded. I looked at them with satisfaction. There was a small piece of earth which I had made more beautiful.

That night when Paul and I went to bed I went right to sleep and the strange thing was when I awoke the next morning, I was still in bed. For the first time in ages I had not gotten up and roamed the night. I glanced over my shoulder and saw Paul was still asleep. What day was today? Perhaps it was Saturday, a day Paul could sleep in. I eased out of bed, slipped on a robe and eased out of the door without waking Paul. In the hallway I smelled the coffee and headed for the kitchen.

"Tracy," I asked as I poured a cup of coffee, "Is today Saturday?"

"No, it's only Friday. I don't think Saturday will ever get here. I'm so thrilled."

"What's so special about Saturday?"

"We're moving into our new house tomorrow. Tomorrow we'll be living right across the road."

I knew she was excited but I didn't think much about what she had said until I was outside, sat down and had four poodles on my lap. 'She's moving right across the road from us?' That would be in the Humboldt house. Hadn't Paul bought the Humboldt house and remodeled it? Then it all came together. What Tracy, Pete, and Paul had been talking about made sense. I quickly set my cup on the table, pushed the poodles from my lap, jumped up and dashed inside. "You're going to be my neighbor!"

"It looks like it," Tracy laughed.

I rushed to her and gave her a hug. "I couldn't have a better one," and I felt tears of happiness in my eyes.

"Thank you, Sharon," she said returning the hug. "But you might not think so with a bunch of kids running around yelling and screaming."

"More the better," I laughed. "But why didn't someone tell me sooner."

"We did, Sharon. Or I thought we did. You see, they like Pete out at the plant. They like him a lot. They have even promised him an executive position once he has his degree. Pete and I will be spending our lives in Stillwater and we will be living across the road from you guys. Stillwater is a nice town to live in and this is a nice area to live. A good place to raise a family. Tomorrow we are moving in and joining the grownup group. We'll have a house and a mortgage to go along with it."

"The house is a beautiful house from the outside," I said as we ate breakfast. "You are going to have to take me over and show it to me, Tracy."

"I will," Tracy laughed. "Can I borrow your vacuum and use it to clean it up?"

"Of course," I said. "I'll even help you."

"That will sure be a change," Tracy laughed. "After five years of me cleaning your house, you're going to help me clean mine."

After I had seen Paul off to work, I went into the utility room and lowered the trapdoor in the ceiling. "What are you fixing to do?" Tracy asked from the doorway.

"Tracy, I've lost weight and all of my clothes are too big. I'm going to look in the attic and see if I have some smaller ones. I know I put clothes up there when I outgrew them. I'm going up and see if some of them will fit now."

"I thought you had lost weight," Tracy said eyeing me. "We could just go shopping and buy you a new wardrobe."

"Why do that," I laughed, "I have Alzheimer's, remember. I can't remember what's in the attic so anything I find that fits will be new to me."

I saw tears in Tracy's eyes and quickly looked away. I unfolded the steps and headed up into the attic. I wish there was some way that I could make other people as comfortable with me having Alzheimer's as I was. Of course I would rather not have it if I had the choice, but the choice was not mine to make. I had Alzheimer's and there was nothing I could do about it.

There were two long pipes fastened to the rafters of the roof, one on each side of the peak. The one on the left side held Paul's old clothes and the one on the right held mine. Below them were stacked black garbage bags. It was one of the garbage bags stacked beneath my clothes that I went to. I opened it and saw it was full of shorts. As I dumped them out on the attic floor I saw that most of them were too small but there were a few that I thought would fit me now. I saw an old chair, took an armload of shorts over and sat down. I went through them and selected eight pair I thought would fit and that I liked. I stood, stripped off my pajamas and started trying on shorts. Of the eight pair, six fit me perfectly and two were a bit too snug. I tossed the six pair down through the trapdoor, put the rest of them back into the garbage sack and put it back where it belonged. Then I went down the hanging clothes and found four pair of jeans that would fit me now. I left the shirts and blouses untouched; nothing had changed in that department. I tossed the jeans down and went farther down the clothes rod. By now I was in the clothes of yesteryear and I saw a couple pair of bellbottoms I thought would fit. I tried them on and they did. Laughing, I tossed them down. It was getting hot in the attic so I put my pajamas back on and left.

Downstairs, I took my clothes to the washroom and began them washing. I could hear Tracy vacuuming in the kitchen so I went to the bedroom and dressed.

When I came out it was quiet so I knew that Tracy had the carpet clean. I found her sitting at the table in the kitchen. "You must have found something that would fit," she said, "I hear the washing machine running."

"I found enough to last me through the summer. When winter comes I'll get fat again. Are we ready to start work on your house?"

"Ready," she said, standing and stretching, placing her hands at the small of her back. "Just remember, I get tired quickly and have to take a break, but after a short one, I'm ready to go to work again. Also, I pee a lot so if you lose me you can find me in the bathroom."

She had the vacuum by the door and she picked it up on our way out. "Want me to carry that?" I asked.

"I can handle it, Sharon. The vacuum is almost bigger than you are."

Inside the house, Tracy went to work with the vacuum while I cleaned the sinks in the kitchen and both bathrooms. It didn't take much as they were all new. Then I started dusting. By noon we pretty much had the house cleaned and ready to move into. When we left, I stopped and looked at her front yard. "Tracy, this front yard is a mess but I'll help you get started on it as soon as you get moved in."

"What's wrong with it?"

"You need to plant some bushes, shrubs and build some flower beds."

Tracy laughed, "Remember, Pete wants to be able to mow with a lawnmower and not a weed eater." Then she grew serious, "But I will ask your help in one thing."

"Sure, what do you want help with."

"It won't take us long to move in tomorrow because we don't have that much. But each month we are going to want to add furniture, you know, a piece here and a piece there as we can afford it. You have such a good taste in decorations that I want you to help me pick it out."

"I'd be happy to. When can we start?"

"This afternoon if you want. The first thing I think we should buy is drapes and I think we have enough money saved to buy them."

So that is what we did. After lunch, Tracy and I went downtown and bought drapes. When we got home I helped her put them up. Before we knew it, it was time to get home and start dinner.

"Sharon, didn't you put some clothes in the washer this morning," Tracy asked when we entered the house."

"Oh, my gosh, I did. I bet they are clean by now." I went into the laundry room, took the clothes out of the washer and put them in the dryer. "When you hear the buzzer go off, let me know," I said to Tracy.

"I will," she promised.

I got a black garbage bag from the utility room and took it to the bedroom. I stripped down and began to try on my shorts. They were all too big so I put them in the trash bag. I left my jeans and other pants on their hangers, put my clothes back on and started hauling things to the attic. I had just finished and shut the trapdoor when I heard the buzzer go off.

"Sharon," Tracy hollered.

"I heard it but thank you," I said and then went to the laundry room and began to hang up clothes. By the time Paul got home from work I had a complete new wardrobe hanging in my closet.

Chapter 30

TRACY WAS LIKE AN anxious teenager on her first date Saturday morning, as she fidgeted around at breakfast. Strangely enough, Pete ate breakfast with us but all he had was a bowl of cereal. He had driven his pickup over, loaded down with a bed and other household goods. It was parked across the street in front of their new house.

"I'd better get over and unload the pickup," Pete said as soon as he had finished, "I'd like to get one more load before the boys get here with their pickups. When that happens things will start to get crazy."

"I'll go help you with the bed," Paul said, scooting his chair back.

"You guys just wait a minute until I get the breakfast cleaned up," Tracy said. "Then I'll go over with you."

"What for, Honey? I'm sure not going to let you lift and tote in the condition you're in."

"So I can show you where to put the things, Mr. Smarty Pants," Tracy said flipping a dishtowel at him.

Tracy and Pete were moving today and tonight they would be living right across the road from us. Suddenly I was very happy and in the mood for some serious furniture arranging. "Let the clean-up go, Tracy. Let's get across the road before these two dump everything in a pile and we'll never find anything."

There were high thin clouds above as all four of us walked across the road. We were in their yard before I remembered so I looked at Paul and said, "You forgot to bring..."

"Shhh, Squirt, it's not time yet. We'll do it this afternoon."

"Do what?" Pete asked suspiciously.

"Never mind," Paul said and kept right on walking.

For a housewarming gift, Paul had bought Pete and Tracy a gas barbecue grill. It was setting out of sight at our house. He had also brought home enough chicken to feed an army and he now had it marinating in plastic bowls in the refrigerator. Tracy had to know that Paul was going to barbecue chicken tonight but I think she assumed that it would be at our house.

The first thing Paul and Pete took in were boxes of dishes. "Just set those on the cabinet by the dishwasher," Tracy said. When they did, Tracy began to unpack them and put them in the dishwasher. "They probably don't need it, but we'll give the dishwasher a workout."

"Let me do that, Tracy, and you show the men where you want them to put things."

"No," Tracy said shaking her head, "If you don't mind, you show them where I want things. You have such an artistic touch in decorating."

"But what if it's not where you want it?"

"Then we'll move it," she laughed. "Trust me, no more than we have we could move it all around today a couple of times and still have most of the day left."

Paul and Pete came back in, each carrying part of the bed frame. They didn't have a headboard or a footboard, just the frame the box springs sat on. They followed me to the master bedroom and when I had shown them which way it should be set up, they went to work putting it together. When the box springs and the mattress were in place, they left after another load. They had just gotten back when two pickups arrived with a couple in each one.

"This is Bob Gerber and his wife, Trina, and this is Ralph Sorenson and his wife, Beth," Pete introduced them to us. "This is the other part of the moving team."

Trina was slim and blonde while Beth was an attractive but a somewhat husky redhead. "Where do you want us to start?" Trina asked.

"Trina, why don't you guys unload my pickup while I take Bob and Ralph over and help load them up," Pete said.

"Hold on just a minute," Bob said, "You promised there was beer included in this job."

"It's in the fridge," Pete said. "Help yourself."

Bob opened the refrigerator and asked, "Is this all there is?"

"No, that's only half of it. The other half is in the fridge over at the apartment."

"Hot Damn! There's a man with a plan," Bob said taking two bottles out and offering one to Ralph.

Ralph shook his head saying "Too early for me."

"It's not too early for me," Bob said putting one bottle back and taking the top from the other. He turned it up and chugged about a third of it down before putting the top back on and placing it in the refrigerator. "Okay, boys, let's go. Beer is waiting on the other end."

It was then things got hectic. With the men hauling, the women helping them unload and me showing them where to put things, the place was a madhouse.

Instead of packing the silverware, the pots and pans, and other things that were kept in drawers, they just brought the drawers over and when Tracy had them put away, they took the drawers back.

When they went after the third load, Paul stayed behind. As soon as the pickups were out of sight, he called to Beth, "Come and give me a hand."

Tracy never paid them any mind but I watched as they went across the street. Soon after I saw them come back, Beth pulling the gas barbecue and Paul carrying a tank of propane. They went out of sight on the east side of the house and Beth came in the back door from the deck. Paul followed shortly.

Just before noon, I asked Trina to go with me and we walked to my house where we made a whole slew of sandwiches and took them back. After lunch it was back to work again.

It was middle of the afternoon when they pulled in with the last load. When the last pickup was unloaded, Paul asked, "Can you guys come and help me?"

"Sure," Bob said, "just give me time to finish this beer." He tipped it up and drained it. It wasn't the first beer he had started on, nor was it the second or third. The four left out across the road and I watched them disappear round the house. It was a short time later that I saw them coming back.

Behind our house we had a small storage building where Paul kept the lawnmower, remnants of camping gear, and fold up lawn chairs. When I saw them coming back, the young men were loaded down with fold up lawn chairs and Paul had a plastic bowl of chicken clutched in each arm.

"I guess we can bake the chicken in an oven," Pete said dubiously as they came in the door.

"Don't worry," Paul said, "we'll figure out some way. Why don't you set up those lawn chairs on the back deck and I'll put this chicken in the fridge. It's not quite time to start cooking it yet."

Paul winked at me as he put the chicken in the refrigerator and the others carried the lawn chairs out. "What the hell!" I heard Pete exclaim from the back deck. "Where did this come from?"

He came rushing back in, "Paul, Sharon?" he said grinning like a little boy who had got just what he wanted for Christmas.

"You think we might be able to cook the chicken on that?" Paul asked.

"Yeah, let me run to the Quick Stop and get a tank of gas."

"Gas is already hooked to it," Paul said. "All you need is for someone to run it and I guess this evening that will be me. Pay close attention, boy, I'm only going to show you how once."

"Will the chicken be purple this time? I don't know that I care to learn how to cook purple chicken."

"Not this time. This time I marinated the chicken in cooking sherry and not Concord grape wine."

The sun was low in the western sky when Paul put the chicken on and the smell filled the air. An elderly lady walked through the house and out on the back porch. "I brought over a cake for you, dear," the elderly woman said.

"Thank you," Tracy said. "You will stay and eat with us, won't you?"

"I don't want to put you out, dear. Are you sure you have plenty?"

"Yes, of course. Have a seat," Tracy said standing up.

"Oh, before I forget it, here is your deposit money back. I checked the apartment over and it is in better shape than when you rented it," and she handed some bills towards Tracy.

"Don't give it to me, give it to Pete," Tracy said.

The elderly woman tottered over to Pete and handed him the money. "It's not mine," Pete said. "Paul put down the deposit for us. Give it to the cook."

"Lawzy me, I've never had so much trouble giving money away in my life," she laughed. "Here Paul, now don't you refuse it."

I saw Paul take the bills from her and put them in his pocket.

Then the woman turned and came to me. She put her arms around me and gave me a hug. "Sharon, how are you feeling? I haven't seen you around much lately."

I hugged her back. Sharon? She knew me. She hadn't seen me around lately? Then she must live in the neighborhood. But who was she? "I'm doing just fine," I answered.

She left, found an empty lawn chair and sat down. Tracy must have seen my discomfort because she came and whispered in my ear, "That is Mrs. Clemens." I thought for a moment, Mrs. Clemens, Mrs. Clemens? Then I remembered. She was my neighbor and Tracy and Pete had lived in her apartment. But I didn't remember her being that old.

Kris and JT came with Jared and I sat down and held him. When he began squirming, Kris went to the car and came back with a quilt. She made a pallet beside my chair and I put him on it.

We ate from paper plates and people kept coming. I didn't know any of them. They would speak to me as if they knew me and I would speak back. They acted as if I knew them, but I didn't. However I never let on. I began to feel uncomfortable. There was a party going on and I was at it and yet I wasn't. It was as if I was hiding in the woods and watching these people have fun. I looked down at Jared and saw his eyes were drooping. "You'd like to go to sleep if it wasn't so noisy, wouldn't you?" I asked.

For an answer, he closed his eyes and then popped them open again at the sound of rambunctious laughter. I stood, reached down and picked him up. I put him over my shoulder.

We didn't go through the house but rather took the steps on the east side of the deck and by the light of the street lights, made our way over to our house. Inside, I turned the lights on low, lay Jared on the couch and sat there with him. He squirmed only a little before he went to sleep. I kept my hand on him so I could feel him should he move and leaned back.

I closed my eyes and thought about my world. Thought about my world and its passing. It happens to everyone. You can see it happening while you are still very young. When you are young you look for a lifetime mate and then you find one. If you are wise and choose well, you know that part of your world has passed. You will look no further. Then you start a family and children are born, but that too, shall pass. For some sooner than others. With me it was the birth of the twins, an infection and the tortured tubes. No more children would Paul and I have. Again a part of my world was passed.

Slowly but surely you do things for the last time, often without even realizing it. You climb your last tree, you run your last mile, and you ride your bicycle for the last time and store it in the garage. You don't notice it at the time, but your world is passing. When you do notice it you want to cry, 'Stop', but the world keeps on spinning and time goes sliding by. There is nothing you can do but pack as much as you can into each day. I had, but still I had regrets. There were things I had never done and now I would never do. But, and I thought back, when would I ever have had time to do them. My days of my life had been jammed packed full.

I knew that tonight an important thing had happened. I had gone to my last party. What was the use in going when you knew no one and therefore had nothing in common. Why should I go when it made me feel so uncomfortable? Uncomfortable when strangers stopped to chat with me.

The door opened and Chris stepped in, "Mom, are you in here," he boomed. I felt Jared flinch beneath my hand. "Shhh," I said, "You'll wake the baby."

Chris and Tiffany came in followed by Kris. "We didn't see you leave the party," Kris said as she sat on the couch beside me.

"Jared was sleepy and it was too noisy for him and---"

"And what, Mom?"

"I didn't know anybody. I know I should have but I didn't."

Kris put her arm around me and pulled me tight. "You know me, Chris, and Tiffany, don't you."

"Of course, though I didn't know Chris and Tiffany were there. I didn't hear or see them come in."

"Well, they have some news for you and I bet you like it."

"What is it?" I asked, first looking at one and then another.

"Jared is going to have a cousin and you're going to be a grandmother again," Chris said his voice just a shade below a boom.

I laughed, jumped up, hugged Chris and then Tiffany. My world was passing but new worlds were coming to take its place.

Chapter 31

IT WAS LATE MONDAY AFTERNOON when Breezy called. "Guess where I am, Mrs. Phillips."

"I have no idea," I said.

"Dad and I have just checked into the Hilton here in Nashville. I have a room for myself, Dad has a room right across the hall and Dr. Griffith and his wife have a room right next door. In the morning at nine thirty we are to be at the RCA studio and go to work."

"Hilton, that sounds pretty expensive to me, Breezy."

"I'm sure it is but RCA is paying for it and is it drop dead gorgeous. Even our meals are free. Well, free to us. We just sign our names on the ticket and put our room number and RCA picks up the tab. I wish you were here. It is so exciting. I think I could get used to living like this."

"Enjoy it while you can, Breezy. All too soon you will just be a poor girl working her way through college."

"I know and I am enjoying it. Just for a day or two I'm being treated like a real celebrity. I'm going to enjoy every moment of it, but you know what?"

"What?" I asked.

"I know it sounds funny, but I miss you and Paul and Tracy. Oops. Someone is knocking on my door so I have to go now. Bye," and I heard the phone click as she hung up.

I sat in the recliner thinking, thinking about this being the first time for Breezy. If RCA management knew what they were doing I doubted that this would be the last time.

Life is full of 'first times' just like it is full of last times. I, and Paul also, had already had our first times but the last times were still ahead of us. I couldn't remember who the people were around me and I couldn't remember yesterday or the day before, but I had vivid memories of my youth, things which had happened thirty-five, forty years ago. I remembered the first times and for some strange reason as I sat there, I remembered my first date.

Mom and Dad had a rule that wouldn't allow me to date until I was sixteen. I thought it was a stupid rule at the time and expressed my opinion frequently, but they stuck to their rule.

Finally it came, my first date. It was the spring of my sixteenth birthday, a beautiful spring Friday and I had a date with Willard Tams.

Willard was husky, redheaded with a freckled faced. I thought he was a hunk. I had flirted with him for the longest time before he got up the nerve to ask me out.

"I know you're in a hurry, Half-Pint, but when you find Domino, you had better bring her in with the milk cows," Dad said as I bridled Stocking, our black horse with a white front foot. "She will be having her calf any time now."

"Okay, Dad," I said as I jumped on Stockings back. I always rode her bareback; the saddle was too heavy for me to manage.

Domino was a black heifer with white spots and this would be her first calf. I left the corral at a gallop, my heart singing. I wondered if Willard would make a pass at me tonight and more important, what would I do if he did. He was sure a handsome hunk.

I found the milk cows right off and sent them towards the barn. I checked the dry cows and found them all; all except Domino. Then I started looking. I wasn't in a hurry, I had plenty of time to help Dad milk the cows and then get ready for Willard.

When I found her, she was in the middle of a sand plum thicket and she was down and trying to have her calf. I wheeled Stocking to go get Dad and then I saw a coyote pacing downwind of her. He paced back and forth, just waiting his chance. "Dad!" I hollered again and again as loud as I could as I rode back to Domino. I knew the chances of him hearing me were very slight. I dropped from Stocking and ran to Domino. The little hooves of the calf were just barley in sight. It wouldn't be long now until the calf would be born. But as I looked at the hooves, my heart sank. They were not the hooves of the front feet, as it should be, but the back ones. I had a breach birth on my hands.

I could do one of two things. I could wait until just before the umbilical cord broke and then pull hard and fast and hope I could get the calf out before it smothered, or I could push the feet back inside and try to turn it in the mother's womb. I decided to do the latter.

I dropped down on my knees behind Domino and began to work the feet back inside. I had never done this before, but I had watched Dad and I did just as I had seen him do. At last the feet were in and I reached in, felt the head, and slowly began to turn it. It took a long time but this was something that couldn't be hurried. At last I had the head facing outward and then I went to work straightening the front legs. The front feet were out when Domino pushed and the head came out.

I heard Dad's pickup and I heard it stop and the door open. "Hey, Half-Pint, where are you?"

"Down here, Dad. Domino is having her calf and I need help." I wiped the sweat from my forehead with my bloody hand and Domino pushed again. I pulled and the calf came out halfway. Only its hips held it back. I was so grateful to hear Dad thrashing through the brush towards me. Domino pushed again and I pulled with all my strength and the calf popped out just as Dad reached me.

He reached down, cleaned the mucus from the calf's mouth, then put his arm around the calf at its belly and lifted. The calf took its first breath of air and billowed.

"It's a little bull," he said as he set it by its mother's head. The mother reached out, smelled it and then began to clean it while I stood there trembling with exhaustion.

"It was about to be a breach birth," I said. "It's a good thing I got here when I did or it would have died for sure."

"You turned it by yourself?"

"Yes, sir," I said proudly. "There wasn't anyone here to help me."

"I'm right proud of you, Half-Pint," he said hugging me. "But there is a young gentleman back at the house waiting for you." Then Dad started laughing, "I don't know what he'll think when he sees you like that."

I looked down at myself and saw what a mess I was in. I was covered with mucus, blood and slime. "What he sees is what he gets," I laughed.

"Jump on Stocking and go get cleaned up. I'll stay here with the calf."

"How about the milking?"

"Your mother and I have already taken care of it. Now get. You've kept the young gentleman waiting long enough."

When I went into the house and Willard saw me, I saw him turn pale. I looked nothing like the girl he had asked to go out. I was a mess. "Just a minute," I said, "Let me get cleaned up and I'll be ready to go."

I would have liked to have taken a bath but I didn't have time for that. I washed up as best as I could, used perfume liberally, a little makeup, put on a dress and I was ready to go.

He took me to *Big Bob's Belly Buster* where we had hamburgers and cokes. I ordered my hamburger without onions just in case, but I needn't have worried. I told him about finding the heifer which was trying to have her calf and when I mentioned that it was about to be a breach birth he asked, "What's that?"

"The calf was about to be born bas-ackwards," I said and then went on to explain what I had to do.

Willard turned green and said, "Please Sharon, not while I'm eating." He was a city kid and not country at all. I doubt that he had ever seen anything born.

Willard was a perfect gentleman that night and my worrying what to do if he made a pass was all for naught. In fact he kind of flinched every time I touched him. I didn't know how boys could be so squeamish.

The next time Breezy called was Friday morning. "I'm in Tahlequah now," she said. "I'm packed and I will soon be heading for Stillwater."

"Did you have fun, Breezy?" I asked.

"You'd never believe how much fun I had. Of course I did a lot of work too, if you call singing work. Again, like Dr. Griffith did, they had me sing with a band and then they had me sing the same songs over again with just me and my guitar. I did thirty songs and I did them over and over. Twenty-six of them were my own songs but I did some old ballads also."

"You mean your album will have thirty songs on it?"

"No," she laughed. "They will edit it down to eighteen or twenty. If people like them and buy them, they will cut the others into singles or make an album with only a dozen songs. They are full of optimism or act like they are and they wanted to know if things went well, could I come back to Nashville again? I told them maybe at Christmas or during spring break, but I was going to school to become a doctor and it didn't make any difference what happened with my singing, I was going to continue going to school *until* I was a doctor."

"How soon will you be heading back, Breezy?"

"I'm in the car now and as soon as I hang up I'm heading for Stillwater."

"Be careful, Breezy. Drive safely."

"I will, bye now," and she hung up.

I sat where I was in the recliner and the poodles jumped on my lap and snuggled down beside me. Soon they went to sleep. Breezy would be coming home! I could all but see her in the red Vibe, her chin jutted out as she headed to Stillwater. I hoped she didn't drive like she did everything else; full speed.

Even though time seemed to drag, before I knew it, Tracy called me to lunch. "Breezy is on her way home," I said to Tracy as we sat down to eat.

"I know, I couldn't help but overhear you talking to her on the telephone. Did she tell you about her stay in Nashville?"

"Yes, she was very excited about it but I also think she is anxious to get back to Stillwater. To be truthful, I'm also anxious to see her."

"You're getting as bad as a mother hen, Sharon," Tracy laughed.

After lunch while Tracy waddled around the kitchen cleaning, I took the poodles and went outside. It wasn't just warm outside; it was hot with the sun beating down from a cloudless sky. It didn't take long for the poodles to scratch on the door wanting back in where the air conditioner was blowing. I stayed outside a bit longer and then went inside to my recliner. When I sat down, the poodles stayed on the cool carpet. As I reclined back and closed my eyes, memories of my childhood returned.

When I was nine or ten years old, we had a black rooster with white spots. Anytime I was around that rooster I made sure I had a stick in my hand. If I didn't, that old rooster would flog me sure as shootn'.

I remember the morning just like it was yesterday, the last morning I saw that rooster. We had milked, separated the cream from the milk and I tagged along with dad to feed the pigs. That's the way we did it on the farm in those days though the year was 1968 and those days were ending. One by one, the small, independent cream stations were closing. We would milk the cows, run the milk through a hand-cranked separator, save the cream to sell at the cream station, and then feed the milk to the calves and pigs.

When dad had poured the separated milk into the pig trough, he handed me the two empty buckets. "Take these to the house, Half-Pint, so your mother can wash them."

I took the buckets, one in each hand and headed towards the house. School had just turned out for the summer and three happy months of vacation lay ahead of me. I was singing and skipping as I went to the house. I had no idea that the spotted rooster was anywhere around until I heard the flutter of wings and the rooster hit me in the back.

He knocked me down. He was half as heavy as I was and I felt his spurs sink into my back. I held onto the buckets, rolled over and started kicking at the rooster with both feet while I swung the buckets at him and screamed. I really wasn't hurt, only scratched a bit, but I was afraid and more than that, I was mad. Darned that old rooster.

I saw Dad running to me, the most beautiful sight in the world. The spotted rooster must have seen him also because he left me at a run. When Dad got there, he picked me up, brushed me off and carried me to the house with me still hanging onto the buckets.

I never saw that spotted rooster again, unless it was that night at the supper table. That night we had chicken and dumplings and I imagined the chicken in them was the black and white rooster and I ate it with enthusiasm.

I must have slept because I suddenly heard the crunch of tires on gravel and a car door open and close. The front door flew open and Breezy came blowing in, a plastic grocery sack in each hand.

"New luggage," she laughed holding up the sacks as she came rushing to me.

Chapter 32

JULY CAME IN HOT as Julys usually are in Oklahoma. Because of the heat and perhaps other things, I had lost any interest in working outside in the flowerbeds. The same with other things, I just lost interest.

It gave me an empty feeling when I looked at a clock and couldn't tell what time it was. I had forgotten how to read a clock and tell time. I had trouble remembering the days of the week. Not what day of the month it was, I had forgotten that long ago, but remembering whether it was Tuesday or Wednesday or whatever. Now my family along with Tracy and Breezy could have made a big deal out of it, but they didn't. I asked them what day of the week it was so much that it soon became a joke. It even went so far that they gave me a Fourth of July present. It was a clock but rather than telling the time of the day, it had only one hand and instead of numbers, spaced around the clock it had the days of the week. The hand of clock only went around once a week.

Whoever heard of getting a present for the Fourth of July? But I was grateful for it. Oh, it wasn't that important that I knew the days of the week, what I was grateful for was their attitude. Instead of pitying me, they treated it as a joke. Pitying gives you nothing, but a good joke gives you a laugh.

The mosquitoes drove Paul and me inside early that evening shortly after sunset. Breezy was back in her room and Paul and I sat and watched television until it was time to go to bed.

Paul was tired, he had had a busy day, and soon after kissing him goodnight, I heard his breathing deepen. I closed my eyes and tried to go to sleep but sleep wouldn't come.

When he began to snore, I eased out of bed, slipped on a robe and padded barefoot into the living room. I started toward my recliner but I felt stuffy, stuffy and closed off inside the house so I went to the door and outside.

The moon was on the wane and in the sky I could see thin streaks of silver clouds drifting to the north ever so slowly. I walked around the yard and the dog with the mangled tail stayed right on my heels. I looked down at the lake gleaming silver in the moonlight and as if drawn by a magnet, I started toward it. It was then the dog took the lead.

When we reached the lake, the dog went romping into the water. I knew what was coming next. The dog would get all wet and then come out and shake water all over me. I beat him to the punch. I waded into the lake and kicked water on him and then the water fight was on.

He and I romped around in the water and the water felt so warm and good that I started wading up the lake the dog beside me. Every once in a while I would kick water at him and he would bark and jump around. For a long time we stayed in the edge of the water and went to shore only when the bottom became so rocky it hurt my feet.

True, the shore was also rocky, but I could see those rocks in the moonlight. I tiptoed through the rocks and when I came to sand, I kept walking. The night air was warm and it was so much fun just walking. Just me and the dog.

When I grew tired, I found a log, sat down in the sand and leaned back against it. The dog lay in the sand beside me and I reached over and scratched him between the ears. Then I leaned my head back and began to count the stars. They were small fiery diamonds in the black velvet sky.

When I had rested, I stood and continued walking up the lake. At last I grew tired and sleepy. I looked down at the dog beside me and said, "Let's go home, dog." He looked up at me and wagged his mangled tail.

I stopped and looked around. Which way is home, I wondered. I looked and looked but still I couldn't tell where

I was. "Well, dog, we have only two choices. Home is this way," I said pointing up the lake, "or it's that way," and I pointed down the lake. Still, for a while I stood looking around. One way is as good as another; I thought and headed up the lake.

Suddenly a gust of south wind hit me and it chilled me. With the chill came fear. I broke into a run, the dog loping along beside me. I ran not paying attention where I was placing my feet. I stepped on a rock and it hurt. Then I stepped on another but I kept on running. I only slowed down when I was out of breath and walked until my breath came back. Then fear drove me on and I broke into a run again.

There came the time when I could run no more. I left the lake when I could see the end of it and went into the woods. I was tired. No I was more than tired, I was exhausted. And I was sleepy. I found a thicket of brush and crawled into it to hide. Dog crawled into the thicket with me. I listened carefully and looked frantically around. There was no one.

"You're safe here, Sharon."

I jumped at the sound of her voice. "Mom!" I said. "Where have you been?"

"Oh, girl, I've been here, there, everywhere."

"Why haven't I seen you before?"

"You did. You just have forgotten. Lie down; think happy thoughts and you will soon be asleep. I'll be near should you need me."

"Happy thoughts? You mean like the time when you and Dad surprised me and bought me a new car?"

"Yes," Mom said with a laugh. "You sure were a happy girl that day."

I lay back in last fall's leaves, pulled the dog down beside me and held him in my arms. I closed my eyes and remembered.

It was just before I started my senior year of high school. We had a bumper wheat crop that year and surprise, surprise we got a record price for the wheat. Dad had gone to Enid for parts the day before and by the time he returned, mom and I had the milking done. That night over the supper table Dad said, "Half-Pint, I know you'll be going to school next Wednesday and you have worked hard enough this summer to deserve a short vacation. But if you'll go with me back to Enid tomorrow to get the rest of the parts, I'll give you the rest of the summer off."

"Sure, I'll go with you. What time do you want to leave?"

"Right after we get the chores done," he answered.

So the next morning we headed to Enid. When we got there I expected him to drive straight to Attwood's but he drove right on by. "Where are we going?" I asked.

"Right here," he said turning right into a car lot.

"Why in the world are we stopping here?"

"We have a new car to pick up. You'll need a car when you start to college and I figured you would like to drive it your senior year.

"A car for me?" I asked, holding my breath. I couldn't believe my ears. Surely I had misunderstood.

"Yep. I see they have it all washed and ready for you to drive."

"I can't believe it. Which one is it?" I asked breathlessly looking around.

"That one right there," he said pointing. "That Volkswagen Beetle."

"Oh Dad! You're the best father in the whole wide world," I said scooting over and hugging his neck. Then I quickly scooted back, opened the door and jumped out. I ran to the dark blue Bug and looked at it. "This one?" I asked opening the door and looking inside. I breathed deep the aroma of the new car smell.

Dad looked in and said, "Darn it, they don't have it ready yet. Let's go inside."

It looked ready to me. It was all washed and shiny. My hands were itching to get in and get a hold of the wheel. Nevertheless I followed Dad as he went inside. He stopped and looked around the showroom until his eyes fell on a salesman and he walked to him. The salesman saw him coming and met us in the middle of the floor.

"This must be your daughter, Sharon," the salesman said, first shaking Dad's hand and then mine.

"It is. I thought you said it would be ready first thing this morning?"

"It is. I'll get the keys for you and she can jump in and drive off."

"But it isn't ready," Dad said, "I ordered and paid extra for seatbelts to be installed and they aren't."

"They're not?" the salesman said in surprise. "Let's go see."

We followed him out to the Beetle where he looked for himself. "I'm sorry, Sir. I'll have them get right on it. It will take forty-five minutes to an hour. If you have someplace else to go you can come back or you can wait here."

"We'll wait," Dad said and soon I saw a mechanic come through the showroom, go outside and drive my Bug away. I was restless and anxious and it seemed to take them forever, but at last I saw the mechanic return with my car.

"I want you to wear the seat belts at all times," Dad said. "The car is small and your face is all but against the windshield."

I drove that car all the way through college and for two years afterwards.

Suddenly the noise, the sun in my eyes, and the heat awoke me. I sat up and beside me, Boomer stood and yawned. The lake was a beehive of activity. "What are we doing out here, Boomer?" I asked. For an answer he licked my face.

"What's going on down at the lake." There were four boats out there, some of them anchored and some of them slowly trolling back and forth. I saw a diver in a black wetsuit and an oxygen tanks go over the side of one of the anchored boats. He made a splash when he hit the water and silver spray flew up.

"I don't know what they're doing but it looks exciting, Boomer. Let's go find out."

I stood, looked around to see where I was. I looked down at my bare feet and saw they had blood on them and when I took a step it hurt. "Boomer, instead of going back down to the beach, there's a road just up the hill and the road goes right by our house. Let's take the road."

Gingerly, I made my way through the trees to the road. Every time I stepped on even the smallest limb hidden by the leaves it hurt. Once I made it to the road walking was much better.

As I walked along I noticed the day was beautiful, only a slight breeze which was enough to cool the heat and the sun was halfway to its zenith. It was one of those golden days and I hummed a small tune as I walked along. Strangely enough, Boomer walked at my side rather than running in front of me as we headed home.

At last we came to the house and I went in the front door while Boomer went around the house. The house was quiet though I could hear people talking in the back yard. "Hello," I called. "Anybody here?" all was silent. There was no answer.

I looked out the back window. The yard was full of people. I saw Tracy sitting in a chair on the back porch with Breezy standing beside her. Both of them had the saddest expression on their faces. Even tears ran from their eyes. They looked as if they had lost their best friend. I wondered why. I knew I should shower and put on decent clothes but curiosity got the better of me. I slid the glass door open and stepped outside. "What's going on," I asked. I swear I never saw two people jump as high as Breezy and Tracy did.

"Sharon!" they both yelled as they flew into my arms.

Chapter 33

"SQUIRT, SQUIRT," PAUL said as he squished me to him. "I thought I had lost you."

I pushed myself back and looked up at his face. Tears were streaming from his eyes. "Lost me?" I asked.

"Yes, I thought you were gone forever. I don't know what I'd do should that happen. My life began when I met you and without you, my life ends."

"Why in the world would you think something like that, Paul?"

"Tracy, Breezy, and I looked for you this morning and you were nowhere to be found. I called 911 and reported you missing. The sheriff came out with a deputy. They found your tracks where you walked down to the lake. Your tracks went into the lake and, and, and…" he pulled me to him again and I felt his shudder. "Squirt," he continued in a whisper, "Your tracks didn't come out."

I tried hard to remember what I had done last night and in a faint fog it came to me. I remembered wading in the water for a while but I couldn't remember what came afterwards. "You thought I had walked into the lake and drowned. That's incredulous. Paul, you should know that I would never leave you." But even as I said it, a dark, ghostly shadow flickered across my mind. I would leave him, I thought. I would leave him. Not in body but the 'me' would one day be gone.

When Paul at last turned me loose, I looked down at the lake. The noise hadn't abated but it had changed. The shouts had turned gleeful rather than grim. Boats which had been trolling, pulled in their ropes with big many tined hooks on them, turned and took off across the lake. Divers came up and when they were in a boat, they took off their gear. Then the boats pulled anchor and with a wave they also left. People were gathering in our back yard and I was beginning to become confused and anxious. I felt an arm go around my shoulder and when I looked, I saw it was big, pregnant Tracy.

"It's time for your medicine, Sharon," she said.

I willingly followed her inside. I anxiously left the crowd that was gathering.

After I took my medicine, I cleaned up and changed clothes. I held up my pajamas and looked at them. They were ripped, torn and ragged. I carried them to the living room where Tracy sat and showed them to her. "There is no need to wash these," I said. "It looks to me that they are done in."

"You're right," she laughed, "I'm sure you have some new ones. I'll help you find them as soon as I catch my breath."

Kris came in from the back yard and handed me Jared. I took him and talked nonsense while he laughed. It was easy to see that he loved his grandma. Love. That's what life is all about. It was great to love and to be loved. Then Chris and Tiffany came in. Tiffany was beginning to show. The kids and, Paul, Breezy and Tracy all seemed to hover around me. Yes, it was nice to be loved, but enough is enough. Finally I looked at Chris and asked, "Don't you have pills to count?"

"Yes, Mom, I do," he laughed. "Come on, Tiffany, let's go."

Kris took the hint, plucked Jared from my lap and left. Breezy, Tracy, and Paul still hovered around me but there was nothing I could do about that. All day they hovered and that evening, Pete ate dinner with us. Then they stayed and stayed and stayed. I was so tired, so dreadfully tired. I finally gave up and left them and let Paul stay with them. I went to bed. Yes, I was tired; I hadn't slept much last night and hadn't even been able to grab a nap during the day. As soon as I had on my new pajamas and my head hit the pillow, I went to sleep. I faintly felt the bed tilt when Paul came to bed and I wanted to ask him if Tracy and Pete had finally gone home but I couldn't wake up enough. He put his arm around me and pulled me close and I drifted off in a warm cocoon of sleep.

When I awoke again, Paul had his back to me so I turned over, scooted up right next to his back and closed my eyes. I could hear the soft rumble of him snoring. My eyes popped open. Try as I might, I couldn't go back to sleep. Finally I gave up, turned over, eased out of bed and headed for the living room. I could see a light on and knew not everyone had gone to bed.

"Having trouble sleeping again, Mrs. Phillips?" Breezy asked. She was sitting at the end of the couch, a spiral ring notebook in her hand and the light at that end of the couch was on.

"Yes, and it looks like you are having the same trouble."

"I know," she grinned, "but this song keeps going around and around in my head so I got up to put it on paper."

"What's the song about?"

"It's a song from a woman's point of view. She loves Willy and she knows Willy loves her. Nevertheless, she flirts with another man. Willy gets jealous as she intended and to her amusement, leaves in a rage. But she knows Willy will be back. The last she sees of him is the taillights of his car as he speeds away. He drives too fast and wrecks and is killed. Sad, huh?"

"Sounds like it. I can see how such a thing would keep you awake. Don't let me stop you. I'll just sit in my recliner and watch."

"That would be okay," she said then turned her attention back to her writing. Occasionally she would stop writing and hum a wordless tune before going back again.

Soon the poodles were on my lap and I petted them as I watched Breezy write. I could see her put something down, study it and often she would scratch it out and start writing again. Every once in a while she would hum a mournful tune. I soon became restless, pushed the poodles from my lap and stood.

"Where you going?" Breezy asked, "Back to bed?"

"No, it's getting stuffy in here. I think I'll go outside."

"If you don't mind, I think I'll go with you."

"But it's dark out there and if we turn on a light so you can write, it'll draw bugs by the droves."

"That's okay; I think I have done enough for a while. Maybe a breath of fresh air will clear my head."

She followed me out and I found a comfortable chair, sat down, and curled my feet up under me. Breezy did the same and the outside dog came to me. Breezy and I talked while I scratched the dog between the ears. Soon there was nothing more to talk about and we sat together enjoying the silence of the night and each other's company. My eyelids grew heavy and I leaned my head back and went to sleep.

"If you two don't look like a passel of wild Indians sleeping outdoors like that," Tracy said as she came out on to the porch.

I opened my eyes and saw the sun was well up. I looked over where Breezy sat and saw her hair was all rumpled as she yawned. "I guess we do at that," I laughed and winked at Breezy.

We had breakfast and Paul had just left for work when a van pulled into the front yard. I opened the door as two men got out and came my way. "Is this the Phillips residence?" the older of the two asked.

"Yes, it is and I am Sharon Phillips. What can I do for you?"

"Your husband, Paul Phillips, ordered some work to be done," he replied. "I just wanted to make sure we were doing it on the right house."

"I don't know anything about it but come on in and get started. If Paul ordered work to be done, then it must be something that needs to be done," I said as I stepped aside and let them in. Paul hadn't said a word to me about getting something done on the house, had he?

"We'll try to stay out of your hair as much as possible and it will only take us four or five hours."

They began to work on the front door, installing boxes and key pads. I grew bored watching so I went outside while the morning was still cool. I had no more than sat down when Breezy came bursting out. "Come quick, Mrs. Phillips," and then she dashed back in. I followed her as she rushed to the radio in the kitchen and turned up the volume. I heard a guitar playing and then I heard Breezy singing on the radio. Of course I had heard Breezy singing many times before but coming from the radio her singing was more beautiful than ever.

"That was beautiful," I said when the song was through.

"Isn't it wonderful what a sound stage will do," she said, grinning at me. "I'm getting some airtime anyway. Isn't it wonderful?"

"Yes, it is," I said, gathering her to me and hugging her.

The younger of the two workmen came into the kitchen. "Who was that on the radio? I have never heard her before and I didn't catch her name."

"Come to Eskimo Joe's Friday or Saturday night and you can listen to her some more. It was Breezy Fox singing and that is me."

"It is a pleasure to meet you, Breezy Fox," he said holding out his hand. I play a little guitar myself. I'm not famous like you; I just play in a local band. My name's Rusty." He and Breezy shook hands and he continued by saying, "I didn't know I was in the house with a real celebrity."

Breezy left the radio on as she started washing clothes and cleaning house. It was while we were eating lunch that they played another of her songs. *"Keep an eye and ear open for this gal,"* the disc jockey said, *"I predict you'll be hearing a lot from her in the future."*

"I sure hope he's right," Breezy said.

"What if you become rich and famous?" Tracy asked. "Will you still speak to us?"

"Now I don't know about that," Breezy said sticking her small nose in the air. Then she laughed and said, "Of course I will. It won't change a thing."

"When you become rich, will you still work for us, go to school, and become a doctor."

"Of course I will, Mrs. Phillips. Becoming a doctor is the important thing and nothing is going to stop me if I can help it. As for continuing my job here, of course I will. I like living here.

I looked at her, saw her chin jut out, and knew that Breezy Fox would one day be known as Dr. Fox.

The workmen finished in the middle of the afternoon, gave Breezy and Tracy instructions and left. It was too hot to be outside and I was sitting in my recliner. Sitting and remembering, remembering the first time I saw Paul. When they left, the house grew quiet. I reclined the chair as far back as it would go, closed my eyes and went to sleep still remembering. I didn't wake up until Paul came home from work.

Tracy went home leaving Breezy to finish dinner. After hugging me, Paul went straight to the kitchen where Breezy was.

"So we have a celebrity in our midst," he said to Breezy.

Breezy laughed as she said, "I sure hope so."

"An Oklahoma City station played several of your songs today and every time they did, I just sort of mentioned the fact that Breezy Fox's real name was Breanne Fox and that she lives with my wife and me and went to college right here in Stillwater. You sounded good, Breezy. I was right proud of you."

"Thank you, Mr. Phillips," she answered.

That evening, Paul and I watched the sunset and, as usual, when dusk came, the mosquitoes drove us inside. We watched television until time to go to bed.

After kissing Paul good night I turned over, Paul pulled me close to him and I went right to sleep. I don't know how long I slept, but when I awoke, Paul was no longer holding me and I could hear his gentle snore. I tried to go back to sleep but I couldn't.

Finally I eased out of bed, out the door, and went to the living room. I sat in the recliner and of course the poodles joined me. I sat there, petting the poodles and remembering when...

Soon I became restless, shoved the poodles to the floor and stood. I walked to the glass door, stood and looked out. It looked so beautiful outside. I reached down, unlocked the door and slid it open. It was then the most God awful clamor I had ever heard broke loose and Paul and Breezy came rushing down the hallway to me.

Chapter 34

IT WAS A BLUSTERY WINTER afternoon and Breezy seemed troubled as she prepared dinner. She was in the kitchen so I couldn't see her very well from the living room but I could hear her, or in this case, didn't hear her. For once she wasn't singing. I sat in my recliner with a lap full of poodles and Tracy sat on the couch facing me. She was nursing Maria, her baby daughter.

Usually when Breezy was anywhere in the house you knew where she was from the sound of her voice as she sang. But not today. Except for the occasional clatter of her cooking, all was quiet in the kitchen. It wasn't like her and I wondered what was wrong.

"Breezy has seemed awfully quiet, Tracy."

"I know and I don't know why. She has been that way ever since she has come back from seeing Dr. Griffith. I wonder what he said to her."

Paul came home and I greeted him. He fixed himself a drink and we went out onto the patio. The sun was low in the west and I knew it would set before dinner.

"It's cool out here, Squirt. I have on a jacket but you might go back in and grab a sweater."

So I did. We went through the usual 'How was your day,' talk which had become our ritual. I listened as he told me about his day and he listened while I told him about my day, or what I could remember of it.

Breezy was quiet all through dinner. At last she looked up and said, "I don't want to work for you anymore."

"What!" I exclaimed. "Why? Have we done something?" I looked at Paul and saw he was in shock."

"No," Breezy grinned. "You guys have treated me wonderfully. I didn't say it right. I want to go ahead, live here, cook, and clean house, but I don't want you guys to pay me. Just let me work out my room and board. That's all the pay I need."

"What brought all this on?" Paul asked. "Are you suddenly rich?"

Breezy ducked her head as if she were embarrassed or ashamed as she said, "Yes."

"You are? How did that come about?" Tracy asked.

"I'm not really for sure myself. You know, I got the phone call from Dr. Griffith and he asked me to come to his office. I didn't know what it was about but you remember he is managing my singing career. I thought perhaps he was going to cancel our management agreement. But that wasn't it. He simply wanted to give me a check for my royalties. He even went with me to help set up an account in the bank. I didn't have the first idea how to go about setting up a bank account. My folks don't have much to do with a bank; never had enough money to worry about it. But now it's different." She stood, reached in her pocket and brought out a rumpled deposit slip. "The radio stations all over the country have been playing my songs and people like them and they're buying my CD. A lot of people must like them. See?" she said passing the deposit slip around."

Paul glanced at it and then he quickly looked at it again. "Congratulations, Breezy. You are rich. You don't have to work for anyone. Are you going to continue schooling and become a doctor?"

"Of course, this doesn't change a thing and I don't want it to change anything. I want things to keep on just as they are. I want to keep on cleaning house and cooking for you. There are only two things that I want to change."

By then the deposit slip was to me and I looked at it. Paul was right; she didn't need to work for anyone. If her CDs kept selling as they were, she would make much more in a musical career than she would ever make as a doctor. "What are the two things?" I asked.

"I've already mentioned one of them; I don't want to get paid because it would make me seem greedy. But I still want to live here. This is my home in Stillwater and I want to live here. I don't want to move on campus."

"Why? Why not move on campus?" Paul asked.

"It's like this, when I walk down the hallway, too many people, even now, recognize me. I feel them staring at me. I was almost late to class one time because so many stopped me and asked for my autograph. I don't mind, in fact I enjoy it if that is what they want. After all, it is people like them that are making me rich. Believe me, I have autographed tennis shoes, t-shirts, notebooks, everything. But this is a place where I can come home to and get out of the hassle. No one knows where I live. I'm always getting my picture taken, and I don't mind, but it is startling to have a flashbulb go off in your face when walking down the sidewalk or the hallway. A few times even in class, which annoys the instructor to no end, as you can imagine. How can I concentrate on my studies with stuff like that going on? I can't imagine what it would be like to live on campus. I'd never get anything done. So please, please, can I still live here until I graduate with a degree in premed and go to OU Medical School? Here I can concentrate on my studies and accomplish the important thing. Here I'm just Breezy. I'll earn my keep, I'll promise you that."

"Of course you can, Breezy," Paul said, reaching over and patting her on the shoulder. "But you know you will never make as much money as a doctor as you are making now."

"And money is important? I prefer to have a meaningful life doing something that is important."

"You mentioned there were two things," I said. "What is the other?"

"You know Tracy and I both work here. She is your nurse and I cook and clean house, anyway that's the way it's supposed to be. But I know how and what time to give you medicine and often to do it when Tracy is busy with something else. In turn, Tracy helps me with the household chores. At times, Tracy and I find ourselves stumbling over each other. I think Tracy could handle everything for three, four, five or six days. I know it would be extra work for her when I'm not here, but she could handle it. She and I could work it out. In return for filling in for me, I could fill in for her and give her a few days off. It would only be during Thanksgiving, Christmas, and Spring Break and we can decide when school is out how much I'd be gone. But during Thanksgiving, Christmas, and Spring Break, I'd like to have a few days off if it is okay with you guys."

"Yes, I'm sure you and Tracy could work it out," I said. "But out of curiosity, what would you be doing on those days?"

"Thanksgiving, Dr. Griffith wants to schedule me a concert in Oklahoma City. At Christmas, he wants to schedule me a concert in Wichita, Kansas. Then during Spring Break he wants me to have a concert in Amarillo, Texas, Santa Fe, and Albuquerque, New Mexico. He claims there is money to be made at concerts and to him, money **is** important. Remember he gets fifteen percent of everything I make as my manager. I like entertaining people and I feel that I owe him that much for what he has done for me. Then this summer they want me to cut another CD in Nashville."

"I suppose you'll want to take the Vibe?" Paul asked.

"No, Dr. Griffith used his money to buy a new van just for that purpose. He showed it to me. It has ***Breezy Fox*** painted on both sides of it. It embarrasses me but it sure looks cool."

"We need to celebrate this," Paul said as he stood. "I wish I had Champagne on ice," he looked into the fridge, "but all we have is Concord grape wine and it will have to do."

He took a gallon jug out of the fridge. It was half full. He got down four wine glasses and started filling them.

"Not for me, kind sir," Breezy said, "Put Orange Crush in my glass."

Chapter 35

"GRANDMA SHARON, GRANDMA SHARON, can I sit on your lap?" the little brown girl said as she ran to me. She came at me so fast that it startled me.

"Oh, my!" I said, catching my breath. "Of course, you can," and I reached down to help her up. I was sitting out on the patio in an easy chair. It was a golden day and the sun shown so brightly it almost hurt my eyes. If it hadn't been such a gorgeous day I think I would have gone inside.

"Maria! Don't run up to Grandma Sharon that way. It startles her," a very tan and a very pregnant young woman said as she sat beside me.

"What is your name, Honey?" I asked.

"Oh, Grandma, you know my name," the little girl said. "You're just teasing me."

"She may not be, Maria," the young woman said. "Grandma Sharon has Alzheimer's and she forgets real easy."

"You have really forgotten my name?" the little girl asked.

"Yes," I answered nodding my head.

"My name is Maria," Maria said. Then she pointed to the young woman, "That is mommy and her name is Tracy." Then she pointed to a toddler with only a diaper on toddling around the yard playing with three poodles. "That is my little brother, Donnie."

I turned to Tracy and asked, "Where's Breezy?"

"She left us several years ago, Sharon. She is at OU in her senior year of medical school."

"Oh." I sat there and tried to remember when she left and I couldn't. I couldn't even remember when I saw her last. I had learned a long time ago that when I forgot something, the best way to find out was to ask someone. "When was Breezy here last?"

"Spring Break. She stopped by here to see us on her way to Kansas City where she had a concert."

"A concert?"

"Yes, our little Breezy is making it big in the music industry. She's really busy with her schooling but she wants to keep her name alive so sometimes she just drops everything for a while and goes on tour."

"Oh," I said and looked out where the toddler was playing with three poodles. "Where is the other Poodle? I thought I had four. What did I do, forget again?"

"No, you still have Lady, Doc, and Elvira, but you gave Snowflake to Breezy when she left."

"Oh," I said. I dimly remembered Snowflake always being around Breezy and under her feet most of the time. Under her feet or in her lap. Those were the good days and I wished I could have them back. But I couldn't and there was no use wishing. I looked around. Where was my cat. I knew I had a cat somewhere, what was her name? Oh, yes, Miss Calico. Where was Miss Calico? I looked and looked and looked. I saw the dog with a mangled tail lying out under a tree, but nowhere did I see my cat. "Where's Mrs. Calico?" I asked.

Tracy looked at me with misty eyes before she said, "Mrs. Calico was put down last winter. She was so very old. She couldn't keep anything on her stomach and grew so weak that she couldn't even walk. Paul took her to the vet and had her put to sleep."

I felt tears in my eyes and I reached up and wiped them away. I felt depressed. The world was spinning too fast and good things were being flung off. If I could only stop the world for a while or at least slow it down. But I couldn't.

The back door flew open and a big, young man stepped out with a small boy following him. "What's everyone doing lazing around out here in the sunshine," he boomed. "How are you feeling, Mom?" and he came at me so fast that I was frightened. Then he bent down and kissed me on the cheek.

"Who are you? I asked.

"I'm Chris, Mom. I'm your son, Chris."

I looked at him, looked him up and down. "You sure grew up to be a big bruiser," I laughed.

"And this is you grandson, Ray."

The little boy came to me and hugged me. "I love you, Grandma."

"Tiffany couldn't come over. Sharon is colicky and fussy. She thought she should keep her at home."

Sharon? Sharon? I was confused. Wasn't my name Sharon? I looked at Chris and asked, "Sharon?"

"Yes," Chris answered. "Your baby granddaughter."

So I also had a granddaughter and she was my namesake. The world began to grow brighter.

"I got an interesting letter today," Chris said. "It was from Breezy. She sent me a check for a sizable amount. She wrote that she knew there were some poor folks around Stillwater who couldn't afford their much needed drugs. She told me to set up an account and go ahead and give them the drugs they needed and pay for them with the money from this account."

"Breezy did that?" Tracy asked.

"She sure did. I don't think she likes being rich and she is trying her best to go broke. She wants to go broke and be poor again."

"How big was the check?" Tracy asked.

"It was the size of a regular check. About this wide and about this long," Chris said, showing her the measurements with his fingers.

"No, you fool," Tracy laughed. "You know what I meant. How much was the check for?"

"Sorry, Tracy, Breezy asked me not to disclose the amount. Let's just say it was enough to help out lots and lots of folks." Then he turned to me, "By the way, Mom, you're going to be a grandmother again."

"You mean your wife, uh, uh…"

"Tiffany?"

"Yes, Tiffany. Is Tiffany pregnant again?"

"No, but my sister, Kris, is. Jared is going to have a brother or sister. Don't tell her I told you. She will probably come over and tell you herself soon and if she finds out you already know, she'll skin me alive."

"When is she coming over?"

"Probably sometime this afternoon or evening."

"Oh, don't worry about me telling her you told me if she isn't coming over until this afternoon. It is easy for a person like me with Alzheimer's to keep a secret. I will have forgotten it by then."

Chapter 36

I LOOKED OUTSIDE THE kitchen window. It was a wonderful, blustery winter day. A wild day like I loved. Occasionally I would see a snowflake, whipped by in the wind. I looked at the woman sitting beside me and a young girl over the stove cooking. "Who are you?" I asked of the woman sitting.

"I'm Tracy, your nurse."

"Why in the world do I need a nurse?"

"You have Alzheimer's. You tend to forget things."

"I guess I do," I laughed. Then I leaned over so I could whisper into her ear, "Who is the young woman cooking?"

"That's Charlotte. She is enrolled at OSU and is working her way through college. She cooks and cleans house for you when she's not in class."

"I thought Breezy did that. Where's Breezy?"

"Breezy is a surgeon now and she practices over at Powder River, Tennessee. She is the only doctor there and she is the only surgeon for miles around."

"So our little Breezy is now a doctor. Does she still sing?"

"Oh, yes. She goes from room to room with her husband, Rusty, singing a song to the patients. Do you remember Rusty?"

"No."

"He is one of the workmen who installed the alarms on the doors of the house. He and Breezy hit it off and started going together. They got married just before she graduated from OSU. He now plays the guitar for her when she sings. He is her band"

"That's wonderful," I said. "Is Breezy still big in the musical world?"

"Oh, yes. Not only do she and Rusty play and sing in the hospital, which she practically built, but she cuts a couple of CD's each year. She is a busy girl and she works long hours, but, as Breezy is fond of saying, 'If you don't have time for music, you don't have time for living'. She works long hours taking care of sick people but she takes two months off every year. A month in the summer and a month in the winter. She uses the first week of each month in Nashville where she cuts a new album and the rest of the month they pack up the kids and they go on tour. Our Breezy is a hot item in the music world. As many CD's as she sells, she could be rich, but I doubt that she is."

"Why?"

"She spends it all on taking care of sick people."

"That's our Breezy," I said, a tear in my eye.

An old man came into the kitchen and said, "Good morning, Squirt. How are you feeling today?"

"I feel great, thank you," I answered and even as I answered, I felt my heart beat faster. But who was he?

He went to the coffee pot with an old man's gait, helped himself to a cup of coffee and then went to the living room. I heard the paper snap as he opened it. Again I leaned over and whispered to Tracy, "Who was that?"

"That was Paul, Sharon," Tracy whispered back. "Paul, your husband."

"No, it can't be! My husband, Paul, is a much younger man."

"Well, it is," Tracy smiled.

"Then he'll have to go to work pretty soon."

"No, Sharon, he won't. He retired four or five years ago."

"Breakfast is on, Paul," the cook said, and began to set plates of bacon and eggs in front of us. Paul came in and sat down. He began to eat heartily while I toyed with my food. I couldn't keep my eyes from him. Yes, I loved him, I loved my Paul, but when had he gotten so old?

Chapter 37

A GOLDEN DAY IN A GOLDEN WORLD. Surrounded by love and laughter. Life. What a great life I had. I was sitting with my feet up and I felt myself smile as I looked at the children playing on the floor. The babies were on their blankets, some of the little girls were sitting on the couch playing with dolls while the little boys pushed cars and trucks across the floor. One little boy was playing with two poodles on the floor. Two? I thought I had three. Where was the third poodle? It was such a beautiful day I was afraid to ask, even if I could ask. Afraid it would ruin the day.

I looked at the walls painted a soothing color, but they were blank. No decorations on them. Why? Why not have flowers or perhaps some other design on the walls. Someone had no taste. A most beautiful young woman came to me. She had a book in her hand. She began to take pictures from the book, one at a time and hand them to me.

"Remember this one, Mom?"

I took the picture and looked at it. It was in color but the color had faded until it was almost black and white. I looked at it and recognized that it was a picture of Chris and Kris, my twin children. The picture was taken when they were very young. I handed the picture back to her, smiled and nodded my head, yes.

She took the picture back and handed me another one. I reached out and took it. It too was old and faded. I recognized it though. It was of Paul and me standing in front of a new car. Were we ever that young? Again I nodded my head, yes, smiled, and handed it back to her and she handed me another one. Even though it was faded, I recognized the people in it. It seemed as if I were looking at a different world, a long-ago world.

Then she handed me one and I didn't recognize it. It was a picture of a middle-aged woman and behind her was the fountain in the lake. For some reason I felt pride in looking at the fountain. I shook my head and handed it back to her.

"That's you in the picture, Mom. You thought the lake needed a fountain in it. You got the city council to agree that if you could raise the money to buy the fountain, they would pay for the instillation. Then you knocked on every door on both sides of the lake until you had the money. I took that picture of you right after they had installed it."

I faintly remembered but most of all I remembered the pride I felt in the fountain.

She continued to hand me pictures and I looked at them. Each time I felt myself smile when I recognized the people and I looked at the picture a long time before I handed it back. If I didn't recognize the people, I would simply shake my head and hand it back to her.

"Thanksgiving dinner is ready to be served," came a booming voice from the kitchen. "That is if JT hasn't burned everything."

"Could've happened with you standing in my way all the time. If it is, then it's your fault. I tried to get you out of my kitchen."

"In your way? If I hadn't been in here helping you, we'd never have Thanksgiving dinner. You just don't appreciate a good thing."

I stood and walked to the kitchen where there was a table all but breaking under the weight of food. Everything looked so good. I sat down and looked around me. Only grownups were sitting at the big table. Two small tables were set up and the children were sitting there. The girls at one and the boys at another. The young mothers were holding the babies in their arms.

When everyone was sitting, one of the young men gave the Thanksgiving prayer. He ended by thanking God for the rich and bountiful life we had. "Amen to that," I heard someone say and looked up startled. It was me, I had said those words. Everyone at the table looked at me in astonishment.

And I had a rich life. I was surrounded by friendship and love. The love I felt was all but overwhelming. For what more could I ask? I lived in a golden world and this was a bright gold day, filled with people I loved.

I ate until I was full. Everything was so good I ate some more. Then, stuffed like the Thanksgiving turkey, I waddled into the living room and sat down in my chair. I sat there and watched the children play with each other and I couldn't help but smile. I closed my eyes and let the sounds wash over me. A baby cried and another laughed. Tracy, Tiffany, and Kris visited with each other in low voices. I felt Paul sit down in the chair next to mine and I opened my eyes and looked at him when he took my hand in his. I heard J.T. and Chris grouse in the kitchen as they cleaned up the Thanksgiving dinner mess. The little boys made motor sounds as they pushed their trucks, cars, and tractors across the floor. All of it was music to my ears.

Yes, it was a happy, beautiful golden day and as I sat there, it was then the blackness came.

Made in the USA
Charleston, SC
16 March 2011